Holy Spear of Magus

Toni Pike

First published in February 2018 – *Kindle Edition*.

This is the first paperback edition: February 2018

ISBN: 9781980209812

www.tonipike.com

HOLY SPEAR OF MAGUS

Jotham and Madena Fletcher remain dedicated to finding the Simonian Sect whose goal is to destroy the Christian Church. They leave their baby daughter at home and travel to Krakow in Poland to investigate a theology professor known as the Guardian of the Spear. Meanwhile, a mysterious Hungarian arrives at the hilltop monastery of Saint Dimitrios in Greece in search of an ancient relic that is rumoured to be buried there.

When a large Pentecostal Church in San Diego is crippled by a cyberattack, Jotham heads there with young computer genius, Eugene Beaudreau, to find out if the sect is responsible. They meet Pastor Silas Conrad and his strange family who are all obsessed with the Holy Spear and its curative powers.

When two monks arrive from the ruthless Brotherhood led by Father Dominic, Jotham is catapulted into a desperate struggle to track down the Holy Spear and stop it falling into the wrong hands. He races to Europe - but his enemies are more diabolical than he could possibly imagine.

About the Author

Toni Pike is an Australian who loves to travel the world doing research for her thrillers. As well as *The Jotham Fletcher Mystery Thriller Series*, she has a book of travel tips and a weight loss book, and enjoys sharing travel photos on Instagram: @authorlovestravel. You can also find her at tonipike.com.

Other works

The Jotham Fletcher Mystery Thriller Series
Book 1: THE MAGUS COVENANT
Book 2: THE ROCK OF MAGUS
Book 3: THE MAGUS EPIPHANY

THE ONE WAY DIET: *The pathway to weight loss*
(a no-nonsense guide to losing weight and coping with the journey)

HAPPY TRAVELS 101 is a short book of travel tips: *Don't leave home without these cruise, flight, safety, packing and sightseeing tips.*

Table of Contents

Chapter 1

Greece

The hilltop monastery of Saint Dimitrios in Greece was more than a thousand years old, perched precariously on top of a sandstone peak in a remote part of Northern Greece. Draco Spiros was seventy years old and he had worked there for more than fifty years. He was like a part of the furniture, ignored by everyone as he went about his work as the maintenance man.

While he waited outside the abbot's office, he tapped a finger on the arm of the chair to hide his shaking hands. He had been summoned there without any explanation and he knew that mean trouble.

At last he heard a creak as the door opened, and he could see inside the austere office. Father Lambros was eighty years old, but his back was straight despite the constant pain of arthritis. Dressed in a rough grey habit, he glared at the visitor. "Come in, Spiros. I have an important matter to discuss."

Draco stood up and shuffled into the timber-lined room. Father Lambros wasted no time in getting to the point but he spoke in his normal, calm voice. "I know that you've been pilfering money from the monastery. Whatever you could get your hands on, for several years."

The game was up. Draco felt as if a hole had opened up beneath his feet and he was falling into a deep, dark pit. "No, Father. There's been a mistake," he said.

"Everyone knows it, Spiros. We've all been watching you for a long time. But I hoped and prayed that you would change your ways and adopt more Godly behaviour."

He tried to plead his case. "Why would I steal from the monastery? I lead a simple life."

Father Lambros shook his head. "Greed is one of the seven deadly sins. You used our meagre funds to pay for your gambling and drinking. Now I've finally decided to let you go. Your work is finished for today. Leave now and don't ever come back.

Draco's head was spinning. "I've worked here all my life. My family has worked here for more than a thousand years."

"I'm aware of your familial ties to the monastery. But you've given me no choice."

Blood rushed to Draco's head. "You'll be sorry, Lambros!" he said with

7

a snarl and then charged towards him.

The old man stepped back in fear and cried out for help.

The abbot had been expecting trouble and two monks were waiting nearby. When they heard the scuffle, they burst into the room and grabbed hold of Draco's arms. Neither of them was young but they were able to manoeuvre the short, stocky man into the corridor. He struggled with them all the way, but they managed to drag him to the front door and throw him out into the cold night air.

He was destined never to return.

***

Krakow, Poland

Jotham and Madena Fletcher were on a three-day trip to Poland and at that moment they were on a stake-out. Their curiosity had been piqued after reading that one young student from the University of Krakow had committed suicide by jumping from the roof of the cathedral. After investigating further, they wanted to find out if the Simonian Sect had infiltrated the Faculty of Theology. The suicide of a student was not that unusual but the young man who had died was popular and loved by his peers; his suicide was completely out of character. Now they were keeping some of the people who worked and studied there under surveillance.

Madena was a former army officer who had come to work for Jotham two and a half years ago. Her job was to help in his quest to stop the Simonian Sect and part of her role was to pass on her martial arts skills. Together, they were a formidable team and she loved her work. But now they were married and the proud parents of a beautiful daughter: little Belle was almost one year old.

Madena was a consummate professional and just as dedicated to their mission as her husband but this was her first time away from Belle for more than one night. They had left her with Cynthia Young, the housekeeper at their estate in the Peak District. She and her husband Felix, the chauffer and handyman, were like the child's grandparents, and they were confident that she was in safe hands.

After inheriting a fortune from billionaire Iago Visser, Jotham Fletcher decided to dedicate his life to stopping the Simonian Sect. He also wanted to

8

stop the deadly Brotherhood, whose members were willing to commit any crime in pursuit of the same goal.

The Simonian Sect was a cult that followed a religion created by their founder, Simon Magus. He was a nefarious magician who was mentioned briefly in the New Testament. He had a small following that endured after his grisly death, but most people believed that his cult had died out by AD 400.

Three years ago, Jotham Fletcher had been an Anglican parish priest in Australia. He visited Rome to give a lecture but ended up uncovering a shocking conspiracy. He found out then that the sect had in fact survived in secret for two thousand years. There were cells around the world and the goal of the organisation was to fulfil the Magus Covenant, a vow to undermine and destroy the Christian Church. Members of the sect had, since the time of the apostles, infiltrated churches and led people astray. They had inspired most of the church's misdeeds.

Jotham and Madena did some research before they left home on their current mission, and decided that they wanted to know more about Professor Walter Kowalski. He was the Head of the Department of Church History in the Faculty of Theology. Although he was not a priest, he also had the honorary title of *Guardian of the Spear*.

"That's sounds like a peculiar role," said Madena in her very proper British accent. Jotham couldn't help gazing at her as she ran a hand through her wavy brown hair.

"I've looked into that," said Jotham. "It's just an honorary title, given to a well-respected member of the church community," said Jotham. "There's a relic on display in Krakow Cathedral that is supposedly the Holy Spear."

She grimaced. "You mean the spear that a Roman soldier used to stab Jesus on the cross?"

"Yes, that's right. To check if Christ were still alive, they pierced his side to see if blood flowed out. There was only a trickle, so they presumed that he was dead. But most authorities claim that the spear in Krakow is a copy of the original. There's no evidence that the relic is genuine and there's no historical trail of evidence. There are several other claimants around the world, including one in Rome."

Jotham and Madena flew to Poland the next day in their private jet. Now they were acting like a couple of lovers, which of course they were, relaxing in a café in the main square of the old town. It was right opposite the faculty building, an elaborate late-Gothic structure.

It was a warm spring morning and Professor Kowalski was loitering outside chatting to a group of male students. He was in his late fifties with fair skin and a serene expression. The exchange appeared to be friendly, but Jotham felt uneasy. The students looked so young and naïve and he saw the older man exchange a knowing glance with one of them.

He turned to look at Madena and, as always, was struck by her tall, lean figure and flawless complexion. "What do you think, darling?" he asked.

"Well, I think he looks innocent enough," she replied, narrowing her wide-apart blue eyes and taking his hand. "But there's something not quite right in his manner. How many members of the sect have we encountered so far who aren't what they seem to be at first glance?"

"So what do you suggest?"

"I think we should stake-out his house tonight."

Jotham nodded. "Agreed. There's something about him I definitely don't like."

Chapter 2

Professor Kowalski lived in a narrow terrace house not far from the old town. It was a cold night, but Jotham and Madena were in luck because there was a small restaurant close by in the cobbled street. The cosy window seat gave them an excellent view of the front door that opened directly on to the footpath.

While they ate dinner, a few people strolled past, probably on their way home from work. It was almost dark and the streetlights had come on, casting an eerie glow. Jotham jumped when one of the students they had seen that morning, a slender young man with dark hair, suddenly walked into the restaurant. He sat down, ordered a coffee and, when it was delivered, he gulped it down in one mouthful. Then he turned and looked around the room as if searching for a familiar face.

They held their breath and lowered their eyes, hoping he didn't recognise them.

After a moment, Jotham looked up and locked eyes with him, wondering if he ought to try and talk to him. But the young man turned away as if he didn't recognise him. Getting out his phone, he appeared to send a text message. With a look of trepidation, he stood up and marched outside.

"Looks as if he needed some caffeine to boost his confidence," said Jotham.

They watched with wide eyes as he walked up to Kowalski's front door and knocked once. The door opened and he looked around furtively before stepping inside.

"What will we do now?" asked Madena.

"How about a coffee? We'll find out if there are any more visitors, but I think we've already seen enough, don't you?

Madena nodded. "Sounds good. That'll help wash down those delicious dumplings."

***

The next day, Madena parked their hire car in a back street only fifty metres from the Faculty of Theology building. Jotham leaned over and put his arm around her. "You're so handsome," she said, pressing her lips on his. "Be careful and remember that I love you."

As he jumped out of the car, Jotham fingered the small audio bug that was attached to his chest and saw Madena tuning in to the listening device. The faculty building was an impressive gothic structure. After walking in through the front entrance he went to the central courtyard that was lined with cloisters. Dozens of students strolled around or huddled in small groups chatting to each other.

Jotham found the right-hand corner staircase and climbed up three flights to the top level. He looked for Professor Walter Kowalski's office and soon found his name on a brass plaque attached to a heavy wooden door. He knew that he ought to knock and wait for an invitation to enter, but his plan was to surprise him.

Jotham took a deep breath. He slowly, silently opened the door just enough to slip through, then stepped inside. Putting his hands behind his back, he locked the door behind him.

Walter Kowalski was bent over paperwork at his desk, but when he heard the door shut he raised his head with a startled look.

"*Tak*?" he asked, meaning *yes*.

Jotham braced his body, prepared to deal with anything that might happen. "I'm sorry, I don't speak Polish," he said. "But I've read that you spent some time at Cambridge and can speak fluent English."

He frowned. "Yes that's correct, but how can I help you?"

Jotham intended to get straight to the point. "My name isn't relevant. I have reason to believe that you're trying to undermine the young men in your charge. Are you a member of the Simonian Sect?

Kowalski's mouth gaped. He stood up and began to tremble with rage. "I don't know what you mean," he said, his accent becoming more pronounced with every word. "But I've just pressed my security alarm, and the police should be here at any moment."

Jotham always lived his life flying under the radar and had no desire to talk to the police, but he knew this would be his only chance to confront Kowalski. "I'll be happy to talk to them about you. My suspicions were aroused when I read that one of your students had jumped from the roof of the cathedral."

"That was a very sad case," he replied. "We were all heartbroken about that tragedy."

"And I suppose that had nothing to do with you? Last night I saw one of your students visiting your house."

Kowalski narrowed his eyes. "You've been spying on me?"

Jotham gulped. Now was the critical moment, and with a member of the sect he knew that he could only expect to be dealing with the unexpected. "You need to hand in your resignation today and sever all professional ties with the university, or you'll be exposed and discredited as a fraud who's trying to corrupt his students."

In response, the professor grabbed a heavy brass paperweight and held it aloft to use as a weapon. "The police should be here shortly. If you're behind bars, I'll have done the Simonian Sect a great service."

"So you admit that you're in the sect?" asked Jotham.

Kowalski charged towards him, raising his arm even higher.

Jotham bent forward, preparing to tackle him and repel his attack. At the last moment he kicked out, striking Kowalski on the arm. He dropped the paperweight and it hit the ground with a thump.

The man looked stunned for an instant. But then he swung his arm around and pushed Jotham hard against the wall.

As Jotham's spine hit the surface, it jarred his entire body. He stepped forward, thinking that he would soon know if he'd been injured by the impact.

But then his eyes widened as Kowalski raised his arms in the air and cried out as if he was demented. "Fly like Simon Magus," he said. He raced to the casement window and opened it wide.

Jotham felt a rush of adrenaline that focused his thoughts. He realised what the man was about to do, and he had to prevent him. "Stop, you'll kill yourself!" he shouted.

Kowalski gave him a wild look as he climbed out the window at a furious pace. "Magic will cure me," he said.

Jotham darted over and grabbed hold of his arm, then tried to drag him back inside. He could feel the strain in his muscles as he tugged, but the momentum was in the opposite direction. The solid man propelled himself forward and he was now suspended in the air.

Jotham tried to hold him, but Kowalski managed to break free and tumbled out. "Fly like Simon Magus!" he yelled again with terror-filled eyes.

What happened next took Jotham totally by surprise.

Instead of falling, he seemed to glide down slowly.

Jotham blinked, trying to understand if he was dreaming or having a hallucination.

Finally, he hit the ground with a dull thud.

Jotham knew that Simon Magus was said to be able to levitate – and he wondered if Kowalski could fly like him. On the day that he died, Magus rose high in the air before suddenly crashing back to earth.

Panic gripped him, but he knew that it was vital to stay calm and his training kicked in. He stood to the side of the window and peered down. It faced the outside of the building, and Jotham could see Kowalski lying face down on the ground below, completely motionless. He must be badly injured or even worse.

Jotham's natural urge was to call the police and then run to help the man. He turned around, but heard the distant, shrill sound of at least two police sirens.

His choice was to escape or risk arrest, and Madena was waiting for him in the car.

He glanced outside again and gasped in shock. Kowalski moved as if he was stirring to life, and then clambered to his knees.

Jotham could not believe it, and couldn't tear himself away from the sight despite the danger. The man stumbled to his feet and limped away.

He was alive, but Jotham felt a chill in his heart as one thought hammered his brain: perhaps it was the magic of Simon Magus that had helped him to survive. He had flown, just like the magician two thousand years ago.

The sirens grew louder, and Jotham knew there was no time to waste. If the police caught up with him, he could be arrested and even framed for attempted murder. He would be separated from Madena and Belle, and unable to continue his mission to hunt down the sect and the Brotherhood.

As he ran out of the office, he took out his phone and texted Madena. "GG." It was their code for: *get ready to go*.

He bolted down the staircase three steps at a time but as he reached the bottom he slowed down so as not to attract attention. Trying to look calm and collected as he strode past a group of students, he then entered the courtyard. Staying close to the wall, he passed through the cloisters, and finally walked into the foyer of the building facing the narrow street.

Once outside, he dashed towards the car. Madena was waiting for him with the engine running. He jumped in and by the time the door slammed shut, she was already halfway down the street. "You've never looked more beautiful," he said.

As she swung around the first corner, he rang his pilot. "Get the plane ready, please, Anthony. We'll be there in twenty minutes, if not sooner."

"Will do, Jotham," he replied, and then ended the call.

Chapter 3

Madena was heading to a farm just outside Krakow that had a small airstrip used by the local gliding club. Jotham had paid the owner a considerable sum to rent it for a few days.

She drove through side streets to avoid attracting attention until they were well away from the centre of town. Once they were on the main highway, she slammed her foot on the accelerator and they were soon approaching the plane. The Beechcraft Premier One was a small business jet that was fourteen metres long and nearly five metres high. It had once belonged to Iago Visser and had been part of the estate inherited by Jotham. He had decided to retain it and it had proven vital in their sect-hunting missions.

Anthony Gillam was standing beside the open door of the plane and he looked immaculate, as always, in his pilot's uniform: a navy jacket with four white stripes on both sleeves. His ginger hair sparkled in the sunlight. The door was lowered, clam-style, and had a dual purpose. The interior side of it served as a set of three steps, known as airstairs.

Jotham and Madena left the car there, to be collected later by the hire car company. A healthy payment would ensure their confidentiality. They scampered up the stairs and into the sleek cream and wood-trimmed interior of the cabin. Anthony followed them, secured the door and strode to the cockpit.

There was no sign of anyone nearby, so it seemed that there was nothing to stop them now.

They sat in two of the four contoured seats that faced each other with small tables between them. There were two more seats behind those and a built-in galley towards the front. As they did up their seatbelts, the plane began to taxi down the runway, and although Madena smiled, Jotham could see her knuckles grasp the armrest.

As the plane took off and they watched the airstrip grow smaller, Jotham breathed a sigh of relief. Looking around the cabin, he was reminded of how much his life had changed since he first met Iago Visser, just three years ago. His home and the jet had belonged to the billionaire, and Anthony Gillam had been his pilot.

Jotham had once earned a meagre salary as a parish priest, but now money was no longer an object – something that still awed and humbled him.

Soon, they were out of Polish airspace and on the way home. As they headed back to England, Jotham opened the polished wood cabinet containing the compact galley and switched on the coffee machine.

Madena relaxed in her seat. "I can't wait to see our little sweetheart again," she said. "But now you better tell me all about Walter Kowalski. I heard most of it in my earphones, and thought for a moment that both of us might be spending the next twenty years in a Polish jail."

***

Vancouver

John Pedersen was watching Kostya Zykov and wondered how he could sit for four hours with his eyes fixed on a computer screen. "Do you need any help?" he asked.

"No, I'm almost ready. Then the timing will be up to you." Kostya was thirty, and had a thick neck and crew cut hair. With deathly white skin, he looked as if he never went out in the sun, and preferred to work at night and sleep during the day. He spoke good English but with a heavy accent.

Pedersen was furious when he heard that an old man had become the new Leader of the Simonian Sect. Instead of returning to the inner circle after his last narrow escape, he'd been sent to the sect's brand new apartment in the centre of Vancouver, and told to work on some special projects along the West Coast.

When he heard about Kostya Zykov and his unusual skill set, he asked for him to be sent there. Kostya had a degree in computer science from Moscow State University and had been a full-time cybercriminal until he joined the sect. He loved to boast that he was a master of the dark net and had quickly built a reputation for dazzling work manipulating international bank accounts. He had been visiting an Orthodox church with his grandmother when a sect member recruited him and broadened his view of where his skills might take him. The Simonian Sect represented both big money and the chance to relocate to the West. It also gave him something to believe in.

He had left his criminal ties behind, but John Pedersen was keen to put Kostya's skills to use. The Russian was happy to oblige, because he believed that he was now working to help the sect.

The two of them now shared the small but modern apartment in Vancouver and they made an odd couple. Pedersen was only thirty-three, but he was a financial genius who had made a fortune on the stock market when he was a teenager. That was before he joined the sect, but he still liked to use his brain rather than his brawn. He regarded himself as a lover rather than a fighter. He had the overwhelming vanity, too, of the highly gifted who have to deal with and take direction from less brilliant individuals.

Now his immediate future depended on the Russian. Together, they were working on a special venture. With Kostya Zykov's help he intended to swell the coffers of the Simonian Sect courtesy of every church in North America. He knew the inner circle would be very grateful for the extra income.

The sect didn't discriminate. It infiltrated every branch of the Christian Church throughout the world, and it was a member in a Russian Orthodox Church who had first recruited Kostya.

"How long before we can start the trial?" asked Pedersen.

Kostya shrugged his shoulders. "Probably within the next twelve hours."

"I can hardly wait."

"All we need is to fool one person in any organisation into clicking a link, and the malware is inserted into their computer system. For the trial we've had inside help from your contact. It's already in their network, waiting to spring to life. Then we'll really know just how well it works."

"A test run," said Pedersen, his boyish face beaming. "My dream is to attack every church organisation in America, starting with the small Pentecostal ones. This will assure both our futures, Zykov. Technology is the way of the future, even for the Simonian Sect. When we've proven what we can do with the Protestant churches, we can make a move on the mega-bucks in the American Catholic Church."

"We should say the mantra together."

"Yes, you're right. This is an important moment."

Kostya stood up and went to the sideboard. He took out an antique dagger from the drawer and held it in his right hand. He raised his arm high in the air and made five downward thrusts in quick succession.

He spoke first because he was younger, using a singsong voice similar to a Gregorian chant.

"All should strive to reach the golden mean
Freedom and moderation gives strength unseen
Between power and thought there is no light
Male female energy all beings unite."

Pedersen spoke next.

"Praise be to Simon Magus for his words.
The Father's mind produced the first thought to create the angels,
Then they created the visible universe.
We must follow the Magus Covenant,
A solemn promise to destroy the Christian Church.
His words will lead you to the truth."

Chapter 4

The Peak District

Jotham and Madena Fletcher lived in the Peak District, an area of great natural beauty in Derbyshire. They saw their private airfield come into view, a concrete strip in the middle of remote farmland. There was a small hangar at the end of the runway and the dark blue Mercedes was parked beside it, but there were no other buildings in the landscape. The only signs of life were some blackface sheep.

The chauffer, Felix Young, was waiting there to take them to the estate. "Belle's been an angel," he said as they got in the sedan. He was a dour Scotsman who was married to Cynthia, the cook and housekeeper. They had originally worked for Iago Visser, and now were even more devoted to the Fletcher family.

Anthony Gillam kept his motorbike in the hangar, and before riding home he would do his post-flight checks and organise re-fuelling.

On the thirty-minute journey home, they drove on narrow, winding lanes past spectacular scenery. At first there were lush meadows and gently rolling hills with stands of ash trees. Soon the landscape changed to heather-clad moors. The road was treacherous, edged on either side by steep embankments or dry stone walls that almost touched the car on both sides. They drove past two farmhouses, but there were no villages.

The Fletcher Estate was a medieval manor house, one of the few still remaining in Britain. It had originally belonged to Iago Visser, who had restored it to its former glory and also added every modern comfort and convenience. He spent a huge amount on the security system, including the addition of a vault in the basement.

When Jotham inherited Iago's fortune, he had been an Anglican parish priest in Australia. But he knew then that his destiny was to give up that role to search for the Simonian Sect wherever it was hidden around the world and also to stop the Brotherhood. That organisation shared his goal of destroying the sect, but they would stop at nothing, including murder, to achieve their objectives. It was led by Father Dominic, who was as obsessive and ruthless as his opponents in the sect.

Jotham had decided to retain the estate because of the impeccable security. By living there, he was able to lead a shadowy and secluded existence, always staying under the radar. So far as he knew, the Brotherhood and the sect did not know his location and that meant he and his family were safe in their own home.

The estate was hidden in a small valley. As the car approached, they saw the massive brick wall that encircled it, and a pair of solid metal gates opened up as if to welcome them home. The gates slammed firmly shut behind the vehicle after it drove in, and Madena smiled with relief. When they were outside those walls, they could never let down their guard.

A circular driveway led to the front door. The house was a vast and forbidding grey stone building that was reminiscent of a castle, with ramparts all around, but it also had the comfortable appearance of a large country home.

Cynthia Young walked outside to greet them with Belle in her arms, and they both smiled at the heart-warming sight. Jotham was struck by how much the little girl looked like Madena, with her wide-apart blue eyes.

They jumped out of the car to run over and Madena was the first one to hold her. "My darling, aren't you a beautiful little girl," she said, covering her face with butterfly kisses. Then she turned to Cynthia. "Thank you so much for looking after her. It looks as if you've done a wonderful job."

'My pleasure, dear," she replied in her resonant Scottish accent. The Youngs had no children of their own, and regarded themselves as Belle's grandparents. Jotham and Madena had lost their own parents many years ago.

The family was enveloped by warmth as soon as they walked through the front door of their home: the comfort of air-conditioning was very welcome in what looked like a medieval palace worthy of a prince. The entrance hall was a vast space lined with wood panelling and dominated by a double wooden staircase. Every piece of furniture was an intricately carved antique made of wood, stone or marble. The walls used to be covered in art that looked as if it would be worthy of the finest museums: religious paintings, icons and mosaics. That was understandable, when the house was owned by a billionaire who dealt in valuable religious artefacts.

Jotham had sold most of these and donated the proceeds to various children's charities. But he had retained most of the furnishings because they suited the building so well. Luckily, the house had been renovated to provide every modern comfort, including en suite bathrooms in all the spacious bedrooms.

There was one work of art that he did retain, and he stopped to admire the painting hung above the first landing of the ornate staircase. The first time

21

he saw it, he had been stunned.

Iago Visser had bought it twenty years ago, although the art databases all stated that its location was unknown. He said that it was one of his most precious possessions, and he admired the chiaroscuro – the use of strong contrast between light and dark. Jotham had seen photographic images of the painting, but never thought he would see the original. It was painted in 1620 by Avanzino Nucci and titled, *Peter's Conflict with Simon Magus*.

When Jotham was a parish priest, he completed a doctorate in theology. His research topic had been Simon Magus, the magician and cult leader who had been reviled by the early Apostles.

He had no idea in those days that the cult was still in existence. When he came to Rome to give a lecture on the subject, he never dreamed that he would become embroiled in a deadly conspiracy and his life would change forever. That was when his crusade began.

***

Jotham soon realised that he needed a partner, and Madena Sutcliffe was the perfect candidate. She had been an officer in the British Army, and she also had an economics degree and an MBA from Oxford. She worked by his side whenever he was on a mission, and was also his fitness advisor, security advisor and financial advisor.

The next morning, they had breakfast with Belle and then she played with her toys in the conservatory with them while they did their morning workout. Madena had state of the art fitness equipment set up there, and she had taught Jotham everything she knew about martial arts and combat. They worked hard to stay in top physical condition, and he was now much better prepared to face the physical challenges of his role. It was a stark contrast to the way he had once lived his life.

As well as caring for Belle and working out, they also continued to monitor the news, social media and any other resources that they could access. They were always searching around the world for any sign of the Simonian Sect or the Brotherhood. If they found something of interest, they would investigate further to see what they could discover.

Jotham was almost forty-three years old, and six feet tall with dark hair. Belle thought he looked very funny on the treadmill and laughed hysterically as he picked up speed. He pulled funny faces for her amusement but, at the same time, he flicked through news channels and watched the screen attached to the wall.

When his phone buzzed, he came to quick halt and turned off the machine.

"Who is it, Jotham?" asked Madena, who was on the rowing machine next to him.

His eyes widened when he looked at the phone. "I don't believe it," he said, and answered the call.

Chapter 5

Wiping the sweat from his brow, Jotham put the phone on speaker mode so that Madena could listen in. He kept his eyes fixed on little Belle, playing with her blocks on the conservatory floor.

"Jotham Fletcher, is that you, yes?" said a woman's voice.

He recognised the Italian accent straight away, and a knot tightened in his stomach. "Yes, that's right," he replied.

"It's Capitana Maria Rinaldi from the Caribinieri," she said. "And how are you these days?"

"I'm excellent thank you, Capitana, and how are you?" Jotham had met Maria Rinaldi on his visit to Rome when he first came face to face with the sect. She had been supportive when her superior, Leo Binocci, had suspected him of murder and chased him across Europe.

"I'm still working in Rome," she replied. "I've just returned to work after maternity leave. We have a little boy now."

"Congratulations, that is great news," he said. "Our little girl is almost one."

"Grazie, and I'm so pleased to hear about your family. But I'm afraid that I'm ringing with an update about Father Dominic, no?"

Jotham's breathing rate rose at the sound of that name. Father Dominic had been incarcerated in a hospital for the criminally insane in Rome, and the last time she had contacted him was to tell him that he had escaped. Fortunately, after committing more crimes, he had been caught and locked up again. But why was Maria phoning him now?

He first met Father Dominic in the Brotherhood's monastery outside Rome, and Jotham had experienced first-hand the lengths that he would go to in pursuit of the sect. He was responsible for more than one murder, but the law had caught up with him. After that first encounter, the Brotherhood had supposedly been disbanded.

But Jotham knew that the members were still at large, and he never stopped trying to track them down. Father Dominic had escaped custody twice, but surely the Italian police would not allow that to happen again.

He clenched his jaw. "I hope you don't have bad news for me."

She paused before answering. "I wanted to inform you that Father Dominic has recently been transferred to a hospice. He's dying from a brain tumour."

Jotham grabbed the handlebars of the treadmill. "You can't be serious," he said. "The man's too dangerous to be allowed out of a high security institution, even if he's ill. You know his reputation."

"Yes I do, but there's no need for you to be concerned."

Dominic had such a tall, powerful presence, it was hard to imagine him succumbing to a disease. "How do you know that's true?" asked Jotham.

"I've seen a medical report. I can assure you that he's harmless now, and he won't last more than a few more months. The hospice is in a remote location in Sardinia. No one could be in danger."

"Why not keep him in Rome?"

"The Catholic church had a hospice there that they felt would be suitable for him."

Jotham shook his head. "So once again, he's under the protection of the church."

He ended the call soon afterwards, but thoughts swirled in his brain all morning. Despite Maria's assurances, Father Dominic was no longer in a state prison, and that thought terrified him.

While Belle was eating her lunch, she delighted in picking up pieces of food in her dainty fingers and hurling them onto the floor. As Jotham watched over her, he thought about the man in black robes who fell to his death from the bell tower of the church of *Santa Francesca Romana*. That was three years ago in Rome.

The strange coincidence was that he died on the same spot where Simon Magus had died two thousand years earlier. The magician was levitating into the air in front of a crowd in the Roman Forum, but then fell to his death.

Jotham was to give a lecture the next morning about Simon Magus. Instead of that, he became a murder suspect - although that matter had been resolved long ago.

Since that moment, his life had taken a new course.

Little Belle reached out to her father and a feeling of joy washed over him. If only he could stay at home with her all the time, leading a safe and comfortable existence, and forget about his enemies.

But he knew that his quest would never end: not until the Simonian Sect and the Brotherhood were defeated. When he inherited Iago's fortune, he took that as a sign from God. His destiny was to hunt both criminal organisations down.

At least he had Madena by his side.

***

San Diego

The San Diego Worship Hall of the Holy Spear Pentecostal Church was a huge, modern edifice with an arched roof and a multi-coloured glass façade. Located just outside the metropolitan area, it attracted a large congregation from all over the city.

The only person inside the building at that moment was Pastor Silas Conrad, the head of the church. He was six feet tall and almost fifty years old, with grey flecks showing through his thick dark hair. Standing in front of the altar, he stared at the gigantic cross that covered the back screen. Made of wood and brass, it was a work of art that conveyed God's power and the stark simplicity of his message.

He knelt down, put his hands together and prayed aloud. "Lord, please give me the strength to face this new trial. I need your guidance. Help me to find a solution so that we can carry on with our work and continue to spread your message. The Holy Spear can heal us."

Taking a deep breath to calm himself, he knew that it was time to face the visitors who were waiting outside.

The first camera flashed as soon as he walked out the door. Silas blinked in response and he felt tears moisten his eyes. His wife, Veronica, was holding court in front of the journalists who were gathered to hear his announcement. He stood next to her and adjusted the microphone.

She turned and gave him a demure smile, and he marvelled at how well she could maintain her professional demeanour under pressure.

He cleared his throat and spoke. "Thank you, ladies and gentlemen, for coming here today at such short notice. For those who don't already know me, my name is Pastor Silas Conrad and I'm the head of The Holy Spear Pentecostal Church. We have ten separate branches along the Pacific Coast and Hawaii, but our centre of operations is right here in San Diego. I'm afraid that I have some bad news. I'm sorry to say that our organisation has been the victim of a cyberattack."

There was a collective stirring in response and one young reporter yelled out. "Pastor Conrad, how long have you known about this?"

Silas raised his hand to call for quiet, then waited for silence before continuing. "We only found out this morning. Hackers have sabotaged our

26

computer system and taken control of our network. Now they're demanding a ransom. I've contacted the FBI and we'll be endeavouring to resolve the situation as quickly as possible."

The message was met first with silence, then it seemed as if every journalist was on their feet demanding answers to questions that Pastor Conrad couldn't answer. Suddenly, the safety that the Holy Spear seemed to promise had vanished.

Chapter 6

The Peak District

Jotham read a story to Belle after lunch and took her for a stroll around the garden. Then he helped to settle her down for an afternoon nap, and she was soon fast asleep.

He joined Madena in the library and put the baby monitor on a side table. It was a large room lined with carved oak bookcases containing thousands of books but there were also desks with computers, and they had online access to libraries around the world. "Belle looks so tiny," he said, glancing at the screen as they continued to scan international news bulletins.

Madena was the first to spot an item of interest, and soon they were watching a recording of Silas Conrad's announcement.

"Mm, the Holy Spear Pentecostal Church," said Madena as she looked up the organisation's website. All they could find was a landing page that showed a black screen emblazoned with a white skull and crossbones, the traditional pirate symbol. The words underneath were in red font, dripping as if the message was written in blood. *This website is currently under siege.*

There was no menu and no way to access the rest of the site. "It would be so frustrating to wake up and find yourself locked out of your own computer system," said Jotham. "I wonder if it's just a regular gang of cybercriminals who are responsible? They say that large corporations are constantly repelling attacks these days."

"Let's see what we can find out," said Madena, her face brightening at the thought of a new challenge. "We should look into this a bit further."

They did some intensive research over the next hour. Jotham found out what he could about the church and its leader, Silas Conrad, while Madena hunted for information about cyberattacks.

They reviewed their findings over a cup of tea on the deck. "So, what did you find out?" asked Madena, stretching her shoulders.

"The Holy Spear Pentecostal Church is an independent evangelical church based in San Diego," said Jotham. "There are several branches down the west coast of America and Hawaii. It was established by Korey Conrad, who had a small congregation outside San Diego. His son Silas took over about twenty years ago and came up with the new name. The organisation has been growing ever since, and Silas broadcasts his Sunday sermon live to all of the

28

churches."

"Look at their motto," said Madena. "*The Holy Spear can heal us.*"

"Strange," said Jotham with a sneer.

"Could the Simonian Sect be behind the attack?"

Jotham raised his eyebrows. "Perhaps we ought to visit San Diego."

Madena nodded, just as they heard a sound emanating from the baby monitor. Belle was stirring in the cot, so they strolled into the nursery, gave her a round of hugs and changed her nappy.

"Did you find out anything interesting about cyberattacks?" asked Jotham as he combed Belle's hair.

"Yes I did," said Madena, pursing her lips. "But let's face it – neither of us is a computer expert. Do you think that we ought to ask Eugene to help us? Perhaps you could take him to the States and I'll stay home with Belle until you find out more."

"I must admit that I was thinking the same thing, but I'm reluctant to call him. He's so young - I don't want to expose him to any danger. I'd love him to work for us again, but he has such a bright future and he should be left alone to finish his degree."

Eugene Beaudreau was a brilliant young computer geek whom he had called on for help the previous year. They had been trying to find the source of a strange series of online messages, and Eugene had done a brilliant job. Not only that, but he had also helped to rescue Madena who had been kidnapped. He hadn't hesitated to put his own life at risk.

Anthony Gillam had heard of him through a relative, and until then Eugene had been a dropout who was wasting his significant talents. Jotham encouraged him to go back to university, and also offered to pay for his tuition and accommodation fees.

Eugene had been keen to work for them again, and with the growth of information technology and cybercrime, Jotham knew his skills were sure to be useful. But he didn't think it was fair to inflict their dangerous lifestyle on the young man. He promised to call Eugene if he were needed and encouraged him to return to his studies.

Now Eugene was back at university and, armed with a ferocious intelligence, he was excelling.

They had last seen Eugene at Belle's Christening celebrations. Because he had helped to save Madena and her unborn child, they had named their daughter after him. Jotham had pointed out that his surname was *Beaudreau* and *Beau* was the male form of *Belle*. They were all delighted with the decision.

"Even if Eugene is able to help us, perhaps I still ought to come with you," said Madena. "I really don't want you to go without me to back you up."

Jotham waved away her concerns. "Belle is still so young - it's really much better if you stay with her this time. This may all have nothing to do with the Simonian Sect."

"Do you promise to contact me if there's any sign of trouble? I'll be there straight away."

He wrapped his arm around her slender waist. "You're the best mother in the world," he said, leaning forward to kiss her tenderly.

***

San Diego

Silas Conrad had taken over his father's humble Pentecostal Church in the outskirts of San Diego and created a small empire. There was nothing humble about the Conrad mansion in a semi-rural development just outside San Diego. After twenty-fours hours, Silas Conrad and all his team at the Holy Spear Pentecostal Church were still locked out of their computers. All they could see on each screen was a white skull and crossbones. Below that were instructions, in tiny font, about how to transfer two million dollars in Bitcoin to the culprits.

Supervisory Special Agent Gary Zickgraf from the FBI had finally arrived. His dyed black hair was a perfect match to his black suit that draped loosely over his rotund body. After a cursory look around the office area, he talked to Silas and Veronica in the living room. "I'm afraid that Bitcoin is untraceable," he explained. "If you pay the ransom, chances are that you'll probably regain access to your system. But that's not certain – and there's no way that you'll ever see your money again."

"So what do you suggest we do?" asked Silas, his face wrinkled up in frustration.

"Officially, sir, I have to tell you that paying the ransom only encourages the criminals to strike again. The reality is that our own record of arresting cybercriminals is not encouraging – and our success rate in returning the extorted money is even worse. Our own intelligence is that most businesses don't take the risk of trusting us; they pay quietly and pass the problem to others. So I have to say pay the ransom, if you ever want your data back. I'm sorry about that - I'd love to be more help."

Veronica put her arm around Silas. "We might just have to do that, sweetie," she said.

"Tell me how big your organisation is, Pastor," said Zickgraf, exhaling as he plonked his generous backside into the biggest armchair.

"We have twelve churches altogether," replied Silas. He lowered his head and massaged his own forehead, suddenly feeling overwhelmed by the situation.

Veronica continued speaking for him. "This is our private home, but we also have our centre of operations in the south wing. Most of our employees work right here, and the other branches have just a handful of staff. Our entire computer network has been incapacitated."

"How many employees in all?"

Just over seventy, and there are thousands of followers who log in to seek guidance every day. Our Worship Hall is just two miles from here – it's similar to a cathedral, although we don't call it that. Silas does his Sunday morning sermon there every week, unless he's paying a visit to one of the branches.

Zickgraf scratched his face. "Can you find the money to pay the ransom?"

Silas looked despondent. "I can find it but our money comes from parishioner donations. How can I tell them that I've given their money to a gang of criminals?"

"I'll see what we can do," said Zickgraf, "but this sort of thing is happening every day now. I always say that it's the modern-day equivalent of stealing the milk money."

"A lot of milk money," said Veronica, patting her husband's shoulder.

Chapter 7

Bristol

Twenty-six-year-old Eugene Beaudreau adjusted his glasses and logged in to the university website to check his latest results.

Emily bent over and planted a kiss on his pale cheek as he pressed the icon. "I didn't tell you, but I already know my score," she said. " I came second, thanks to you."

"A man should be able to help his own girlfriend," he said, his eyes widening when he saw his grade.

"You're the best tutor in the world. Perhaps you should become a lecturer. Head of Computer Engineering at the University of Bristol."

"Or maybe Harvard or Oxford," he added without any hint of conceit. He was always surprised to find that he had done well.

Emily, a petite brunette, glanced at the screen. "Looks like you came first, once again. Maybe you should change your strategy? You're being too consistent and those extra subjects haven't done you any harm."

"I want to finish my degree in half the normal time so that I can work with the Fletchers."

"I know that," she said, pecking his other cheek. "And I have no doubt that you'll succeed – wherever you end up working."

Eugene thought again about Jotham and Madena, although he knew that he couldn't tell Emily about all his exploits the previous year. That had been the most exciting time of his life - and Jotham had said he would consider employing him if he returned to university and finished his studies.

Now he was beginning to wonder if that had just been a ploy to encourage him to turn his life around. He had been a brilliant school student but had opted out of university in his first year there. After that, he spent his days in front of his computer, becoming a self-taught hacker. His activities had only been for fun and he never engaged in anything illegal, but now he regretted the time he'd wasted.

At least he had mastered certain skills and, since then, had put them to better use, including his work helping Jotham Fletcher a year ago.

Now he was back at university and topping the class, exceeding his wildest expectations. He even had a girlfriend, a fellow student who thought that he was cute and funny. He thought that she was beautiful.

His phone chimed a loud peel of bells, and he fumbled in his bomber jacket to find it and answer the call. "Jotham," he exclaimed straight away. "It's gobsmackingly good to hear from you."

"Hello, Eugene," he replied. "How is everything?"

"Frighteningly good. But how's Belle? She must be almost one." He cast a glance at Emily and noticed her look of alarm.

"Yes, she's wonderful," said Jotham.

"That takes the biscuit. I can't wait to see her again. But what can I do for you today?"

Jotham's tone grew serious. "There's a job that I thought you may be able to help me with but only if you can spare the time. I don't want to interrupt your studies."

Eugene stood up, his words tumbling over one another as he spoke. "You know you can count on me. I have a two-week break starting right now and I want to help."

"That's good news. Anthony Gillam can collect you in the helicopter."

"I'm packing my bag right now," he replied, hugging Emily with excitement before ending the call.

After he put the phone down, she glared at him. "Eugene, this is your study vacation."

He gave her a high five in response. "My friend has a special project for me and I'll be gone for a few days. But don't worry, there'll still be plenty of time for study."

"I'll miss you," she said, pretending to pout.

"Me too."

"Do you know where you're going?"

"Jotham lives near Manchester, but that's all I can tell you. I'll be back before you know it."

***

Greece

The heat of the day began to ease just after sunset. The thickset man in

33

his early thirties walked towards the Abydos Taverna in the village of Dimitrios. All the lights were on and the tables were occupied by locals chatting about the day's gossip. Looking up, he could just make out the monastery of Saint Dimitrios, perched on the peak that towered over the village. The building was renowned but the remote location meant that there were few visitors.

He could hear conversations in the taverna, but all he could understand was the sound of his father's voice inside his head. "*You'll always be a failure, Goran. No matter what happens, you'll always be a disappointment to me.*" The harsh tones wouldn't go away, although his father had been dead for nearly ten years.

There was only one person who was alone, a man of about seventy perched at the bar. Perhaps he might be able to help him, and while they talked that would help the voice to go away. The bartender in front of him didn't look happy, and was pointing an accusatory finger at a long tab. He appeared to be telling him that the drink he was holding would be his last.

That gave Goran the perfect opportunity to introduce himself.

As the bartender served another customer, Goran walked up to the bar and sat on a shaky stool next to the man. "Are you having problems, my friend?" he asked in English.

"You have no idea," he replied gruffly.

Goran was relieved to find that he understood the language. "Can you speak much English?"

"Enough to get by. I learnt at school. It helps with the occasional tourist we have in the monastery – Saint Dimitrios, the building on top of the hill."

"I'd like to visit that. Do you work there?"

He lowered his head. "I used to - all my life until they sacked me today - at my age! Now I can't even afford to drown my sorrows. The owner here wants me to pay my tab and gambling debt. How am I meant to do that when I don't have a job?"

Goran looked sympathetic. "I'm sorry to hear that. Let me buy you a drink."

"Thank you, I'd like that very much." He waved to the bartender and spoke to him in Greek. "Ouzo. Ouzo for me and my friend, he's paying."

The bartender scowled and turned to Goran. "Are you sure? Let me see the money first."

"Sure," said the stranger, flashing his wallet. Then he looked at the old man. "My name's Goran Novak."

"I'm Draco Spiros."

"So you really worked at the monastery?"

Spiros grabbed the new drink and gulped it down. "That's right."

"Let me buy you another," said Goran, waving the order.

"All my life I worked there. And not only that, my family has worked there for more than a thousand years. We've played an important part in the history of that place."

Goran shook his head. "An amazing story. I'm touring Greece looking for historical objects. My boss is a dealer in Budapest."

"So you're from Hungary. Who do you work for?"

"A very wealthy man. One of the wealthiest in the country."

His face lit up. "I see. Do you know there are laws about exporting ancient objects?"

Goran leaned close to his ear. "I work outside the law, and I'm sure that you're just like me."

Spiros squinted and gave the matter some thought. "I know about an artefact. You've come to the right man."

"Is it in the monastery? There's an old legend."

He answered with a low voice. "My family passed on the knowledge about the location, and it's worth more than you could imagine. You wouldn't believe how much. Our role was to keep it hidden, to protect it."

Goran could not believe his luck. "Does anyone else know about it?"

"No one else knows, there are only rumours. But my wife left me decades ago and I don't have any children. Now they've kicked me out of the job I had all my life."

"So what do you need?"

Spiros locked eyes with him. "I need to fund my retirement."

"Sell it to me and you can have what you want," said Goran. "Believe me, your future will be changed, and it will be our secret."

A look of sublime contentment washed over the Greek man's face. "It's lucky that you're young and strong, because two men are needed to retrieve it."

"I have tools in my backpack. Can we go there in the dark?"

"Yes, that's the best way, so that we have cover."

"Then finish your drink and let's go."

Chapter 8

Bristol and The Peak District

Jotham had purchased a new Bell 49 light twin helicopter the previous year after Anthony Gillam obtained his helicopter licence. It had proven to be very useful for short flights.

Anthony took less than an hour to fly the helicopter to Bristol to collect Eugene Beaudreau. He climbed aboard with an enthusiastic smile. "Great to see you again, old buddy," he said, settling into one of the red leather seats. "Thanks for picking me up. I could get used to this, as I always say."

"It's good to see you again, Eugene. Make sure you do up your belt."

"How's my favourite girl? I haven't seen her since she was two months old."

"Belle is gorgeous. She looks so much like Madena and she's crazy about me."

"When are you going to have your own family?" asked Eugene.

"As soon as I find the right woman."

"I'm sure you're working hard at that. I've got a girlfriend now. She's in my year and we study together."

"I bet you do."

They lifted off and Eugene gazed out the window admiring the landscape. But after thirty minutes, he grabbed a paper bag from the side pocket of the seat. "All these vibrations," he yelled over the noise of the blades. "I'm feeling a bit green around the gills. That happens every time I get in this thing."

Anthony turned his head. "It affects everyone, don't worry about it," he shouted.

They landed at the airstrip and Felix Young was waiting for them. He was delighted to see Eugene again, and whisked him back to the estate in the Mercedes.

As soon as he saw Belle, he ran towards her and she reached out her arms almost as if she could remember him. "Belle, you're beautiful, I'm in love," he said, lifting her high in the air. She responded with squeals of delight.

"Thank you so much for coming," said Jotham, shaking his hand.

"It's gobsmackingly great to be back. I was really chuffed to hear from you."

"Tell me how well you're doing," said Madena, giving him a hug.

36

"I've been aceing every subject," he replied, and opened the photo album on his smartphone. "This is Emily."

"She looks like a stunner."

"She is, and she's smart too."

Cynthia Young had a hearty lunch prepared for his arrival. "Now, tell me about the job," he said while he ate dessert, bouncing Belle on his knee.

Jotham locked eyes with him. "There's been a ransomware attack on the Holy Spear Pentecostal Church, a big evangelical church based in San Diego."

"*The* San Diego?"

"That's the one. I want the two of us to fly there and see if we can find out who is behind it. Hopefully, we might be able to unlock their system for them."

"So you think the sect might be responsible?"

"It's a possibility. What's your professional opinion?"

Eugene massaged his chin. "Those attacks are often random. Criminals produce the malware, and then someone is careless and allows it to get into a computer network. The next thing you know, they see the telltale screen with a ransom demand. And they always want payment in Bitcoin or the equivalent. Not long ago, our health system was attacked and hundreds of peoples lives were put at risk."

"So do you think that's what happened in this case - just a random attack?"

"Not necessarily. But I'll know more when I can see their computer system. The police don't have a clue what to do about it, and people often end up paying the ransom. The sad fact is that the police can't afford to pay for the best people. It's the criminal gangs with the deepest pockets."

"Well," said Jotham, "you're the best there is and my pockets are mercifully deep. Do you think you could help?"

"I'll give it my best shot. Have you told the people in charge of the church that we're coming?"

"I want to surprise them. It's a long flight there; we need to do it in two legs. On our way over, I plan to phone and say that we might be able to assist them."

"Sounds good. So when do we leave?"

"Straight after dinner. Anthony wanted some time to prepare the plane."

"And we need to make some travel arrangements," added Madena. "A transatlantic flight and then across to the Pacific coast will really test Anthony

37

and the plane."

"That's wicked," said Eugene. "I love Cynthia's cooking, and I can play with Belle until then."

***

Greece

The ascent began just outside the village. Though Spiros was over seventy and had arthritis in his knees, Goran Novak was surprised by the speed at which he led him up the steep, narrow track. Halfway up, he turned off into an area of dense bush. "There are caves here, quite a few of them," he said. Towering above them, he could make out a few dim lights in some of the monastery windows.

Goran was pleased that they both had a torch or they would have been walking in almost total darkness. He trod carefully, knowing that one small mistake could see him fall off the edge of the cliff and probably to his death.

Spiros strode with confidence and knew precisely where he was headed. He stopped beside a dense stand of bushes, and pushed some branches aside to reveal the opening to a cave.

"Here we are. There are about ten caves around here, but this is the one we want. No one else knows about it."

"You can tell me about the object now," replied Goran, beginning to wonder if the old man had lured him here to rob him. He snapped a thin branch off the shrub next to him, just in case he needed to defend himself.

"All in good time," said Spiros.

"So there's some truth to the old legend?"

The old man didn't reply.

They both crawled through a narrow tunnel a metre long. After taking a few steps inside, he found that the small cave was about one and a half metres in height. They both had to bend right over and Spiros, who was short and fat, found it a struggle. "This is killing my knees," he said.

They were in darkness, apart from the narrow shafts of light cast by their torches. Goran shone the beam around and saw that a pile of small boulders blocked the way ahead. "We've got no hope of going any further," he said.

"Don't worry," replied Spiros. "That's why we need two men. The object is buried under that lot. I hope you had a good dinner, you're going to need plenty of energy."

That reminded Goran of the fact that he hadn't eaten since lunchtime. "Have you ever seen it?" he asked.

"Never, but my father told me where it was buried, and his father told him. It's tiny, but more powerful than you could possibly imagine. My family has guarded it for a thousand years. All through the generations, passed on from father to son. That's why we stayed in this godforsaken village and worked in the monastery. We regarded it as our duty."

Goran gulped. He knew that this could be the chance of a lifetime. After tonight, the voice in his head might be stilled forever. He would prove his father wrong once and for all. "Let's get to work, then," he said.

They lifted most of the boulders together, as they were almost too heavy for one man. Goran was thickset with rippling muscles, the result of swimming training when he was a boy. In recent years he had become an expert in Baranta. That was a new form of martial arts in Hungary that involved traditional weapons, including whips and axes, and he knew that one day, those skills would come in very handy.

Spiros glared at him every time they lifted a rock and tossed it out of the way. Goran shone the beam in his face, and his sinister look convinced him that he was planning something. "This is going to take a couple of hours," he said.

Spiros wiped the sweat from his forehead. "You're lucky to be so young and strong. Think how I feel."

"So, tell me, did you ever want to have children?"

"My wife left after a couple of years, and that was the end of that. I'm too much of a loner."

"But what about your family's heritage?"

"A thousand years of tradition ends with me. All I care about is making sure that I have some money for my old age."

"How old are you?"

"Seventy-two. My father died when he was fifty, after driving my mother to an early grave."

The rock pile was growing smaller and a few minutes later they saw bare earth. Spiros pulled out a pocketknife.

"I've got a trowel in my backpack," said Goran.

After an hour of cautious digging, Spiros yelped. "That's it, we've done it," he gasped. A few minutes later, they uncovered and lifted out a small wooden box about eighteen centimetres long, devoid of decoration and grey with age. The old man dusted the surface, then pushed the simple iron latch and opened it.

Chapter 9

Goran's heart thumped as he shone the torch inside the box. There was a piece of iron with a sharp point that resembled the tip of an arrow. "Is this what we've been working hours to retrieve?"

Spiros was breathing heavily. "Believe me, it has heavenly power," he said.

"Is it worth dying over?"

"Several people in my family have died trying to protect it over the centuries. The Turks came here as conquerors but my ancestors refused to say where the treasure was hidden."

Spiros touched the object with the tip of his finger.

Energy surged through his body like an electric shock, and the throb in his arthritic knees vanished. He clutched his forehead and lowered his eyes, letting out a deep sigh.

Then he looked up with his face twisted in panic. "I've made a terrible mistake. I shouldn't have brought you here."

"Is this the Holy Spear?"

"You can't just sell it to the highest bidder. Go away, and leave me alone. Forget that you ever saw it."

"No way, you old fool," replied Goran. He grabbed the box and stood up, crouching over because of the low height. "This belongs to me now."

Spiros turned and wrapped his hands around a boulder, unseen in the darkness. With the agility of a much younger man, he whiplashed around and tried to strike him.

He hadn't counted on Goran's speed and strength. The young man used his arm to deflect the blow then punched Spiros in the throat. It was enough force to cut off the blood supply and knock him out. He collapsed onto the hard ground.

Goran gave him one swift and vicious kick to the head. Then he grasped his neck and twisted it as if he was turning a valve.

Spiros was dead, his mouth agape as if in shock at his own mortality.

Goran dragged his body to the far corner of the cave. Working hard for the next two hours, he covered it with the boulders they had just moved. His arms ached and his hands were bleeding by the time he finished, but the body was hidden.

He doubted that anyone would miss Draco Spiros.

41

Goran picked up the box and stuffed it in his backpack. Leaving the cave, he followed the narrow track that led back to the village.

***

Vancouver

The shrill ringtone woke John Pedersen from a deep sleep. He reached out to pick up his phone from the bedside table, and was surprised to see that it was almost one o'clock in the morning. He recognised the number and sat bolt upright as he pressed the answer button. "Hello, John Pedersen here," he said, slowly stirring to life and trying to add some dignity to his voice.

"Pedersen, I have some news for you." He recognised the Leader's voice straight away. The old man was probably calling from his new retreat that was rumoured to be somewhere in France.

"Yes, my Lord?" he asked, hoping that he was about to hear some good news.

"Listen carefully. I'm sending someone to come and work with you. A man from Poland, who was forced to leave his previous position at short notice, unfortunately."

Another person in the apartment was the last thing that Pedersen wanted. "What's his name, my Lord?" he asked.

"Walter Kowalski. Don't worry, he speaks fluent English. He was a Professor in the Faculty of Theology at the University of Krakow."

Pedersen was not impressed. "I don't think that I'd have any use for someone like that."

"I'm sure you'll find something for him to do. I'm afraid he outwore his usefulness, and anyway, he was close to retirement age. He'll be staying with you for a while. Just tell him to keep a low profile - and keep him occupied. When I find a more permanent position for him, I'll let you know."

John gulped. "When will he arrive, my Lord?"

"He caught a train to Frankfurt and flew straight to Vancouver. His flight arrived an hour ago so you can expect him at any moment. I know I can count on you."

John was almost shaking with fury. He and Zykov shared a small two-bedroom apartment, and he didn't need an ex-academic with a haughty attitude moving in with them. But the Leader always expected his orders to be followed without question. "I'll try my best," he said, just as the Leader abruptly cut off the call.

He woke Kostya Zykov and told him the bad news. They were both waiting in the living room when, half an hour later, the entrance intercom rang.

Pedersen pressed the talk button. "You better come up," he said brusquely.

When they opened the door to Kowalski, he strode in and gave them both a firm handshake. "How do you do, I'm pleased to meet you," he said with an ingratiating smile.

"I'm afraid that we've only just heard you were coming," said Pedersen. "Luckily, there's a spare bed in Zykov's room. You can sleep there."

Kowalski sneered. "That will do for tonight, John, but after that I think you better move in with Zykov. I'm grateful for everything you've achieved here so far, but tomorrow you can hand the reigns over to me. I know my unexpected arrival must have come as a shock to you, but I'm sure we'll get on very well."

Pedersen had to admit that the man had plenty of nerve. "I'm sure we'll get on like a house on fire," he replied. "But let's get one thing straight, Professor Kawasaki, or whatever your name is. I'm in charge around here, and you won't be taking over anything except the spare stretcher bed. We're working on some very complex IT projects that require technical expertise. You'll be sharing with Zykov until we can move you on somewhere else."

Kowalski narrowed his eyes to thin slits. "We'll talk more in the morning," he said. Then he turned to Zykov. "Are you Russian?"

Kostya took a step towards him. "Yes, is that a problem for you?"

"No, not at all," he replied with a tight voice. "It's been a long night, I really should get some sleep."

**

The Peak District

Madena was talking to Jotham in their bedroom as he rubbed her shoulders. "I'm pleased to be staying home with Belle," she said, "but our work's important and I want to be by your side."

"This may have nothing to do with the sect at all," he replied. "And it's great to have Eugene's input."

"It sure is, but promise me that you'll call if there's any sign of trouble."

Jotham nodded. "I'll miss you."

"I'll continue my research. You never know what might turn up."

They made love in the enormous four-poster bed, both aware that there was always the possibility that he would not return. Afterwards, they held each close and Jotham ran his fingers through her wavy hair. "I know you'll never forget your first family," she whispered.

"You and Belle are everything to me, but Jane and William are always deep in my heart."

"And that's the way it should be," she said, gently kissing him.

Although he didn't discover the truth until three years afterwards, Jotham's first wife and baby had been killed by the Brotherhood. He thought at the time that a random hit-and-run driver caused the accident when he was a parish priest in Canberra, Australia's capital city. He had never heard of the sect or the Brotherhood, but he was completing a doctoral thesis on the topic of Simon Magus, a character mentioned briefly in the Bible. Three years later, he was invited to give a talk in Rome on that subject, and his life changed forever.

That was when he learned about the Brotherhood, and discovered that they had tried to kill him because they suspected that he was in the Simonian Sect. He was the intended victim, but instead his wife and baby had been killed when the car exploded into flames.

Straight after dinner, Anthony Gillam left to prepare the plane. Before driving to the airstrip, Jotham walked over to the tiny chapel just twenty metres from the house. The original church burnt down in 1840 when there was a small village nearby. The replacement was built in 1845, so it was much newer than the house. When he had first seen it, he was amazed at the remarkable resemblance to his own parish church in Canberra, which had also been built in 1845 and was the first church built in the region.

Whenever he saw the chapel, it reminded him of his former home in Australia and the church where his first wife and child were buried in the small graveyard. He prayed that God would watch over Madena and Belle while he was away, and that he, Eugene and Anthony would return safely. Once his life had been devoted to watching over his parish, but now he had a new vocation. His new life was calling him into danger to protect a very different congregation to the one he had served in Canberra.

Chapter 10

A few minutes later, Jotham kissed Belle and Madena good-bye and he watched them disappearing from view as Felix drove away. As they sped along the narrow roads to the airfield, he remained alert for any signs of danger and discussed the travel plans with Eugene. "We'll have to stop at Newfoundland en route to refuel," he explained. "Anthony will need some rest to break up the flight."

"Wow, I never thought I'd be visiting Newfoundland," he replied. "But I guess it's the most direct route, as the crow flies."

"Precisely. Meanwhile, we can try to find out a bit more about Pastor Conrad and his organisation.

"I can look into whether there are reports of any similar attacks on any other churches."

"Good idea, though I haven't heard about any. It's great to have you with me, Eugene."

Anthony Gillam had the plane ready when they arrived, and a few minutes later they were airborne. Eugene gazed at the sunset as they flew over the beautiful landscape of the Peak District.

"Perhaps I'll be back home in just a few days," said Jotham.

"Why is it called the *Holy Spear Pentecostal Church*?" asked Eugene, eating some cookies he'd found in the galley. "I know the meaning of *Pentecostal*, but what's the Holy Spear?"

"I'm glad you asked," said Jotham. "When Jesus was crucified, a Roman soldier used a spear or lance to pierce his side to see if he were still alive. Have you heard of that?"

"Yes, I have," he replied. "Now I remember."

"Madena and I did some research recently. No one knows for sure, but there are stories about what might have happened to the weapon. At the end of the sixth century, the Holy Spear was supposedly in Jerusalem. In AD 615, that object was captured by the Persians and fell into the hands of pagans. The pointy tip had broken off, but both parts were given to a man who took them to Constantinople."

"Now called Istanbul."

Jotham nodded. "Correct. The tip was deposited at Saint Sophia Cathedral. But in 1244 it was presented to Saint Louis and placed in Saint Chapelle. That's the royal chapel used by the kings of France. During the

French Revolution it was moved to the Bibliotheque Nationale, but then it disappeared."

"So it could be anywhere," said Eugene.

"The shaft of the spear remained in Constantinople and was seen there, but fell into the hands of the Turks in 1492. The Sultan sent it to Rome as a gift to the Pope, and it's preserved under the Dome of Saint Peter's Basilica."

"But what about the tip? Was that last seen in France?"

There are several claimants, and it could be any of them, or none of them. One is in a tiny church carved out of stone in Armenia. Another one is preserved with the imperial insignia in Vienna. There's a third one preserved in Krakow, and that's a strange coincidence. Madena and I were recently there on a mission, looking for a member of the sect who worked at the university. The man had the honorary title of the *Guardian of the Spear*. But that has no relationship to this incident, as far as I can make out."

Eugene opened his eyes wide. "So you heard about the cyberattack later?"

"Yes, but that's why we jumped on the incident so quickly, when we heard the name of the church. I forgot to mention, there's also a legend that the genuine tip of Holy Spear is hidden somewhere beneath the hilltop monastery of Saint Dimitrios in Greece.

***

Anthony Gillam stopped at Gander International Airport in Newfoundland and they caught a few hours sleep at a nearby hotel. They headed off early the next morning and, when they were halfway to San Diego, Jotham took out his phone.

"It's eight o'clock in the morning there now, so time to contact Silas Conrad," he said as he finished a cup of coffee.

"Have you got his direct phone number?" asked Eugene.

"Only the office number."

Eugene raised his hand. "Let me find it for you." He picked up his smartphone and set to work, busily pressing the keyboard. Two minutes later, he grinned. "Here's his private mobile number," he said, sending it in a text message.

Jotham was stunned. "Thanks Eugene, that's very clever of you."

He dialled the number and heard the crisp Californian accent. "Hello, this is Silas Conrad, how can I help you?"

"Good morning, this is Jotham Fletcher," he replied. "I'm sorry to disturb you, but I've heard about your current problem on the news and I might be able to help you."

The man paused before answering. "You're not the person responsible, are you?" he said with more than a hint of suspicion in his voice. "Or perhaps a journalist?"

Jotham spoke firmly. "No, certainly not. I can assure you that my intentions are honest."

Silas softened. "What do you mean by help?" he asked.

"I'm a wealthy businessman. At the moment I'm flying to San Diego with my computer expert who may be able to find a solution. We don't want anything in return."

"That's very kind of you."

Jotham could still detect wariness in his voice, as if such an offer was too good to be true. It was time to come in for the kill. "I'm an Anglican priest originally from Australia, so you can rest assured that we can be trusted. We'd be pleased to help."

"I'd be grateful. So you're a believer?

"I certainly am."

"Then I'm sure that God must have sent you."

"We'll be arriving this afternoon," said Jotham, "and we'll come straight to your office."

**

Sardinia

Sister Alicia always wore a modern white habit with mid-calf hemline and short white veil. She was in charge of the Convent of the Immaculate Conception, just outside the village of Mare in Sardinia. It was a haven of peace surrounded by rolling hills, but the small hospice had never had a patient like Father Dominic before. He was sent to them from a hospital for the criminally insane in Rome.

Alicia was told to make sure he didn't escape so his room was always kept locked. But even if he did manage to break out, in his condition he would not get far. Over the last few weeks he had become increasingly weak and tired and his balance was poor. That meant he needed to spend his days resting.

She knocked once before unlocking his door. "Good morning Father Dominic, and how are we feeling this morning?"

"Just the same as yesterday, Sister Alicia. My whole body is aching." He was propped up in an armchair. Now that he was in the hospice, he was allowed to wear his long black cassock instead of a prison uniform. It had once been a perfect fit for his tall, powerful frame but now he was thin and there were loose folds of fabric.

"I'll get you something for that, and then we'll pray together."

"I should be out of here, serving the Lord. All my life I worked for one cause, and now my fear is that I've been a failure."

"You were a very determined man, Father, from what I hear. Just be grateful that you're still alive. Now is the time for you to prepare for the final phase of your journey."

"I tried my best, but it wasn't enough." His eyes closed as if he was falling asleep. "Our enemies are all around us, but perhaps God will perform a miracle and cure me."

"I have a surprise for you, to cheer you up," she said. "You have a visitor, and we expect him to arrive later this morning."

Dominic opened his eyes. "Who is it?"

"Father Benjamin is coming from Rome. The Vatican wants him to help care for you and give you counsel."

Dominic's eyes darted from side to side, but he maintained a steady composure and didn't speak. Sister Alicia wondered if he understood what she told him, or if the effects of the disease were clouding his thoughts.

Chapter 11

Father Benjamin drove through the open gate of the convent and parked the small car that he had borrowed for the duration of his stay. He was dressed in a black suit and priest's collar, and Sister Alicia greeted him with a warm smile. Women were always impressed with his tall, slim build and kind demeanour. His mother told him that he had the face of an angel.

She ushered him into Dominic's room. "Here's Father Benjamin," she said as if the patient were a child. "I'm sure you'll like him very much."

"I'm honoured to meet you, Father Dominic," he said with a gentle voice. "I've worked at the Vatican for many years"

"I'm pleased to meet you, Father Benjamin," replied Dominic.

"I'll leave you two alone," said the sister, handing Benjamin a key to the room. "Let me know if you need anything. I'll be in my office."

She walked out and locked the door. Benjamin sat down and gazed at Dominic as if he was an insect under a microscope. "My family used to bring me to this area for vacations when I was a child."

"Where did you grow up?"

"In Milan, but I studied and then worked for several years in America. I've heard so much about you from our few remaining friends in the Vatican, though always in the strictest confidence. They can't openly support a body with extreme methods, but they understand the need for action to preserve the Church. Your most senior colleague there asked me to be with you now in your time of trial and make sure that you were comfortable. I'll be staying here in the Convent."

"You must be ambitious if you were in the Vatican." Dominic tried to adopt his most charming, honey-toned voice, although that effort made him feel more fatigued.

"Not everyone who works for the Vatican is ambitious. Our Pope is only concerned with doing good in the world. I've worked in a policy role there for many years."

He narrowed his eyes. "I know why you've been sent here," he said, and followed that with a cough.

"There's no need to tire yourself, Father Dominic. We have plenty of time to get to know each other."

Dominic leaned forward in his seat. "Have you been sent here to replace me as head of the Brotherhood? While there's breath in my body I'm determined to complete my mission."

"I've been sent to help you through the final stage of your earthly life."

"Has the Vatican already chosen you?"

Benjamin eyeballed him. "I know that would be a very challenging role."

"Only I know how difficult. But unless there's a miracle then my life will soon ebb away. I need to pass on my skills to a new person."

"That's very good of you, Dominic. The work of the Brotherhood needs to continue, even after both of us are dead."

"My dream was to overcome and destroy the Simonian Sect, but now that goal seems as far away as ever. For two thousand years they managed to survive in secret, and their goal has always been to destroy the Church. They haven't just infiltrated the Catholic Church, but every branch of Christianity, including Protestant and Orthodox branches. We have to root them out wherever they are."

Father Benjamin adopted his standard look of kindness and serenity, one that he had mastered to a state of perfection. "They would have succeeded by now if it were not for you. The church owes you a great deal." He reached out and put his hand on the older man's arm. Dominic nodded and his breathing rate slowed, as if the hand of Jesus had touched him.

Weariness overwhelmed him and he closed his eyes.

***

San Diego

After landing in San Diego, Jotham and Eugene left Anthony Gillam at the airport to look after the plane and get some rest after the journey. An Audi sedan was waiting there for them, with the keys on the bonnet as instructed. Jotham set up the satnav system and soon they were driving through the heart of the city.

"San Diego," said Eugene, looking in all directions. "Cal-i-forn-i-a. I always wanted to see this place."

"Maybe you could get a job here one day, or further north in Silicon Valley."

"That would be cool, but only if I can't work for you."

"Just remember to keep all your options open," he said, hoping that he

50

had really done the right thing by bringing him here.

"I will," he replied with a sigh.

They headed north, out of the metropolitan area and into the semi-rural fringe. "The Holy Spear Pentecostal Church should be just up ahead. All their branches have a church, but this is their main one."

"Are we meeting Silas Conrad there?"

"We're going to his house, two miles away. That's where they have their office."

Jotham stopped to have a quick look at the church. The sign at the front said:

San Diego Worship Hall
Holy Spear Pentecostal Church
Everyone welcome

Below that was their motto: *The Holy Spear can heal us*

That is something," said Eugene at the sight of the huge arched structure with a multi-coloured glass façade. "That looks like a stained glass window."

"Yes, it's impressive, but not too ostentatious," said Jotham.

"It's beautiful. Can you see the spear?"

Jotham squinted in the sunlight. Sure enough, the shape of an enormous spear could be made out in the glass, extending down its entire length. "I'm afraid I find that rather disturbing," he said.

Eugene nodded. "Yes, so do I. Let's get going."

Jotham sped on, and they had no trouble finding the house further down the road. It was a stunning contemporary mansion clad with timber panels and cream stucco, set on a five-acre block. The immaculate front garden had a central water feature, and there was a small parking lot along the side, surrounded by a hedge.

"Now that is ostentatious," said Eugene.

The building had a central section that was the size of large house, and two separate wings on either side. They were connected by two glass-enclosed walkways on the ground level, and they saw a young woman with a folder walking towards the one on the right.

"I want a house like this when I grow up," said Eugene.

"Perhaps you could start your own church," said Jotham.

They parked and strolled past the manicured lawn. After ringing the doorbell, they were surprised when Silas Conrad answered the door himself.

Almost fifty years old and the same height as Jotham, he was buttoning his shirt and his curly hair was wet.

"Hello, are you Jotham Fletcher?" he asked.

"I certainly am, and this is my colleague, Eugene Beaudreau."

"The computer expert. An honour to meet you." His eyes sparkled as he gave them a warm smile.

"An honour to meet you, Pastor Conrad," said Eugene.

They shook hands. "Please call me Silas. Do come in. Excuse my appearance, I've just had a shower after a workout."

Jotham thought that he seemed charming, the sort of person to whom others would gravitate.

The vast entrance hall was artfully simple. "This is my humble home," said Silas. "Our office space, where all the staff work, is in the south wing. Our private living space is in the north wing. Right here on this level we have our reception area and library and, upstairs, my wife and I have our own offices."

"That all sounds very well thought out," said Jotham.

Silas invited them to sit on a huge sofa and he sat opposite in an armchair. "I'm the Director of the Holy Spear Pentecostal Church, as you know. I really appreciate your offer of help. With our computer system locked up, things have been extremely difficult. We can't access our files and financial records, or our personnel and parishioner records. Even our diaries. We're completely dependent on technology and online interaction."

"What have the police said?" asked Jotham.

"I'm afraid they haven't been able to help me at all. First they tell me not to pay the ransom because I'll be giving money to criminals, but in the next breath they tell me I have no other choice."

"That's where we come in," said Eugene.

"My apologies, I've been doing all the talking. Tell me about yourselves."

Chapter 12

Jotham smiled and locked eyes with Silas. He knew this was the moment when he really needed to sound convincing. "Eugene is my computer expert, and if anyone can help you, he can. I'm very concerned about the increase in cybercrime, so when I read about your church in the news, I wanted to help.

"Do you live in the United Kingdom?"

"I'm an Anglican priest from Australia, but I've been living there after coming into an inheritance."

"Whereabouts?"

"In Cornwall," said Jotham, with a pang of guilt about lying to a fellow priest.

"At the furthest point, near Land's End," added Eugene for extra colour.

"I see." Silas raised his eyebrows as if he was dubious, but Jotham could tell that he trusted them. His face relaxed. "I was intending to pay the ransom, as much as possible from my own funds so that the church wouldn't be disadvantaged. Then I received your call."

"I just hope we can help you," said Jotham.

A slim, attractive woman with short blonde hair walked in, and Silas stood up. "Here's Veronica," he said. "Jotham and Eugene, I'd like you to meet my wife."

"How do you do? Very pleased to meet you," she said, shaking their hands. She was in her early forties, with subtle makeup and dressed in a smart skirt and blouse. "I'm the Manager of Youth Education, as well as being Deputy Director of the church."

"And she does a wonderful job," said Silas. "I don't know what I'd do without her."

"Thanks for your offer of help," she said, "although I must admit that I'm feeling nervous about all this."

"Don't worry about a thing," said Eugene. "Just put me in front of a computer. I have to warn you, though, that if I can't help you, then there'll be no alternative other than to pay the ransom, or else abandon your current system and start again from scratch."

Veronica frowned. "Are you sure what you're doing is safe?"

"Yes, don't worry about that," he replied.

"This been has been a terrible blow. Did Silas tell you that every week he broadcasts his sermon online to all our churches? With no computer system, that's out of the question. And all his sermons over the years are stored in there. He's worked so hard to make the Holy Spear Church a success."

Silas turned to Eugene. "Why don't we go to my office? You can work in peace there."

"Sounds good," he replied.

They led the two guests upstairs and into a huge office. It was the perfect ultra-modern office space, with white sofas, mood lighting, a sleek wooden desk and a chrome and metal bookcase that covered one wall. Books related to Silas's work crowded the shelves. "Veronica did the interior design, and from my desk there's a lovely view of the garden and the hills in the distance."

Eugene sat in the office chair and stretched out but then sat upright and examined the computer. "So is this connected to the rest of the system?"

"It certainly is, unfortunately. All our computers are on a single network."

Eugene raised his hand. "Leave it to me but give me a couple of hours."

"Would you like some coffee and cookies?" asked Veronica.

"Yes please," he replied. "You can read my mind."

"Coming right up," she said with a smile.

She strolled out of the office as Silas turned to Jotham. "Will you be helping Eugene in here?"

"No, he needs peace and quiet. His work involves intense, focused concentration."

"Then why don't I show you around our office area and after that I'd like you to meet my father and brother."

"I'd be delighted." Jotham was pleased to have the chance to see if there was anyone who looked suspicious.

He turned to glance at Eugene as they walked out of the room. He had removed his glasses and appeared to be hypnotised by the skull and crossbones symbol on the computer screen. Then his professional skill kicked in and he was already hard at work tapping the keyboard.

***

The open-plan office area occupied both levels of the south wing. Silas introduced Jotham to some of his staff, who seemed polite and friendly. "We try to provide job opportunities for young people, both college graduates and others from a disadvantaged background. There are also quite a few senior citizens here who often turn out to be our best employees."

Jotham scanned the scene, searching for any sign of unusual behaviour but there was nothing that attracted his attention. It seemed like a happy and well-run workplace, although it was strange to see so many computers turned off and people working with pens and paper or small hand-held devices.

As they walked back to the reception area, he turned to his host. "Is it possible that any of your staff could be involved?"

"You sound like the police," replied Silas. "No, I'd be astonished if anyone here were to blame.

Jotham nodded. "I read that your father was the one who founded the church."

"Yes, right here in San Diego. It was just a small congregation then, on the spot where we've built the Worship Hall. He had a healing ministry in those days."

"Did your father choose the name?"

"No, that was our idea. I took over from Dad twenty years ago. Veronica read a book about the Holy Spear and it was her suggestion. I believe that God whispered into our ears and inspired us. We changed the name to the *Holy Spear Pentecostal Church*. The Holy Spear then became a focal point of our beliefs."

Silas sounded so proud of his achievements, but Jotham felt a chill down his spine as he listened to his strange views. "Your church expanded after that?" he asked.

"Yes but I could never have done it without Veronica. The growth has been exponential since then, and now there are twelve churches down the west coast, plus Alaska and Hawaii. Korey continued his healing ministry but he tried to heal in the name of the Holy Spear. That stopped when he became ill and couldn't heal himself."

"That's very sad," said Jotham.

"Yes, but he has faith that one day he'll be cured."

"How is your father now?"

He shook his head. "Not good. He's in a wheelchair and almost completely blind. He lives with us and my younger brother, Noah, is his carer. They've always been close. Do you have a family, Jotham?"

"I'm married with a baby girl," he replied, flashing a photo on his

55

smartphone. "This is Belle."

He gave a warm smile. "She's gorgeous."

"And you, Silas?"

"My son and daughter are at college back East. They adore Veronica." Silas Conrad seemed like the perfect family man and dedicated pastor, but there was something about him that made Jotham feel uneasy.

***

Sardinia

Father Benjamin returned to Father Dominic's room early the next morning. "How are feeling this morning?" he asked. "Can I get anything for you, perhaps a cup of tea?" The patient was already sitting in the armchair, propped up with pillows.

Dominic stared straight at him and tried to sit upright. "How old are you?" he asked.

Benjamin smiled, wondering what game he was playing. "Forty-nine."

"And I suppose you're in excellent health, unlike me."

"Yes, I've always worked hard to maintain my fitness."

"Good, you're going to need it. I was a great athlete in my younger days, and much younger than you when I became head of the Brotherhood." He slumped back in the chair, exhausted.

"Don't tire yourself, Dominic. You need to preserve your energy."

He waved his fist. "I don't have time to worry about that. Did you know that I've been in the Brotherhood for most of my adult life? I was a parish priest for just two years. Since then my only goal was to find the Simonian Sect."

Benjamin patted his arm. "Perhaps we should talk about a new approach for the future."

Dominic clenched his teeth. "We don't need a new approach. I've done unpleasant tasks that no one else has wanted to do, terrible deeds, but we're fighting a determined enemy."

Benjamin maintained his calm demeanour. "Don't upset yourself, Father Dominic. I want the same as you: to wipe the sect from the face of the Earth."

"We also have another enemy."

"What do you mean?" he asked.

"Jotham Fletcher."

Benjamin paused before answering. "Yes, while I was in the Vatican, I heard about him."

"At first we were sure that he was in the sect, but I was wrong. He also wants to stop the sect but he wants to take the honour away from me - my lifelong goal. It's because of him that they locked me in that prison. Without him, I'd be free."

Benjamin leant over and put both hands on Dominic's shoulders. "If God is with us, then we can do anything. We can overcome our enemies with love."

Dominic shook with barely suppressed fury. "Yes, that's certainly a new approach. You're a fool! Despite my weakness, I still long to complete my life's work."

Chapter 13

San Diego

Silas led Jotham to the north wing of the house. "We all live here, but Dad has his own apartment on the ground floor. He spends every morning in prayer but he should be finished by now. He's always been a difficult man."

They found the eighty-year-old in his own cosy living room. He was in a wheelchair and facing out the window, soaking up the sun's rays. A tall man with a muscular physique and curly brown hair was on the sofa next to him, reading the newspaper aloud.

"I have someone for you to meet, Dad," said Silas. "Jotham Fletcher, from the UK. This is my father, Korey Conrad, and my brother, Noah."

Noah stood up and turned the wheelchair around. "Pleased to meet you," he said, extending his hand to the visitor with only a hint of a polite smile.

Jotham was taken aback by his handsome features, and he looked as if he were ten years younger than Silas.

"Who is this, why are you interrupting me?" asked Korey, and Jotham noticed his obvious visual impairment. He seemed to be gazing into space.

Quickly, Silas jumped to placate him. "I'm sorry, Dad," he said with a tight voice. "I thought you'd be finished by now."

Jotham took the old man's hand and shook it.

"Dad's name is spelt K-o-r-e-y. In Celtic that means spear holder. That was one of the reasons we came to include the Holy Spear in the name for our church.

"After all, it was me who established it first," said Korey.

"Yes, it certainly was, Dad," said Noah. "None of us are liable to forget that, but you know that the name was Veronica's idea."

Silas gestured for him to be quiet with an angry look. Jotham expected that Noah would react, but instead he just gave a resigned shrug as his brother tried to change the conversation. "Jotham's colleague is helping with our computer issues," he said.

"Really, and how did you hear about that?" asked Noah.

"Through the media. I happened to be coming to San Diego and thought I might be able to lend a hand. My computer expert is very talented."

Silas walked up to his brother. "How has Dad been this morning?"

"The same as usual," he replied, rolling his eyes.

"You could ask me how I feel," said Korey. "I've had a headache all morning. No doubt Noah is pulling a face. He's always been a disappointment to me. I suppose Silas has been showing you around and trying to impress you with everything he's achieved. So much more than me."

"You know that's not true Dad," said Silas

"He told me that he's very proud of you," said Jotham.

"So he should be. Noah, bring me something for my headache."

"I'll get your medication, but please be polite to our visitor," said Noah, skulking away. Jotham was struck by his innocent expression and couldn't help feeling sorry for him.

Straight after he left, Veronica walked into the room. "Hello, Korey, how are you?" she said, walking up to him and planting a kiss on his cheek.

He sighed. "Much better now that you're here."

She knelt down beside her father-in-law. "I heard what you were saying. None of this would have been possible without you. You know that. Faith in the Holy Spear and the Lord Jesus - that's what led to our success." She got to her feet again and stood behind him to gently rub his shoulders. That appeared to relax him and he closed his eyes.

"The Holy Spear," he repeated as if he was in a reverie. "It gives us our strength and can heal us."

Veronica continued. "The tip of the spear pierced the side of Jesus. Drops of blood fell on the soldier's eyes and cured him of a terrible inflammation."

"I wish that could happen to me," he said.

Jotham looked at Korey. It was likely that he had always been a dominating bully who wanted to control everything around him. But there was also a chance that this was the result of senility or another health problem. Being a minister, he was used to dealing with personal and family issues, and he noticed that Silas seemed frightened of displeasing his father and short-tempered with Noah.

Noah returned with a pill and a glass of water that he gave to Korey. After one sip, he thrust out his hand. "This isn't cold enough," he snarled.

Noah lowered his eyes. "I'll get you some more ice."

"We'll leave you to it," said Silas, leading Jotham out of the room.

As they retreated down the corridor, Jotham ensured that they were alone before he spoke. "When did your father lose his sight?" he asked.

"Six years ago. There was a single vehicle accident. Noah was driving and he ran off the road. That put Dad in a wheelchair and led to his vision loss."

"How tragic for Noah, and your father."

Yes, it's sad, and that's why my brother is so devoted to him."

Jotham had seen cases like that before. Noah had become a victim of those awful circumstances and now he allowed his father and brother to take advantage of him. Perhaps it was a way to punish himself. Even stranger was the way Veronica encouraged Korey's faith in the Holy Spear, as if he was a child hearing a familiar song that lulled him into a reverie.

***

Sardinia

Father Benjamin could see that Dominic was struggling to stay awake. His eyelids fluttered but somehow he found the inner strength to focus on their conversation. "Have you looked at the news today – is there any sign of the sect?" he asked.

"These are modern times, Dominic, and we're in the midst of a technological revolution. There's been a cyberattack on one of those evangelical churches in the United States. The computer system has been immobilised and the church has to pay a ransom to have it restored. It's called a ransomware attack."

Dominic coughed but then his eyes glinted. "I've read about cybercrime, it's a big problem everywhere. The Simonian Sect might be behind the attack - that might be their new modus operandi."

"Yes, that could be the case," said Benjamin. "The same thought occurred to me. But would we really concern ourselves with an attack on a Protestant church?"

"Yes, no matter what branch of Christianity it is, no matter how far removed from our one true faith," said Dominic emphatically. "It's a domino effect – if we don't repel them wherever they are, soon the sect will be beating down the door to St Peter's."

Benjamin nodded. "Then we really have an enormous task ahead of us."

"What's the name of the church?"

"The Holy Spear Pentecostal Church."

"Strange name. Where is it?"

"The headquarters is in San Diego."

Dominic suddenly grabbed his head and moaned as if he was in distress.

"Are you all right – do you want me to call someone?" asked Benjamin, jumping to his feet. "Do you need some medication?"

A minute later, he calmed down and sighed. "That's better now. A spasm of pain, it was very bad," he said. "But my work is too important to let that stop me. He leaned forward and took hold of Benjamin's arm, so hard that he recoiled. "You have so much to learn, so much that I need to teach you."

"Yes, Dominic."

"I want to contact two members of the Brotherhood: Brother Sean and Brother Paulo. They were sent to a contemplative order in Northern California, but they were with me in the monastery outside Rome. They were very young then. That was before it was dismantled and we were all forced into hiding, sent to the four corners of the Earth."

"I was informed about that."

"That was Jotham Fletcher's fault. He ruined everything, almost led to us being wiped out. Sean and Paulo managed to get to America. They'll know what to do and what's expected of them."

"You're going to send them to investigate?"

He squeezed his hands tight. "Exactly. I have complete faith in them."

"Will they be allowed to leave their order at such short notice?"

"They won't let anything stand in their way."

***

The Sonoma Valley

Saint Michael's Abbey was in the Sonoma Valley, thirty miles north of San Francisco. The Spanish Mission style building was surrounded by rolling hills, providing a haven of beauty and tranquility for the monks who lived there. The simple interior of the small chapel had white stucco walls and a timber ceiling. At that time of day, it should have been empty but there were two men in their late twenties standing near the altar.

Brother Sean, who came from Ireland, was more than six feet tall and even in a full-length monk's tunic it was easy to see his thick neck and the bulk of his muscular torso. He lowered his hood to reveal short-cropped fair hair and eyes as green as his homeland. Brother Paulo, from Italy, was tall and thin, but he was just as strong.

Sean watched with a reverent look as Paulo stood beneath the crucifix and lit three votive candles on the old wooden table. When he had finished, they fell to their knees and raised their arms in prayer, gazing at the angst-filled face of their saviour.

"Help us to do the work you've set for us," said Sean. "No matter what it takes, no matter how hard it becomes. For two thousand years the work has never ceased."

Paulo continued the Brotherhood's litany. "Let the battle end before our lives are over, if that is your will, dear Lord. Give us the wisdom and strength to do our duty."

They stood up and looked towards Heaven, twisting and turning the rosary beads in their fingers. Sean had tears in his beady eyes. "We of the Brotherhood are the only ones who know the truth," he said. "When will the struggle ever end? When will the sect ever be defeated?"

"Lead us as we go out into the world and guide us in the way we should go, because you know that they are everywhere."

When they finished their ceremony, they snuffed out the candles and strode out of the chapel.

Chapter 14

San Diego

Jotham and Silas left Eugene alone at the computer for more than two hours; by then they were both keen to find out how he was progressing.

"Would it be okay to interrupt him?" asked Silas.

"I'm sure that'd be fine," replied Jotham. "I'm desperate to know what he's found."

"Not as desperate as I am."

They walked back to Silas's office. Jotham knocked and quietly opened the door, but then his jaw dropped. Eugene was slumped over the keyboard, looking as if he was sound asleep.

It had been a long flight over and they were both exhausted, but a flash of fear swept over Jotham. Perhaps something more sinister had happened. "Eugene, wake up," he cried as he dashed over. "Are you all right?" Tapping him on the shoulder, he gasped with relief to see that his skin was a healthy colour and he was breathing at a normal rate.

Eugene sat up with a start and spluttered as he straightened his glasses. "Oh, oh, sorry about that," he said. "I must be jet-lagged. I just felt so tired. Or maybe it's all this intense concentration."

"Are you sure there's nothing wrong?" asked Jotham.

"Absolutely," he said, wiping his eyes. "Now, where was I?" He tapped the keyboard to bring the screen to life.

"Have you had any luck?" asked Silas.

"Maybe. In fact, I think I've done it."

Jotham grinned. "You have? That's great news."

"Yes, just a minute." Eugene pressed another key and they all saw the black screen, still adorned with skull and crossbones. Silas pursed his lips in disappointment.

"Why don't we give you a bit more time to work on it," said Jotham.

"Don't worry. I remember now. I must've fallen asleep before I reached the final stage. Let me try that one more time." His hands danced across the keyboard, typing a series of letters and numbers while he yawned. "Sorry about that. Now, look at this. Oh – hold on a jiffy."

"What is it?" asked Jotham, hoping that Eugene was feeling okay.

He looked up from the screen at both of them. "I'm just about to try something new. That's the good news. The bad news is that it might completely wipe out the entire computer network."

Jotham patted him on the shoulder. "I have complete faith in you, Eugene." He silently prayed that the computer system was not about to die a terrible death.

Silas grimaced and appeared to be holding his breath.

"This is it, then: here goes nothing," said Eugene, and pressed the final key.

They waited for thirty seconds.

The skull and crossbones vanished, leaving only a black screen.

Which then turned blood red.

Eugene tapped his fingers on the desk and looked at his watch.

Forty seconds passed slowly by.

And then the homescreen sprang to life. *Welcome to the Holy Spear Pentecostal Church*. The banner included an image of the San Diego Worship Hall and the smiling faces of Silas and Veronica Conrad.

Silas raised his arms in a victory sign. "Praise the Lord! I'm so happy. I can't believe it. You're a genius, Eugene, a real genius."

"Well done, my friend," said Jotham, laughing.

"Let's see if all the pages open," said Silas. He leaned over and tried pressing a few of the items in the menu, as well as other documents.

They all opened on cue.

"That really takes the biscuit," said Eugene, beaming as he leaned back in the chair and stretched his aching limbs.

"Look, my sermons, this is wonderful," said Silas, pointing at the screen. "I thought I may have lost them forever.

"I'm glad we were able to help," said Jotham.

"Is it really all over?"

"I think so," said Eugene.

"Thank you so much, both of you."

"My pleasure," said Eugene. "I'm just as pleased as you are. To tell the truth, I thought I'd blown it."

Veronica strode into the room after hearing the commotion, and Silas gave everyone a high five. "It's over, sweetheart," he said, giving her a hug. "Everything's working again."

She stepped back with a stern look, and then inspected the computer for herself. Only then did she break into a reserved smile.

"That's phenomenal," she said. "Congratulations, Eugene."

"It was no trouble at all. I've managed to remove the ransomware and release the data, but there's no way of seeing where the hack originated from."

"Never mind. They never seem to arrest those criminals anyway," she replied, and Jotham noticed that her eyes were narrowed. "I truly thought that we'd have to pay the ransom. Even the FBI couldn't help us."

"Are you all right, sweetheart?" asked Silas, sitting at his own desk as Eugene walked towards Jotham.

She glared at the visitors. "How's it possible that you were able to do this?"

"I told you he was clever," said Jotham.

She took a deep breath. "Are you sure that you weren't the ones who put the ransomware into our network?"

Eugene stepped back towards the door.

Silas locked eyes with his wife. "It was very kind of you to help us," he said.

"That was our pleasure," said Jotham. "I'm glad that everything turned out well."

Silas made a slick movement with his hands, opening his desk drawer and then leaping to his feet.

He was holding a handgun, a SIG Sauer P320, and it was pointing straight at them.

"Put your hands up, please," he said. "I think we should call the FBI for a little chat."

The visitors complied with his instructions, and Jotham tried to recall how often he had been in a similar situation in the previous few years. Nothing chilled his blood more than staring at the barrel of a loaded pistol. His knew that his first priority was to stay calm and protect Eugene. "Why do you have a gun?" he asked. He inclined his head towards the door to indicate to Eugene that he should head there while he covered him. The young man took two paces towards it.

"Everyone has one around here," replied Silas.

Jotham tried to his keep his voice steady. Having been a parish priest, he was used to dealing with overwrought people at times, and the best approach was always to defuse the situation. "You're making a mistake. We only wanted to help. Do we look like arch criminals?"

"Not really, but appearances can be deceiving."

Veronica watched on, looking pleased that she had managed to cast suspicion on them. "I'll call the police," she said.

Eugene blurted out a response. "I advise you not to do that."

Jotham was stunned, once again, at his inexperienced colleague's courage.

"Really, and why not?" she asked.

"You'll ruin my future, I'm a student," he replied, and turned to Silas. "As a pastor, you should think about that. And Jotham Fletcher is the nicest person I've ever met."

Silas continue to hold the pistol, but Jotham thought he detected a slackening of his resolve. He knew there was a chance that Silas belonged to the Simonian Sect, that his own church was a front, and even that he had kept that secret hidden from his own family.

He decided to hit him with some more emotional ammunition and gauge his reaction. "There's a group I'm searching for," he said, "and I suspect that they might have been responsible for the cyberattack."

Silas loosened his tight grip on the weapon. "So now we have the truth. What sort of group?" he demanded.

"A type of cult. That's all I'm prepared to say."

Jotham knew that one option Silas had was to kill them both and claim that it was self-defence. No jury would convict him and his fame would grow.

Veronica was defensive. "That can't be possible, it sounds like a fantasy."

"So that's the reason you came here?" asked Silas. He looked incredulous. If he was lying, then he was a great actor.

"Yes," replied Jotham. "I still don't know if they were responsible, but at least your computer system is safe now."

"You must believe us," said Eugene, taking another step towards the open door. "We've repelled the attack. Why would we do that if we were the cause? Now put that down before you hurt someone."

Silas lowered his arm and put the gun back in the desk drawer. "I'm convinced that the power of the Holy Spear brought you to me," he said.

The look on Veronica's face appeared to soften. "We should thank God and his Holy Spear for bringing them here," she said.

That was one of the strangest things that Jotham had ever heard. "I don't share your faith in the Holy Spear, I'm afraid. I believe in the word of God that's written in the Bible."

"Forgive me, Jotham," said Silas. "I know that you came here to help me. We shouldn't have doubted you."

"That's okay, I understand," he replied.

"I don't," said Eugene.

Silas exhaled. "Would you like to stay for tomorrow's morning service? Now that the computer system has been unlocked, I'll be able to broadcast my sermon to all our congregations as usual."

"We're planning to leave first thing in the morning. I want to get back to my family and Eugene has his studies."

Veronica gave a restrained smile. "Have some lunch at home with us after the service and then leave."

Jotham couldn't resist the chance to investigate them further. He wanted to know more about the family's strange faith in the Holy Spear, and this would give him an opportunity to do just that. "Thanks for the invitation," he said, and then turned to Eugene. "Would that fit in with your study commitments?"

"I have exams in a couple of weeks but I can wait until tomorrow."

"Then we'd be delighted to accept. But we want to be strictly incognito, just blending in with the crowd. Please treat us like strangers, and don't acknowledge or tell anyone about our help in any way. We always keep a very low profile."

"Certainly, we understand," said Silas. "Would you like to be our guests at home tonight?"

"No, thank you," said Jotham, who felt they'd spent enough time in that house for one day. "We've booked a hotel suite, and Eugene needs a rest."

"I understand."

"We'll see you in the morning, but we have to leave straight after lunch. I can't wait to get back to my daughter."

Chapter 15

Anthony Gillam was staying in the city centre, and Jotham phoned to let him know about their plans for the next day.

"I'll get the plane ready in the morning and be waiting for you," said Anthony. "Call me straight away if you need any help. I'm just about to ask a very charming lady out to dinner."

"What a surprise," replied Jotham, with more than a hint of sarcasm. "Have a great night."

"Will do, over and out."

Jotham ended the call just as he and Eugene arrived at their destination. One advantage of his wealth was that their security and privacy could be assured whenever they travelled – at a price. They had found a resort hotel only five miles from the Conrad house, and before leaving the UK they had reserved the Presidential Suite. After booking in under his favourite alias name of John McDonald, they were planning to dine in their room.

"This really takes the biscuit," said Eugene as he waltzed into the lavishly appointed two-bedroom suite and looked out over the extensive garden. The dense grouping of plants and shrubs made it appear lush despite the dry climate. "I really like your style, Jotham. I was born to be one of the super-rich, you know."

"You deserve a special bonus after today. Let's order some food," replied Jotham, grabbing the menu.

"Awesome, I'd like a big, juicy steak, and a dessert with plenty of whipped cream."

"I'm sure that can be arranged."

Eugene checked out the bathrobes in the closet. "I'm going to try one of these on for size," he said. "Do you think we might have been in danger if we stayed in the Conrad house?"

Jotham looked up. "I don't trust many people these days, and I wasn't about to put it to the test."

"And I don't want to stay too long in the same house as a loaded gun. Do you think the sect might have infiltrated the church?"

"It's a possibility and the service tomorrow should be enlightening. Their obsession with the Holy Spear seems very misguided, to say the least."

Eugene danced around as he wrapped himself in the robe. "What were the rest of the family like?"

"I met Silas's father, Korey, and younger brother, Noah. He was responsible for a car accident that left his father blind and in a wheelchair. But the father treats him like a slave."

"That doesn't sound like a happy home. I might have a shower now."

Jotham stretched out on the huge sofa and ordered dinner. Although it was almost midnight in the UK, he texted Madena.

She videophoned him a moment later. After telling her everything that had happened, Madena tiptoed into the nursery and focused the camera towards little Belle, who was fast asleep. "We can't wait to see you again," she whispered. "Sleep tight, my love."

As he put the phone away, Jotham heard a knock on the door.

"Room service," said a woman's voice.

As always, he was alert to danger. He darted over and stood to one side of the door. Slowly, he twisted the doorknob and, with a push, let the door swing open.

A plump, middle-aged woman in a crisp checked uniform greeted him with a polite smile as she pushed a trolley into the room. "How are you this evening, sir? I'll just get this set up for you. Would you like to dine out on the balcony? It's a lovely evening for a romantic dinner."

With Eugene, romance was not high on his agenda. More importantly, their safety came first. He was not about to linger out in the open like a sitting duck. "The table inside would be great," he said.

"Certainly," she said, deftly arranging the meal.

***

Brother Sean and Brother Paulo drove to San Diego dressed in civilian clothes, jeans and shirts, so as to avoid attracting attention. Silas Conrad's house was on a five-acre block in a semi-rural area, but they were relieved to find an enclosed gazebo in a corner of the front garden. They sneaked inside before dawn and, safely secured there, were able to keep the house under observation for the rest of the day.

In the late afternoon, they followed Jotham Fetcher's car when he left the residence and drove to the hotel. Now, under cover of darkness, they were sheltering amongst some thick shrubs in the garden. Lights were on in most of the suites and many guests had the curtains open. That gave the monks a dress circle view, but they were only interested in one of the rooms.

69

"It's like watching a movie, yes?" said Paulo. "That old Alfred Hitchcock one."

"Now I know why the Lord brought us to California," said Sean. "For the past two years I've prayed over and over that we could help the Brotherhood again."

He nodded in agreement. "Yes, we've been longing for this chance."

"And God has answered our prayers."

***

After dinner, Jotham looked outside and opened the french doors to enjoy the cool breeze. He scanned the leafy, manicured garden, searching for any sign of trouble - and thought he detected an almost imperceptible stirring in a thick hedge.

He narrowed his eyes to sharpen his focus and listened carefully. The silence was broken by a peel of laughter from what sounded like a young woman.

There was a knock on the door, and Jotham jumped. He was ready for a fight if that was necessary but just at that moment, Eugene walked out of his bedroom dressed in a bathrobe. "It's probably my hot chocolate," he said.

Jotham waved his hand to indicate that they should stand to either side of the door as he opened it.

"Room service," said a woman, and Jotham recognised her voice straight away – the same woman who had delivered dinner less than two hours ago.

He relaxed and opened the door. "Hello again," he said.

"Here's your nightcap, sir." She walked in with two steaming mugs on a silver tray.

"I thought you might like some too," said Eugene.

"Thanks Eugene, that's very considerate of you," he replied.

The woman left a moment later.

Eugene yawned as he took the first sip. "Well, I'll go back to my room now," he said, "and see you in the morning, unless you need help. Don't hesitate to wake me up."

"Good night Eugene, and thanks for your work today. If that was a Simonian Sect attack, then you've single-handedly managed to repel it."

"You're the best boss ever, Jotham. Have a good night." He cast his eyes around the room one final time. "This hotel suite is the answer to my prayers."

"I thought Emily was the answer to your prayers."

"Yes, she is too."

He sashayed into his bedroom and shut the door.

Jotham approached the window and gazed out with his back pressed against the wall. There was nothing unusual, so he shrugged his shoulders and started to draw the curtains.

But he stopped dead when he saw a branch of the suspect hedge move.

He turned around. Eugene's bedroom light appeared to be out. He was safe in bed and he wanted him to stay that way. The young man had resolved the cyberattack issue, and a year ago he had been courageous and put his life in danger to help save Madena. But he did not want him to risk his life again.

Jotham tiptoed towards the door of the suite. Trying not to make a sound as he opened it, he slunk into the corridor.

Chapter 16

Like a phantom trying not to be seen or heard, Jotham headed into the garden, shielding behind plants as he approached the area of interest. He had almost reached the hedge when he jumped back in shock. A young man and woman, as if from nowhere, appeared from a side path and strolled in front of it.

The woman laughed, and he recognised the sound that he had heard before.

He knew they were probably the only people in the garden, and what could be more idyllic than a stroll in the moonlight? He thought about Madena and wished that he could be with her at that moment, in love and without a care in the world.

To satisfy his curiosity, he looked around to make sure no one was watching and checked behind the hedge. But there was no sign of anyone, or anything, suspicious. Satisfied that there was no danger, he stood up and breathed in the night air.

Then a cold hand grabbed his left shoulder.

Adrenaline surged through his body as he swung around, ready to defend himself.

But he looked straight into the face of Eugene Beaudreau.

"What's happening?" asked Eugene in a soft tone. "Do you need help? I was worried about you."

Jotham slumped with relief. "Sorry, Eugene. It's nothing; I just wanted some fresh air. Let's go back inside now, and we better make sure we lock the room securely."

"Did you see anything strange?"

It was no use trying to hide the truth from him. "I thought I did, but it was nothing."

"That's good, but remember that I'm here to help."

"I know, thanks Eugene. Maybe I just need some sleep."

Jotham peered out the window several times throughout the night, but saw nothing unusual. He finally decided that he had only been jumping at shadows.

When he woke up in the morning, he picked up his phone and flicked through his favourite photos of Madena and Belle. Their daughter had grown so quickly and she was on the verge of taking her first steps.

***

Vancouver

John Pedersen received a message at midnight and stormed into Kostya Zykov's bedroom. "Wake up sleeping beauty, we have a problem," he said. Walter Kowalski was snoring loudly on the stretcher bed near the window.

Kostya sat up with a jerk, banging his beefy head on the bedside reading lamp. "What's going on?" he asked as he jumped out and headed towards the living room. He perched on the seat in front of the computer and pressed some keys. A minute later, he glared in disbelief at the screen.

Pedersen scowled. "Well?" he asked.

Kostya narrowed his beady eyes. "This can't be happening," he said.

Walter Kowalski was now wide awake, and wandered into the room. "What's all this noise about?" he asked.

Pedersen ignored him and glared at Zykov. "Well - how bad is it?"

"They've found a way to decrypt the ransomware. Someone's removed the encryption."

Pedersen stepped back and punched his own fist. "So how long did your brilliant work last?" he asked with bared teeth. "After seventy-two hours they find a way to remove the ransomware. You're an incompetent idiot."

The blood rushed to Kostya's head. "This was foolproof. No one is that clever. I tell you, I know what I'm doing."

"This is your fault. I'm not taking the blame. You even had inside help to access the system."

"It was the perfect weapon. Don't ask me what happened."

Kowalski rolled his eyes. "I'm going to make a cup of tea. It sounds like someone has outsmarted you two."

"That's none of your business, Professor," said Pedersen, his face reddening. "But I think I know who did this. A stranger offered to help Silas Conrad, a man called Jotham Fletcher. He brought his own computer expert with him."

Kowalski switched on the electric kettle and smiled smugly. "And they foiled your plan?"

Pedersen paced the floor. "It sure looks that way."

Zykov grimaced. "Do you know him?"

"Fletcher. I suspect he's the man who interfered with our plans before, more than once. The previous leader sent me to kill him in Rome and I failed."

Kowalski squinted as a thought struck him. "What does he look like?" he asked.

"Six feet tall, slim with dark hair and about forty."

Kowalski slapped his own forehead. "That sounds like the man who ruined everything for me at the university."

The others stared at him in disbelief. "Are you serious?" asked Pedersen.

"I certainly am. He's clearly working against us – he has to be eliminated."

"Do you want me to do it?" asked Zykov.

Kowalski glared at him. "Have you ever killed anyone before, Zykov?"

He shrugged his shoulders in reply. "I'm a hacker, not an assassin. But if it's necessary, I'll do my duty for the sect."

"You'd be doing us a favour," said Pedersen, "but there are other ways to get rid of him. If any of us encounter him again, we should be prepared to make it his last day on Earth. Meanwhile, we need to make sure that the Leader doesn't hear about all this."

Kowalski crossed his arms. "I suppose you expect me to lie for you?"

Pedersen pointed a threatening finger at him. "You stay out of it, Professor, this has nothing to do with you. We're sick of your constant sniping."

His eyebrow twitched but he tried to maintain his air of superiority. "I'll stay quiet for now. Remember, things have been difficult for me, and we're meant to be on the same side, you know."

***

San Diego

Jotham drove Eugene to the San Diego Worship Hall to attend the morning service, but he was stunned to see a group of about thirty people jostling with each other outside the entrance.

He parked the car down the road and approached on foot. It soon became obvious that it was a media pack armed with cameras. Six police officers were trying hard to keep them under control and out of the church.

Jotham turned towards Eugene. "Perhaps the police are finally trying to be helpful, but I don't really understood why they're here."

Eugene pursed his lips. "Maybe they're here to arrest us. My parents won't like that."

Jotham had secretly been wondering the same thing. The invitation to the service might be a ploy to hand him over to the police. Silas and Veronica had every reason to suspect that they were the ones who planted the ransomware. It must have seemed odd to have strangers turn up on their doorstep like two white knights to the rescue.

His priority was to protect Eugene.

"Why don't you make a hasty exit right now," he said. "If they arrest me, then inform Madena and ask Anthony to get you out of the country fast."

Eugene looked at him with his chin held firm. "There's no way I'm leaving you, but maybe we should both get out of here."

Jotham could tell that it would be no use arguing. "We'll try to sneak past and sit in the back, just as we planned."

He had run a media gauntlet like that before, but this time he and Eugene were just faces in the crowd, anonymous and unknown. The journalists weren't likely to be waiting for them, even if the police were.

Parishioners filed into the church, trying to ignore the scrum. Despite that, they were blasted by a barrage of questions.

"What do you think of Silas Conrad?"

"Who do you think is responsible for the cyberattack?"

"Any comments to make about the situation?"

They were met with curt rejections as people turned away from them.

There were more people filing into the building, and the police officers were distracted by the increasingly vocal media contingent. Jotham and Eugene kept their heads lowered and cut into the midst of the crowd.

A second later they were inside the church, and sat at the end of the aisle in the back row. From there, it would be easy to make a hasty retreat.

Jotham scanned the interior of the worship hall. It was certainly impressive. The altar looked more like a stage and the backdrop was an enormous, brightly coloured painting. It depicted people of all nations listening to Jesus giving his sermon on the mount. The hall was filled almost to capacity, with steeply tiered seating like a theatre. Families and younger people sat towards the front. They had excited expressions, as if they were looking forward to a show.

The large choir was seated on one side of the stage, facing the audience.

There were five musicians on the other side, including an organist who was playing rousing hymns.

Jotham and Eugene did not go unnoticed. Many people turned and waved to them with a welcoming smile. "You better look downwards, Eugene, we seem to be on show," he said.

Eugene did as he was told, but glanced up furtively. "Maybe that's how they greet strangers here," he muttered.

"I hope that's it," he said. "Any more attention and we'll have to leave."

Jotham thought about the services that he led when he was a parish priest in Canberra. That small church was the first one built in the region, so it was one hundred and fifty years old. His approach to worship had been of a traditional kind, and his congregation was more reserved. He wanted to know more about Silas and his peculiar faith in the Holy Spear, and he wondered if the people gathered there were being subjected to a form of brainwashing.

Veronica entered through a side door near the altar, waved to the congregation and sat in the front row. She was wearing a modest blue floral dress, perfect for a clergyman's wife. Noah followed, pushing his father in the wheelchair and they sat on either side of her. Korey nodded and smiled, but Noah looked in the other direction.

The organist struck a loud chord and everyone fell silent. Applause erupted as Silas Conrad walked on stage with outstretched arms.

Chapter 17

The morning service, broadcast to all the branches of the church, was more like an entertaining stage show than any act of worship Jotham had ever conducted. He had never heard such enthusiastic hymn singing, led by the choir of over thirty choristers in yellow smocks.

Silas gave his sermon like a talented performer, strutting around the stage to engage the audience at just the right moments.

He played them like a violin.

"The Holy Spear can heal us," he said. "I have much to give thanks for because of the help I received from two strangers." The audience clapped and cheered for at least a minute. "The power of the Holy Spear led them to me."

Jotham cringed at being included in that statement.

"Praise the Lord," cried a woman in the front row.

After that, Silas held nothing back as he revealed his obsession. "You know how much I believe in God expressed through the power of the Holy Spear," he said. "But whereabouts is it located? Can we find it anywhere? It's likely that the shaft of the spear is secured under the dome of St Peter's Basilica in Rome. The tip of the spear was broken off and no one really knows what has happened to it. Some say it might be in Greece, Armenia, or Vienna.

"After Jesus took his last breath, a Roman soldier pierced the side of his chest with the tip of the spear. It was their way of confirming that he was dead. Only a few drops of blood flowed out. They fell onto the soldier's face and cured him of a terrible inflammation of the eyes. Why is that important to us? Because it reminds us of God's power."

Jotham could hardly fathom what he was hearing.

Eugene looked at him with eyes agog. "I think he's lost the plot," he whispered. "I never learned that in Sunday School."

"No, nor did I," replied Jotham. "And I didn't learn it in Theological College, either."

Silas Conrad had invented his own set of beliefs about the Holy Spear, and his congregation seemed to be lapping it up like manna from heaven.

He continued the sermon. "That is just one example of God's power that we can experience through faith in Jesus Christ. Our church has chosen to remember that small miracle beside the cross. If you have faith in the Holy Spear, then you can believe that God is able to perform a miracle in your life."

Jotham knew that it wasn't his job to set him on the right path, or to challenge the belief system of another church. His job was to find the Simonian Sect. As the service continued, he thought about the time he encountered the Leader of the Simonian Sect and the words he said to him. *"The Simonian Sect is a secret worldwide monastic group that has sent missionaries out to infiltrate the church since its earliest days, to instigate its most infamous deeds. We don't do bad things ourselves, at least not very bad; we just inspire the church to do bad things. And they don't need much encouragement."* The Leader then explained that they were trying to fulfil the Magus Covenant. That was a solemn vow taken by every member of the sect to destroy the Christian Church.

Silas's erroneous beliefs were a distortion of the facts. That was precisely the sort of misinterpretation and misrepresentation that the sect liked to propagate.

Jotham wondered again if Silas might secretly belong to the sect, or if he had come under its influence at some time in the past.

At the end of his sermon, there was a round of applause – something that never happened in Jotham's church. He saw Veronica pat her father-in-law on the arm, and then Noah gave her a polite hug. The family looked as if they were close, but that might only be the image they presented in public.

The congregation stood up to sing a lively spiritual song. That was when Jotham saw the police officers at the front of the church. They proceeded to walk down the centre and side aisles, scanning the faces in each row as if they were searching for someone.

His heart thumped as they approached. It was the same raw fear that he experienced when he climbed up the chimney and down from the roof of the Brotherhood monastery outside Rome. He loathed that sensation, but he was never meant to be a man of action. That role had been forced on him.

He glanced at Eugene, who looked sharp but lowered his head.

When two of the officers reached the back row, they stopped and looked straight at them.

But then they looked away and moved on, heading out the door.

Jotham dared to take a breath as the song came to an end.

***

En route to Budapest

His father's voice always reminded him that he was a fool, that he

78

would never amount to anything. But for once the relentless noise inside Goran Novak's head had gone silent.

Staring straight ahead, he leaned back in the comfortable business class seat, ignoring the talkative executive next to him and the air steward who offered him a drink. He focused his concentration on trying to listen for the voice that had tormented him for years, but all he heard was a faint ringing sound.

Perhaps the voice would never come back.

The object was safely secured in his backpack, and that was now stowed in the overhead locker. Throughout the short flight, he kept an eagle eye on anyone who sauntered past, just in case they dared to go anywhere near it.

When the plane landed in Budapest, he was the first passenger to stand up and he felt relieved to have the bag in his hands again.

A limousine driver was waiting when he exited the airport and whisked him to his apartment. He lived in the heart of Budapest, in a turn-of-the century building close to the Grand Boulevard. As he walked up the wide spiral staircase to reach the third floor, Goran comforted himself with the knowledge that his dear, departed father could never have afforded the rent on such a spacious and elegant apartment.

When he opened the front door his grandmother greeted him with a tearful embrace, followed by a kiss on both cheeks. She was so petite that he had to bend over so that she could reach. "How are you, my precious?" she asked. "I missed you so much, but I've made roast duck for dinner."

Goran always felt like a giant when he stood next to her. She was almost eighty with wispy grey hair and pencil-line eyebrows, and had looked after him since he was seven years old. "I'm good, Grandma. My trip was a great success and I've found something valuable."

Her eyes lit up. "Can you sell it?"

He nodded. "It should be worth a fortune."

She beamed with pride. "You're such a good boy. Where did you find it?"

"Hidden in a cave in Greece." They locked eyes and he held her wrinkled hands. "I'm sure that it's the tip of the Holy Spear."

Her mouth gaped open. "Really, precious? You can't be serious."

Goran grinned. "Take a look for yourself."

He opened his backpack and took out the old wooden box. As if afraid that it might escape if he wasn't careful, he slowly lifted the lid. She gazed in

79

astonishment at the small piece of iron. "It does looks like the end of a spear."

His eyes sparkled. "A man sold it to me in a village. His family guarded it for centuries, but he doesn't have any children and needed the money."

"He won't talk, will he?"

"No, he can be trusted." His knew that his grandmother had always possessed an almost supernatural ability to read his mind. They exchanged a knowing glance, and he could tell that her skills were not dimming with age.

"Good, precious, but how do you know this thing is genuine?"

"Because it's already changed my life," he said. "I've stopped hearing Papa's voice."

Tears welled in her eyes. "That's wonderful news, but you shouldn't worry about your father. He was no good. Would you like a shoulder rub?"

"That would be good, Grandma," he said, sitting on the brocade sofa. She kneaded his tight muscles and he felt his tensions ease. He cast his eyes around the luxurious apartment, which she had decorated in a classic style.

"We should go the Gellert Baths tomorrow," she said. "The thermal waters are so good for my old bones."

"Your favourite place, of course we can," he said. "When I was little, we couldn't afford to go there."

She planted a kiss on the top of his head. "I'm so proud of you, Goran."

"After dinner, I have some work to do."

Chapter 18

San Diego

Jotham and Eugene made a hasty retreat as soon as Silas Conrad indicated that the service was over. They strode down the side aisle and were the first out the door, scampering around the corner before the media pack had a chance to react to their presence.

Before most of the congregation had strolled outside, they were in their car and driving away. On the way to the house, Jotham pulled over and parked in a deserted side road. Getting out his phone, he called Madena to tell her about the church service.

"Why do you think the police were there?" she asked, bouncing Belle on her lap.

He waved to his little girl and she responded by blowing him a kiss. "I was afraid they were there to arrest us."

"I was very afraid," added Eugene.

Jotham gave him a lopsided smile. "I think the police wanted to appear to be doing something, or seeing if anyone suspicious turned up. And the media were desperate for a story."

"We kept our heads down and sat at the back," said Eugene, vigorously fluttering his fingers to attract Belle's attention.

Madena gave Jotham a tender look. "I can't wait till you get home."

"Love you both around the universe and back," said Jotham as he ended the call.

They continued on to the Conrad house, and the family had just arrived home. "There you are," said Veronica, ushering them inside. "We wondered what had happened to you."

Jotham did the talking. "We wanted to keep a low profile. I must admit we were a bit taken aback by the media and police there."

She led them into the spacious kitchen in the north wing where the family lived. "I made some lasagne last night. I'm just going to heat it up and toss a salad."

They were all gathered there, including Noah and Korey.

"So how did you like the service?" asked Silas.

"It was fascinating," replied Eugene "Almost like going to the theatre."

"I'm glad you enjoyed it. And you, Jotham, what did you think?"

81

"Very impressive," he replied. "The congregation was so enthusiastic, but I hope there won't be a police presence from now on."

"That was because of the cyberattack, and I don't expect them around next week," said Silas. "I had no inkling they'd be there, and I certainly wasn't expecting the media. Before you arrived, I made a brief announcement outside, to say we were delighted that the situation had returned to normal."

Jotham wanted to test Silas and see if there was a reaction. "So it's business as usual, in your own, unique way," he said. "You seem to have an unusual set of beliefs."

Silas narrowed his eyes. "Yes, I think the people who join my church are looking for something different."

"I have to be honest with you. I don't support your faith in the Holy Spear. In my view, that object doesn't have a role to play in the Christian church. My beliefs are based on the teachings in the Bible."

Eugene Beaudreau looked from one man to the other as if he was watching a tennis game.

Silas seemed unperturbed by Jotham's remarks. "I can assure you, we follow the teachings of Jesus. But I do believe in miracles. The Holy Spear is just an embellishment, a symbol of hope."

"I believe that God has the power to perform miracles," said Jotham. "Embellishments can be dangerous, and might lead to the undermining of the church."

He searched the other man's eyes to see any sign of a reaction, or any indication of guilt. Silas maintained his pleasant demeanour, but Jotham knew that a member of the Simonian Sect could spend their lives in senior roles in a church organisation, keeping their true goals and beliefs well hidden.

Noah helped Veronica to serve lunch in the dining room, opening the french doors there to enjoy the San Diego sunshine. Jotham thought that she was probably the only member of the family who didn't bully him. Silas suffered from a moderate addiction to his smartphone, so it was not surprising that he placed it on the table next to him while he ate.

"This is brilliant," said Eugene, cutting his next mouthful of lasagne.

"I'm glad you like it," said Veronica.

"Veronica's a wonderful chef," said Silas. "She was thinking of teaching a class in the church." The sudden blare of organ music announced that he had a phone call.

"Silas, you shouldn't bring that to the table," said Korey gruffly.

"Sorry, Dad, it's Jacob, he's on duty so it might be something serious," he replied, pressing the answer button. "I'll use the speakerphone."

Everyone at the table could now hear the young man's voice. "Hello Silas."

"What's happening, Jacob?"

"I have a man on the line who's trying to contact you. He says he some important information that you need to know."

Silas and Veronica exchanged puzzled looks. "Strange. In that case, put him through."

***

Everyone at the table could hear the phone call. "Hello," said a heavily accented voice. "Is that Pastor Silas Conrad?"

"It is, and who is this?"

"My name is Goran Novak, and I live in Budapest."

Jotham listened intently, wondering if the call might relate to the attack on his computer system. He cast a sly glance at Eugene, who looked as if he was paying rapt attention. They both knew that many cybercrime attacks originated from central Europe.

Korey Conrad was about to blurt out a comment, but Veronica leaned towards him with a finger across her mouth. "Quiet, please, Dad," she whispered.

"From Hungary?" continued Silas on the phone. "That's a long way from here. How can I help you?"

"I've been reading about your church, and the name is so distinctive," said Goran, putting the emphasis on the first syllable of his words.

"Yes, it is unusual," said Silas.

"I have an ancient artefact in my possession, the tip of an iron spear."

Jotham nudged Eugene under the table, who responded by nervously adjusting his glasses.

Silas, the whites of his eyes bulging, leaned forward in his seat. "What do you mean by that?"

"The tip of an iron spear: what Roman soldiers called a *pilum*. For centuries it was hidden in a cave under a monastery in Greece."

Silas coughed as his throat tightened. "Do you mean Saint Dimitrios?" he asked.

"Yes, a remote area."

"I know that legend. Why did you contact me?"

"Your church is wealthy and I read about your faith. My goal is to sell the object if the price is right. I don't want to put it on the open market."

"Tell me what you want."

"Let me be frank. Are you interested in having first right of refusal?"

Silas seemed unable to speak, and his face was contorted into a look of astonishment. Veronica rushed over to him, loosening his collar as if concerned that he might be having a heart attack.

Goran continued. "You do understand what I mean, don't you?"

Finally, Silas responded. "Yes, definitely, but can you deliver it to me?"

Veronica went back to her seat.

"I'm in Budapest, a long way from you," he said, pronouncing *way* like *vay*. "But you'll need to collect it in person and I'll be staying in a hotel on the Pest side of the riverfront. My plan is to contact you again in forty-eight hours. That gives you plenty of time to get to here."

"Can't you bring it here? I can pay your expenses."

"Please understand, they don't want me in the United States. Are you prepared to come here, or not?"

Silas shrugged his shoulders. "Yes, if you insist, but I need to see the object before making you an offer."

"That's understandable. Give me your personal phone number. I'll contact you in Budapest and tell you where to meet me. My phone number's private."

After Silas recited the number, Goran Novak abruptly hung up.

Eugene was the first to speak. "That is gobsmackingly incredible," he said, as Silas sat in shocked silence.

"That's the perfect way to describe it," said Jotham. This was a turn of events he could not have predicted. "But you need to be cautious. This could be a huge hoax."

Veronica put her arm around Silas. Slowly, he rose to his feet. "I need to make some travel plans," he said, looking at them with moist eyes. "We may have found the Holy Spear."

Chapter 19

Sardinia

Father Benjamin arrived to find Father Dominic picking at his breakfast, and it occurred to him that he seemed to look thinner every day. The sick man was already dressed in the black cassock that he loved so much, a symbol of his precious identity.

Dominic looked up at him with dull eyes. "I'm determined to eat as much as I can, to keep up my strength," he said.

"How did you sleep?" asked Benjamin as he sat down.

"Not well, not well at all. My leg muscles twitched all night, and there's an ache in my head that keeps getting worse. But it's God's will, so I shouldn't complain."

"Shall I ask for some pain relief? There's no need for you to be brave."

"No, I want to remain alert," he said with a clenched jaw. "So long as there's breath in my body, I'll be ready to seek and destroy the evil sect."

Father Benjamin cleared away the tray when he finished. "You're remarkable, the way you continue to make an effort," he said.

Dominic closed his eyes and focused on his breathing to suppress the unrelenting throb in his head. "I'm sorry. You'd better pray for me and then we'll talk about the work of the Brotherhood."

Benjamin jumped as his phone buzzed, and he retrieved it from the pocket of his suit. "It's your colleagues in California," he said, switching to speakerphone as he put it on the table between them.

Dominic's eyes sharpened. "Thank you for helping me to contact them," he said. "I couldn't have done it without your help." He coughed with the exertion of leaning towards the phone.

"Hello, Brother Sean," said Benjamin. "I'm here with Father Dominic."

"Hello Fathers," he replied. "And I'm with Paulo."

"What have you found out?" asked Dominic.

"We did as you asked, we've been watching the Conrads, but the problem has been solved. They somehow managed to decrypt the ransomware."

"What does that mean? I don't understand."

"The church's computer systems are working again, but there's been an interesting development. They had outside help and we saw the man who helped them."

"Who was it?" asked Benjamin.

Brother Paulo joined in. "Do you remember the man we were holding in the monastery in *Italia*? The one who escaped that night and we chased him, but he managed to get away."

Dominic threw himself against the back of the chair as if he was apoplectic. He answered him with a hoarse voice, slurring the words. "Jotham Fletcher?"

"Yes, that's the man," said Sean. "We both saw him that night."

"I've heard about Fletcher," said Benjamin. "But what was he doing there? Perhaps he attacked the computer system."

Dominic was still agitated. "He's always hunting for the sect, so he might suspect that Silas Conrad is a member. We have to find out and stop Fletcher."

"Do you want us to kill him?" asked Brother Sean.

Dominic spoke in a thunderous tone, as if he'd found new strength. "Stay in San Diego. You need to talk to Jotham Fletcher and the priest."

"Do you mean Pastor Conrad?"

"Yes," bellowed Dominic, trying to focus his thoughts despite a surge of pain. "The sect is behind all this and Fletcher is there to stop them. Unless he's finally become a member – that wouldn't surprise me."

"I should go to San Diego to investigate for myself," said Benjamin. "This sounds too important to be left in the hands of two young monks."

Dominic waved his hand. "No, Benjamin." The news had enlivened him, taking his mind off his own suffering. "You should stay here with me. There's a great deal that you need to learn about the Brotherhood." He leaned towards the phone again. "Sean and Paulo, you need to find out the truth. You know what that means."

Brother Sean paused before replying. "Are you sure?"

"Yes, you know what you learned at the monastery. Our work isn't easy, but it has to be done because there's so much at stake. Find out what's going on, and don't let me down."

"Yes, Father, we'll do what you ask," said Paulo. "God bless you."

When Father Dominic ended the call, Benjamin glared at him. "Why have you left that in their hands, without any supervision? I really think that you're not thinking straight and need to hand over the reigns to me as soon as possible."

Dominic's face tightened. "How dare you. Listen to me. Sean and Paulo

86

were with me in the Brotherhood's monastery outside Rome, and they understand what's required of them. They know the survival of the church is at stake."

"I understand that."

Dominic tried to adopt a more solicitous manner. "Prepare yourself, Father Benjamin. When my monks find out more, then you may need to travel and look into this further. I thank the Lord for bringing you here to me. We'll work on finding a solution together." He suddenly clutched his hands. "Please let me rest for a few minutes. When the pain eases we can pray and talk further."

Benjamin stood up and left the room.

***

San Diego

Jotham could hardly wait to see Madena and Belle again and had been about to leave for the airport with Eugene and return to the UK. But the phone call had disrupted everything, to say the least.

Despite the old man's protests, Noah took Korey to his apartment for his regular afternoon nap. After they left the room, Silas paced the floor in a lather of excitement. "God works in mysterious ways," he said.

"He certainly does," said Veronica.

"This is thanks to you, sweetheart. Somehow, I feel as if our lives have been leading up to this moment."

Jotham was dubious about the phone call and tried to bring him back to some sort of sober reality. "Silas, have you considered that the item might be a worthless piece of junk? All over Europe, it's possible to find Roman coins and other relics in the soil. Battlefields can be littered with old weapons."

Silas shook his head. "No, I feel in my heart that this is something special. Don't you believe in God's will, in his Hand leading you to go where he wants?"

Jotham knew that he had been led to his own quest thanks to a long series of coincidences. "Yes, I can understand that," he said, "but you have to be cautious."

"I really think that something extraordinary is out there waiting for me."

"You should at least do some background checks."

Silas was in no mood for restraint. "It's been my lifelong dream to be in possession of the spear for the sake of the church, but that was just a fantasy. I never thought it would happen. After Dad's accident, I dreamed that the Holy Spear would be able to cure his blindness. That would be a miracle, right here in San Diego."

Veronica was frowning, but her eyes were bright as if she wanted to believe the claim. "We need to be sure that we can trust the man," she said. "How can we prove that it's the genuine article?"

"We'll put it to the test, that's how," replied Silas.

Jotham sensed that they were letting their emotions take control and they were already convinced the relic was genuine. "Have you considered that this could be some sort of trap?" he asked.

Silas locked eyes with him. "I have to find out for myself."

Jotham had no idea if the phone call from Hungary had anything to do with the Simonian Sect. But he felt that he needed to help Silas Conrad and knew that he couldn't let him undertake this journey by himself. If he went with him, he could encourage him to rethink his belief system and return his church to a more traditional dogma. If Silas was secretly in the Simonian Sect, then he might find a chance to discover the truth. "I could help you get to Budapest," he said. "We could fly there in my jet."

Silas's eyes widened as he stared at Jotham. "You'd be willing to take me to Hungary?"

Jotham nodded. "You shouldn't go alone."

His whole body seemed to relax. "I can't thank you enough, Jotham."

"We can be on our way within a couple of hours. I'll notify my pilot, Anthony Gillam, right now."

Eugene stepped forward. "I should go with you," he said. "You'll need my help."

Jotham could not predict what might be waiting for them in Budapest and had no intention of putting Eugene in any more danger. "You've done more than enough already, and you do need to get back to university."

He looked deflated. "Will you ask Madena?"

"I'll tell her about our plans but there's no time for her to get here and she may not be needed. The two of us will be leaving within a few hours, and you can take a commercial flight back to the UK later today. First class, of course: you deserve it after your excellent work here."

Eugene adjusted his glasses. "That would be gobsmackingly good,

Jotham," he said.

Veronica narrowed her eyes. "I'm not so sure about all this," she said. "You've helped us, Jotham, but Silas and I should travel together. This is our dream."

"Out of the question," replied Silas in a firm voice that surprised Jotham. "I need you here to run the church. You're my second in charge and we'll be back in a couple of days. Don't say any more to Korey about all this. He may not even notice I'm gone."

"I won't tell him anything," she said. "But I'd still rather go with you."

"Please, Veronica," he said, putting his arms around her.

She nodded reluctantly.

Silas turned to Jotham. "We should pray together in the Worship Hall first."

"Yes, we should," said Jotham, "and then we'll leave straight after that."

Chapter 20

Vancouver

At seven in the morning, John Pedersen was staring out the living room window. He turned around when Zykov emerged from the bathroom, dressed and combing his wet hair. "Have you ever heard of the Holy Spear?" he asked.

Zykov shrugged his heavy shoulders. "I think so. A Roman soldier stabbed Jesus when he was on the cross."

"Correct. You're smarter than you look."

"I did some background reading. We've been dealing with the Holy Spear Pentecostal Church, remember? No one really knows where it is now - just like the Holy Grail."

"Well, perhaps that's all about to change."

Walter Kowalski strolled in from the bedroom, still buttoning up his shirt. "Did someone mention the Holy Spear?" he asked.

Pedersen had a glint in his eyes. "Yes, as a matter of fact. Someone in Hungary contacted Silas Conrad, claiming to have the tip of the Holy Spear. He says he found it in northern Greece."

Kowalski's jaw dropped. "In Krakow, I was the *Guardian of the Spear.*"

Zykov raised his eyebrows. "Who or what was that?"

"I was a professor of theology at the university. The Guardian of the Spear is an honorary title, bestowed on a highly respected figure. There's a relic in Krakow Cathedral that's said to be the tip of the Holy Spear. It's more than a thousand years old, but everyone knows that it's only a copy. I've given quite a few lectures about it."

"Very interesting," said Pedersen, with more than a hint of sarcasm. "But now it seems Silas Conrad might be able to get his hands on the original."

A smile slid across Kowalski's pudgy face. "There's a legend that the genuine relic is hidden beneath the monastery of Saint Dimitrios in northern Greece. If that's where it came from, it could be genuine. We should procure it for the sect."

"Why would we do that?" asked Pedersen with a sneer.

Kowalski's eyes opened wide. "Because of the magic," he said. He sat down and tapped his fingers on the dining table. "The Spear has a supernatural aura. Our founder, Simon Magus, understood the power of magic."

90

"I still don't know what you're talking about."

"Me either," said Zykov, scratching his head.

Kowalski spoke in a measured tone. "You know that Simon Magus was a magician who offended the early Christians. The Apostles said they were able to bless people with the Holy Spirit. Magus wanted to know how to perform that magic trick because he understood and believed in the overwhelming power of magic."

"Yes, I understand," said Pedersen, sitting at the table with him. "After that, he came to realise that he was the true Messiah."

"That's right. If our sect has the Holy Spear, we'd be in control of that magic. Simon Magus wanted to buy the ability to impart the Holy Spirit. The Apostles, Peter and Paul, ridiculed him and plotted his downfall, but that's not going to happen to us."

"Are you sure that the spear has magical powers?" asked Zykov.

"We need to have faith, just like Simon Magus did. John, I know you want to be the Leader of the Sect one day."

Pedersen narrowed his eyes, aware that Kowalski was trying to charm him. "One day, perhaps," he said. He tried to appear relaxed, but his heart was pounding.

Kowalski continued. "If the Simonian Sect had the Holy Spear, we'd have immeasurable power. We could finally fulfil the Magus Covenant and destroy the Christian church. You could become the next leader of the sect, and perhaps I could be the deputy by your side, the Lord Surrogate."

Pedersen walked over to the window again and looked out at the North Shore Mountains in the distance. "This could be a turning point," he said. "The greatest moment in our history."

He sent a message half an hour later and received a phone call a few minutes later from the Leader of the sect. Zykov and Kowalski listened in to the brief conversation. Pedersen kept his voice low as he explained the news.

The elderly leader was silent for over a minute before he responded. "I want you to procure the tip of the Holy Spear for us, no matter what it takes," he said. "You'd better not fail, or expulsion from the sect won't be the only consequence."

Zykov stared at Pedersen after he ended the call. "What about Jotham Fletcher?" he asked.

He gave him a sly smile. "He's going with Silas Conrad to Hungary. We'll be able to kill two birds with one stone and get rid of him for good.

91

Luckily, we'll be keeping our own hands clean."

Then Pedersen noticed the look of joy on Kowalski's face. As the truth struck him, the pulse in his forehead pounded and his head began to spin. Kowalski was not about to let him take the glory for finding the spear. At the very least, he would never let them forget that it was his idea. But more than that, he wanted it for himself, and he wanted to become the next Leader of the Simonian Sect. A former professor, he would be the perfect choice.

If he had the chance, he would probably kill them both so that they wouldn't stand in his way.

Pedersen exchanged a knowing look with Zykov to flash him a warning. If he wanted to take all the credit for finding the Holy Spear, then they would have to kill Kowalski.

As thoughts hammered his brain, beads of sweat broke out across his brow and his breathing rate started to soar.

Zykov wrinkled his face in concern when he noticed, and he took a step towards him. "Are you all right, John?" he asked. "You seem to be breathing heavily."

"I think he's hyperventilating," said Kowalski. "Sit him down, I know what to do."

Zykov led Pedersen to the small sofa. His face was reddening as Kowalski grabbed a paper bag full of apples on the kitchen bench. After up-ending the contents, he raced over. "Here, breathe through this," he said, handing him the empty bag. "Hold it over your mouth and nose, to reduce the oxygen to your brain."

Pedersen took several slow breaths as instructed. As he returned to normal, the fog in his mind lifted. After a few more minutes, he was breathing steadily and put the bag down.

"Now what?" asked Zykov.

"We should say the mantra," said Pedersen.

"Yes, you're right," said Kowalski. "This is an important moment."

Zykov opened the sideboard drawer and took out the antique dagger that they always used for the ceremony. The three men stood together in a line as he held the scrolled handle and raised the weapon high in the air. He closed his eyes as if he was in a reverie, and made five downward thrusts in quick succession.

Because he was the youngest, Zykov was the first to speak. He used a singsong voice to recite the words that he'd committed to memory.

"All should strive to reach the golden mean
Freedom and moderation gives strength unseen
Between power and thought there is no light
Male female energy all beings unite."

Pedersen spoke next, trying to adopt the same monotonous tone.

"Praise be to Simon Magus for his words.
The Father's mind produced the first thought to create the angels,
And then they created the visible universe.

Kowalski's turn came last.

"We must all follow the Magus Covenant,
A solemn promise to destroy the Christian Church.
His words will lead you to the truth."

They opened their eyes, and stood in silent meditation for two minutes.

Pedersen cast a sly glance at Zykov. Kowalski narrowed his eyes as if he could tell that they were plotting something. The others moved forward and he suddenly realised that he was under threat.

He swung around and raced towards the door. He threw it open and dashed out, and as they ran after him, he slammed it hard in their faces.

When Pedersen opened the door, Kowalski was nowhere to be seen. The elevator was already descending.

"Fire stairs," snapped Zykov.

They ran to the fire exit door at the end of the corridor and tore down the steps, two or three at a time. They reached the bottom and pushed open the door, stumbling out into the street.

Thirty metres away, they saw Kowalski bolt out the front entrance of the apartment building at an incredible speed.

They were determined to catch him, and Pedersen had always been a fast runner. He had managed to escape from more than one tricky situation thanks to that skill.

He began to close in on Kowalski as the ageing man sprinted across the road without stopping.

Just then, a bus came like a bolt from the blue and hit him full force. Kowalski fell under the wheels and it was all over for him in a fraction of a second.

The bus came to a screeching halt.

A few people in the street came running over and tried to help, while others gathered around and looked on.

Pedersen and Zykov were standing twenty metres away, gasping for air and in shock at what they had just seen. No one realised that they were connected to the victim.

Pedersen waved his arm to indicate to Zykov that they should retreat back to the apartment. Sticking close to the wall, they walked back into the quiet lobby and stepped into the elevator.

Zykov was looking subdued, but Pedersen slapped him on the back. "We're in luck, Kostya. Our dirty work has been done for us, and we can tell the Leader that it was all a terrible accident."

Chapter 21

San Diego

Although it was early in the afternoon, the curtains were drawn and the bedroom was in darkness when Veronica tiptoed in, shutting the door behind her.

"I knew you'd be here," she said.

In the dim light she could just make out his figure near the bed. "I've been waiting for you."

Tossing her shoes away, she undid the buttons of her floral shirtdress and let it slip over her shoulders and fall to the ground. "We need to say good-bye before you leave."

"You're wearing a pink lace bra, my favourite."

"Can you really see me in this light?"

"I can see you everywhere. Wherever I am, I won't be able to stop thinking about you."

She undid her bra and tossed it aside. "Be careful in Hungary. I don't want anything to happen to you."

"Come over here and tell me all about it."

***

The abbot at the monastery in Northern California was not pleased when Brother Sean and Brother Paulo asked for temporary leave. Somehow, they also managed to convince him to lend them the rusty van that everyone used for running errands.

The two monks drove to San Diego in civilian clothes, and had been keeping Silas Conrad and Jotham Fletcher under surveillance for nearly thirty-six hours. They sneaked into the back of the Holy Spear Pentecostal Church's worship hall for the morning service, and later followed Jotham Fletcher to Conrad's house.

Now they had tailed the two subjects back to the Worship Hall and this time they were sure that the two men were the only people in the large building.

"We should pray that God will be with us," said Paulo. "This is the best chance we're ever going to have."

"Agreed," said Sean, tapping his leg. "But we need just the perfect moment to strike."

Three minutes later, the old van turned the corner outside the church, moving so slowly that there was no sound as it pulled up next to the side door. "May God help us and forgive us," said Paulo. They put on their habits and exchanged a nervous look. Then they slid out of the vehicle, leaving the doors open.

Inside the hall, they could see Jotham Fletcher and Silas Conrad on their knees in the front row, their heads bowed in prayer.

***

Silas and Jotham had walked into the Worship Hall in the middle of the afternoon, planning to leave for the airport straight afterwards. With no one else there, their footsteps echoed as they walked to the front row and sat down.

Jotham gazed at the colourful painting that formed a backdrop to the altar. "Let's pray," he said as they knelt down.

Silas cleared his throat and then began. "Thank you, dear Lord, for giving me this chance to find the Holy Spear. With the blessings that flow from its power, I beg you to restore my father's sight."

Jotham wanted to be the voice of reason and try to dampen Silas's enthusiasm. He seemed convinced of the relic's veracity. "Whatever happens, we pray that you will protect us and keep our families safe while we're away."

"Amen," said Silas.

Jotham hadn't finished yet. "Help us to follow your word and trust in you. Lead us closer to the truth, down the right path where you want us to go, and help us always to accept your will. Watch over Eugene as he travels back to England." He thought about Madena and Belle, and wished they were in his arms at that moment.

"Help me to find the Holy Spear," said Silas, his voice now choked with passion. "I implore you to lead me to your precious relic."

Jotham always tried to stay on the alert for any sign of danger, but he was finding Silas's weird ranting hard to tolerate and that was starting to wear him down. He wasn't sure where this mission would take him, but he couldn't wait for it to be over.

Through the haze in his brain, he heard an almost imperceptible sound. Perhaps it was Eugene or a staff member from the church.

He swung his head around, just as he felt a stab of pain in the muscle

96

mass at the base of his neck. A man in a dark grey habit was right behind him, a hypodermic needle in his bulky hand.

Jotham cried out as the needle pierced his skin, and Silas screeched at the same moment. There was another robed man standing behind him.

He tried to identify them before he passed out but his brain was already whirring in wild circles. Although he reached out to grab the dark-haired young man behind him, his strength had evaporated and his arms were like jelly. As he blacked out, his head hit the seat and he crumpled to the floor.

The two monks stepped back to let the sedatives take full effect. Jotham was still barely conscious, although he was as helpless as a baby. He blinked and could see Silas sprawled across the floor beside him.

He felt his feet being lifted and then a jarring pressure though his body as one of the men dragged him by his ankles. His back scraped along the floor as the man pulled him towards the side door. Jotham tried to call out and tell them to let him go, but he couldn't make a sound.

"I'm glad we're parked close by, yes?" said the man who was holding him, and even in Jotham's fuddled state, it sounded to him as if he were Italian.

The sunlight hit his face as the door was kicked open, and finally Jotham fell into deep unconsciousness.

As if waking from a slumber for just a moment, he stirred as the van drove off. He sensed that he was probably lying in the back of a vehicle. "Silas," he muttered, but there was no answer and then he drifted off again.

***

Sean and Paulo loaded Jotham and Silas in the back of the van and secured the door, then sat in the front cabin and looked in every direction as they drove away. They were confident that the prisoners would be out to it for at least three hours. A couple of monks travelling along the road should not attract any suspicion, but they wanted to get to their destination as quickly as possible.

Brother Paulo was from Rome and had learnt to drive there, so he was now able to put that experience to good use. He took the wheel and proceeded to bolt along as fast as he could, while at the same time trying hard to avoid attracting unwanted attention.

Brother Sean kept a firm hold on the grab handle and tried not to look at the road ahead.

97

They were headed further into the countryside, and after twelve miles reached a very small town comprised of just a few streets plus a gas station with a convenience store. A mile outside the limits was a dilapidated building that looked as if it had been abandoned for decades. Built from grey concrete blocks with just a few tiny windows, it resembled a one-level warehouse. The structure was daubed in fading graffiti and surrounded by a dense and wildly overgrown hedge.

There was one decaying sign at the front, but only two words were still legible.

Insane Asylum.

Paulo drove to the rear of the building and stopped the van. "Looks perfect, yes?" he said.

Sean nodded. "Now let's get these two inside."

Chapter 22

The shock of an icy blast stirred Jotham to consciousness. He blinked twice and opened his eyes, but soon realised that his head and upper body were saturated.

"Good morning," said a man's voice with an Irish accent. "Time to wake up, to be sure."

Jotham was hit by a second freezing bucketful, and that brought him to his senses. Now he was wide awake, but his body was hit by an involuntary spasm of shivering. It took all his considerable self-control to avoid screaming. "Who are you?" he asked, looking around.

There were two young monks standing there, both in dark grey habits. One was slim with Mediterranean appearance, and the other had fair hair and a solid build. They both appeared strong and capable of putting up quite a fight. The room looked grim to say the least, with bare concrete walls and floor. The only illumination was a camping light on the floor in the corner. It cast a dull light on all of them, adding to the impression of decay and ruin.

Jotham automatically tried to raise his arms and launch an attack. But the spasm of pain in both wrists soon alerted him to the fact that his hands were tied to the arms of a wooden chair with duct tape.

"Where am I?" he asked. "What do you think you're doing?"

The Irishman grinned. "Welcome to the Sisters of Healing Mental Asylum. Of course, it hasn't been used for quite a while, not since the county shut it down three decades ago. Some nasty things were going on here, it seems."

Jotham noticed that there was only one small window high up on the wall, and it looked as if it was dark outside.

The last thing he could remember was being in the worship hall with Silas after lunch. They had been planning to leave for Budapest straight afterwards. He'd had a hearty lunch with the family but could now feel the pangs of hunger and thirst. That meant it was probably late in the evening.

He licked his lips to take in some water from his drenched face. There was an unrelenting ache in his arms and a sharp pain in his wrists where the duct tape pressed into his skin.

The fog in his mind began to clear. "Where's Silas Conrad?" he demanded. Jotham realised that he was almost certainly being held by the Brotherhood, although there was always the possibility that it was the Simonian

Sect or even another group.

The dark-haired man walked towards him, the hem of his tunic scraping the dusty floor.

Jotham frowned. "What are your names?"

"We should introduce ourselves," said the Irishman. "I'm Brother Sean and this is Brother Paulo, and we're on God's side. Very pleased to meet you, but enough of that. Now it's my turn for questions. What do you know about the evil sect?"

Jotham felt a surge of anger. "Let me guess – you two are in the Brotherhood."

Sean repeated his question. "Jotham Fletcher, what do you knows about the Simonian Sect?"

Both men had wide shoulders, and there was something about them that looked familiar. As he eyeballed one and then the other, Jotham had a sudden insight. "I saw you in Italy," he said.

A knot tightened in his stomach as he recalled the night in the monastery outside Rome. Held prisoner by Father Dominic, he had been interrogated and later managed to escape. A group of monks had chased him, and he had glimpsed their faces. He had woken up many times since then, remembering the horror of that night.

Sean and Paulo exchanged a knowing look.

"You were with Dominic, in that monastery near Rome," said Jotham.

"Very good, Signor Fletcher," said the Italian.

"Don't you know that Father Dominic is only using you to do his dirty work?"

"We're doing the work of the Lord. The sort of work that no one else wants to do, or even knows about." With the bucket in hand, he turned and strode out of the room.

Jotham watched as Brother Sean moved over to a plastic bag on the floor next to the portable light. His head pounded as he wondered what was in store for him.

Leaning over, the Irishman pulled out a towel and looked at Jotham with eyes narrowed to thin lines. He charged forward, raising the towel in both hands, and threw it over his head.

Jotham was powerless, although he tried to shake his head to throw off the shroud. Adrenaline surged through his body so that all his senses were on high alert. In a world of darkness, he heard the heavy footsteps of the Italian as

100

he walked back into the room.

Sean broke into his broadest Irish brogue. "You can be telling us now. What do you know about the involvement of the evil sect? Why are you here in San Diego?"

"I came to help the Conrads," he said.

He felt a sudden drenching shock as Paulo poured a bucket of cold water over his head. This time he needed to contend with more than just shivering cold. The towel absorbed the water and the effect was to block his nose and mouth.

He was struggling to breathe.

The terrible sensation of suffocation, of feeling as if life was slipping away, overwhelmed Jotham.

He gasped for air, only to find the damp towel forming a seal over his lips and nostrils.

He was blacking out as Sean pulled the towel away. "Well?" he cried.

Jotham sucked air into his empty lungs. "I don't know anything about the sect," he said.

"We've been given our orders to kill you," said Paulo. "We can bury you here and your body will never be found. The Brotherhood will be rid of you for good, yes?"

The chilling effect of the water resulted in hypothermia. Jotham began to shiver as every muscle went into spasms. The reflex movements were an effort to heat up his body so that it returned to homeostasis. At that moment he felt completely helpless, but he only knew one thing.

He needed to think of a way to escape.

***

The Peak District

Madena was at home with Belle in their estate in the Peak District, but Jotham and Eugene were never far from her mind. She did her afternoon workout in the conservatory, much to Belle's amusement. The little girl loved to do her own dancing to the music and tried to imitate her mother's exercise movements.

While Belle had an afternoon nap, Madena continued her research into the early origins of the Holy Spear Pacific Church. She found some old photographs of the founder, Korey Conrad, and references to a small congregation in an outer suburb of San Diego. Korey had been a handsome man back then, with piercing green eyes. Late in the afternoon, she gave Belle a bath and then dried her. After wrapping her in a towel, they gazed at the mirror in the nursery as they sang their favourite songs.

Late that night, Madena received a phone call from Jotham. He told her about the mysterious phone call and the object that might possibly be the tip of the Holy Spear. She agreed that he should travel with Silas Conrad to Budapest, while Eugene returned to the UK to resume his studies. "I'll send you my latest research notes," she said, "But for all we know the man who rang could be a fraud, or this could be another attempt at extortion."

"That's why I think I need to look into it," replied Jotham. "But I don't want to take any risks."

"Keep me posted, and get out of there at the first sign of trouble. If need be, we'll go there together to investigate further."

That night, Madena slept fitfully. At two in the morning, she woke up with a strange sense of unease and sent Jotham a text message. She lay there listening for a beep, but there was no reply and the urge to sleep overwhelmed her.

At four o'clock in the morning, the phone chimed and she jumped to answer it, her heart pounding when she saw that the caller was Eugene. Glancing at the time, she knew that it was early evening in San Diego. "How are you, Eugene?" she asked, rubbing sleep from her eyes.

The young man didn't waste any time in getting to the point. "Madena, I've got bad news. Jotham's vanished, along with Silas Conrad."

Chapter 23

Madena sat bolt upright in bed as she listened to Eugene on the phone. "What! When and where did this happen?" she asked.

"They went to the Worship Hall to pray before they left for Budapest and never returned," he said. "I can't find any trace of them and they don't answer their phones. Silas's car was left outside the hall, but the keys were missing. They were probably with him when he disappeared."

"I'm so sorry, Eugene. I should've gone with you to San Diego. So where have you looked?"

"Anthony and I have been searching everywhere. It's obvious that someone has taken them both, there's no other explanation."

Madena's breathing rate rose as the frustrating reality struck home. She had to support and encourage Eugene and Anthony, and somehow find a solution. "Are there any clues in the Worship Hall?"

"There are signs of a disturbance inside, drag marks on the floor. There were tyre tracks near the side door. Anthony thinks it might be some sort of small van or truck."

"Have the police been called?"

"Silas's brother is with Veronica, and they're trying to keep it a secret from the father. They don't want to call the police because of the publicity, and I assured her they were better off letting us handle it."

"That's good, Eugene, as always we want to stay under the radar," she said, trying to sort out every detail in her head. "I'm heading straight to the airport to charter a jet and get to San Diego as soon as possible. Obviously, that's going to take quite a while, but I'll see what can be arranged. Keep searching for clues, look around the area and let me know if you hear anything."

When Madena ended the call, her head was spinning. It sounded like the work of the Brotherhood, but then again it could also be the Simonian Sect. There was even the possibility that it might be regular criminals who were also responsible for the cyberattack. Perhaps they had decided to try a more traditional crime like kidnapping.

Madena hated to disturb Cynthia Young in bed, but there was no alternative. Her housekeeper was quick to respond when she heard about the emergency and only too willing to look after Belle until she returned.

"I have complete faith in you to look after her, thank you so much," said

Madena. "I better be going; there's no time to waste." Cynthia put a comforting hand on her shoulder as she gazed with tearful eyes at her child sleeping in the cot.

There was no way of knowing whether both her parents would return home.

Felix drove Madena to Manchester, which was the nearest major airport. Speeding along, he took every opportunity to get ahead of the traffic and managed to make it there in record time.

While in the vehicle, Madena was on the phone trying to book a private charter jet. By the time they reached the airport, a plane was waiting for her on the tarmac. It would fly her straight to Montreal, and then another jet would be waiting to take her the rest of the way to San Diego.

The journey should take less than fourteen hours. She prayed and hoped that Jotham might be standing there to greet her when she arrived.

She approached the small plane at a jog and ran up the stairs into the cabin, feeling as if she were walking into the jaws of hell.

***

San Diego

Brother Sean and Brother Paulo stood over Jotham after his latest drenching, but when he stopped shivering they turned and walked out of the derelict room. "Where's Silas Conrad?" he yelled after them, but they didn't answer him.

Now he was alone, he struggled to devise a plan to make his escape. He tried to stand up, but was still tied to the chair. That meant he was straining his back with the weight of the chair and forced into a half-bent-over position. He made a few shuffling movements towards the door just as the two monks returned, this time holding Silas Conrad between them.

"You can sit down again, Fletcher," said Brother Sean, kicking the chair between Jotham's legs. When the wooden legs landed on the ground, he knew that he was back to square one. "Stay right where you are, or we may have to kill you sooner rather than later."

Silas's darting eyes showed that he was overwhelmed with confusion and fear. As they pushed him into another chair and bound his arms, he turned towards Jotham. "Do you know these men? I don't understand what's happening."

"Don't tell them anything, Silas," said Jotham. "They're in the Brotherhood."

"Who are they?"

"Bad people. Trust me, they're not on our side."

"Shut up," said Paulo, slapping Jotham across the cheek.

Silas looked up at Sean with an imploring look. "What are you doing?" he asked.

"This," he replied. He pulled a plastic bag out of the pocket of his habit and deftly slipped it over the man's head.

"No!" screeched Silas. Jotham felt an upswell of anger against these brutal men, so typical of those who worked for the Brotherhood. They were willing to commit any heinous crime in the name of their cause.

"What do you know about the sect?" asked Sean with a snarl.

"What sect?" implored Silas, shaking his head from side to side and struggling against his bonds.

He could still breathe, but only just. The bag expanded and contracted with every breath and he started to heave.

Although obscured by the grey semi-transparent bag, Jotham could see the terror on Silas's face every time the plastic was sucked into his gaping mouth.

Paulo reached out and pulled it off his head. "Do you want to tell us now what you know about the sect, yes?"

Silas gulped for air while he had the chance. "I don't know what you're talking about."

"Leave him alone," said Jotham. "He doesn't know anything, and nor do I."

A minute later, Sean snatched the bag from his friend and roughly replaced it over Silas's head. This time they kept it on for longer, despite the fact that Silas denied any knowledge of the sect.

Jotham felt overwhelmed with rage and pulled at the tape around his wrists.

"Well, what will you be telling us?" asked Sean as he removed the bag.

Silas heaved in a desperate series of gasps, his eyes wild. "Someone hacked into the computer system, but that's been resolved. Jotham brought his computer expert."

Paulo glared at him. "We know that you're hiding something. Are you a

105

member of the sect?"

"No, that's a lie. I don't know what you're talking about."

"Then you need something to help you think!" said Sean.

"I know what you need," said Paulo, delving into the bag on the floor. There was a small culinary blowtorch in his hand. "Some encouragement, yes?"

The monks laughed.

"Do you like cooking?" asked Sean as Paulo switched on the torch. "Brother Gaspar loved cooking. Do you remember him, Dr Fletcher? He was an excellent chef, but he was killed because of you."

"He was killed in a bomb blast. That had nothing to do with me."

Revulsion erupted deep inside Jotham as he recalled Father Dominic standing by the fireplace in the monastery. He had toyed with a poker in the red-hot coals then walked towards him, bringing the weapon ever closer to his bare chest. His stomach churned to think of the searing agony as the tip burned his skin.

Now Paulo walked towards him, leering with his arms outstretched. Jotham braced his body, ready for the onslaught.

"No!" cried Silas in a frightening, unnatural voice. "What are you doing?"

Paulo brought the small, intense flame close to Jotham's face. "You're very handsome, did you know that, Fletcher?" he said. "But not for long."

Brother Sean scowled at Silas. "Do you have anything to say now, Pastor Conrad? Your friend shouldn't have to suffer."

Tears flowed down Silas's sweaty face. "We don't know anything. You have to believe us."

Jotham's mind raced, and he knew it was time to act. Plan A was to use the element of surprise, swing his chair around and knock Brother Paul off his feet, then kick Sean where it really hurt.

If that failed, there was no Plan B.

Brother Sean turned suddenly towards Silas. "I think you know about the sect, both of you. What are you hiding?"

"Stop this," whimpered Silas.

Paulo darted forward and brushed the blowtorch against Jotham's forearm, only for an instant but he flinched and recoiled at the dreadful pain.

Jotham tensed his legs, preparing to jump, when Paulo suddenly swung around and leapt over to Silas. He pressed the flame into the man's bare forearm, close to the duct tape ties. Contact lasted for half a second, and Silas let out a piercing scream.

"What aren't you telling me?" yelled Brother Sean as Paulo withdrew the flame.

Silas shook his head from side to side, wild at the torment. "Someone claims to have found the Holy Spear."

Sean's face lit up like party lights. "Where are they and what's their name?"

"He doesn't know what he's saying, leave him alone," said Jotham.

Now was the time for action. He sprang to his feet, half-hunched over and still tied to the chair, and lunged at Paulo.

The weight of the chair knocked Paulo to the ground, and Jotham landed on top of him.

Brother Sean's features twisted in shock and panic. He pulled a hypodermic needle out of the pocket of his cassock and aimed it high. As Jotham tried to struggle back on his feet, the monk jabbed him in the neck muscle.

Jotham kicked out at Sean and then Paulo, but didn't have a hope of gaining the upper hand. Instantly weakening, he could hear Silas screeching but that sound grew faint as he drifted into unconsciousness.

His eyes were shut and he couldn't respond as he felt them cut the cords around his wrist, nicking his skin in the process. One of them dragged him by the feet out of the room and down a dark corridor. The odour of death filled his nostrils.

The last thing he heard before everything went dark was the clang of a metal door slamming.

Chapter 24

Jotham felt as if he were lying at the bottom of a deep, dark hole, but he could hear a small voice deep inside his head, encouraging him to wake up. He stirred a number of times and realised that he was lying on a cold concrete floor, such a painful contrast to his own soft bed at home. His damp clothing made his body shiver and waves of nausea brought him almost to the point of vomiting.

He opened his eyes but could only see a bright light in the distance.

Jotham called out for Jane and William, his dead wife and baby, and he could almost see their faces but then they faded away. He coughed as he recalled the driver who slammed into his car and the blinding flash as it burst into flames. That was the last moment of their lives.

Wrapping his arms tight around his legs, he curled his body into a foetal position and thought of Madena, the lean firmness of her body, her wide apart blue eyes and dazzling smile. Belle's enchanting little face appeared in his dreams and he longed to hold her once again.

A man whispered in his ear but it sounded as if he was speaking through a tunnel. "Wake up. Please wake up. This is my room. What are you doing here?"

***

Sardinia

Father Dominic slept fitfully and spent most of the night trying to cope with the relentless throbbing in his head.

He prayed earnestly for relief, and at four in the morning he finally drifted off to sleep. When he woke up three hours later, Father Benjamin was sitting beside his bed.

"What time is it?" he asked.

"Seven o'clock. Sorry to wake you, but you have a phone call."

"Sean and Paulo?"

"That's right, here's my phone," said Benjamin, handing it to him. "They're keen to talk to you."

"Turn it on so that we can both hear."

Benjamin placed it on the side table.

Sean's voice came over the speakerphone. "Father Dominic?" he asked.

"Yes. Is Brother Paulo there?" he replied.

"Right beside me."

"What news do you have?"

"Silas Conrad and Jotham Fletcher were about to travel to Budapest, in Hungary. They were going to meet a man who claims to have found the tip of the Holy Spear."

Dominic sat up, though the sudden effort made him grimace. "That's incredible. What's the man's name?"

"His name's Goran Novak. When Silas Conrad reached Budapest, he was going to get a call from him to find out his location. But now we have Conrad's phone. What do you want us to do?"

Dominic clutched his head. "Where does Novak say he found the relic?"

"Buried close to a hilltop monastery in Greece."

"Saint Dimitrios?" asked Father Benjamin, his mouth agape. "I once visited the site. There's an old legend that the tip of the Holy Spear was buried somewhere nearby, but no one really believed it."

Dominic buried his head in his hands and was silent for half a minute.

"Do you want us to go to Hungary and try to find the man?" asked Paulo.

Benjamin leaned towards the phone. "Where are Conrad and Fletcher now?"

"We have them locked up."

Dominic cocked his finger and spoke in a calm voice. "You've both done well. All I want you to do now is kill them both. Father Benjamin will go to Hungary for the Brotherhood."

"Yes, Father," said Sean, sounding disappointed.

"As soon as you've done that, you can return to your monastery but keep Conrad's phone by your side."

"We've disconnected the location services, so they can't trace it."

"When Novak calls that phone, find out where he is and report the arrangements to Father Benjamin straight away. Do you understand what I've said? And make sure you use an American accent when you're speaking to him."

"Yes, Father," said Paulo. "Sean will answer it, he can impersonate him."

"Father Benjamin will be waiting in Budapest to hear from you."

"You can rely on us," said Sean.

When the call finished, Father Benjamin locked eyes with Dominic. "That's incredible, if it's true," he said.

"You know what has to be done, don't you, Benjamin?" replied Dominic "This is your chance to prove that you're really worthy of leading the Brotherhood."

"You want me to get that relic?"

"You're a genius. There's no time to waste, you need to book a flight and leave as soon as possible. Let's just hope that Mr Novak tries to phone Conrad, or you'll be looking for a needle in a haystack."

Benjamin stood up and looked down at the dying man. "You can count on me, Dominic."

***

When Sean put the phone away, he noticed Paulo was looking pale. "Something wrong?" he asked.

"I've never killed anyone before," he replied. "Not by myself. Are Fletcher and Conrad really so evil?"

Sean scowled. "Living in California has made you soft. This is our duty."

"I know it's an honour to be trusted with a task like that, but Father Dominic has a brain tumour. That might be affecting his judgement and we're the ones who have to answer to God."

Sean massaged his own chin. "Perhaps you're right. We could be making a mistake."

"What will we do, stay here and keep them prisoner?"

He gave that some thought before answering. "No, we don't have to do anything. They're both locked up and there's no way they can get out. No one's going to find them here. We'll just return to our monastery and let nature take its course."

He nodded in reply. "That's a good idea. Have you got both their phones?"

"Yes, I'll smash Fletcher's and toss it over a cliff, and keep Conrad's phone with me to wait for that call."

Paulo gave a sly smile. "Then let's go home. This asylum is giving me

110

the creeps."

***

Jotham opened his eyes and felt his head ache as if he was being pounded with a hammer. Stretching out his limbs, he slowly woke up to the realisation that he was laying on a cold concrete floor and the only furniture in the room was one metal bucket. The only source of illumination came from moonlight shining through a small window high on the wall.

He tasted vomit in the back of his throat, but then became aware of his parched mouth and gut-tightening pangs of hunger.

A man appeared in a corner of the room, gazing at him with wide eyes and Jotham blinked to make sure he was real. "Who are you?" he asked with a hoarse voice.

But there was no answer and then he disappeared from sight. It must have been his imagination, or perhaps only a shadow. Dehydration or drugs could easily have a strange effect on the mind.

Slowly, he came to his senses and gingerly rose to a sitting position. He felt dizzy but that eased, and then he tried to stand up.

Jotham was in what appeared to be in one of the cells of the old mental asylum. He felt a chill in his core at the thought of what life must have been like for the former patients.

Checking the heavy metal door, he found it was locked tight, and he wondered if Silas Conrad might be in the adjacent room. He didn't want to shout and alert his captors, so he knocked repeatedly on the two side walls.

There was no answer, and he realised that he had no idea what had happened to him. Silas might be in another part of the building; he might still be undergoing interrogation - or even worse. The last time he saw him, his situation with the two monks did not look good.

Then he remembered being jabbed in the neck by Brother Sean, and that was his last memory.

Jotham felt the throbbing pain on his arm from the encounter with the blowtorch, and there were bruises and cuts on his wrists that were caked in blood.

His eyes adjusted to the dim light and he looked around. There was no food or water in the room, only an empty bucket. It also occurred to him that his watch, a wedding present from Madena, was missing. Fumbling in his pockets, he soon realised there was no sign of his phone, either, but his wallet was still in his back pocket.

He had no way of knowing the time, but knew that it was night and, judging by his ferocious hunger and thirst, he'd been there for a long time. His mind slowly cleared and he tried to focus his thoughts on formulating a plan.

Chapter 25

Jotham stared at the small window more than two metres above the ground and saw that it was a single pane of glass. It might just be possible that he could squeeze through, though there was every chance that he might become stuck like an oversized cork in a bottle.

His heart pounded. He knew what had to be done, but he was terrified of heights and he hated climbing, so why, he wondered, was he always finding himself in these situations? At least he had a bucket to stand on. He upended it on the ground, then stepped on top and rose almost to his toes. He could just reach the windowpane and punched it with tightly closed fists.

There was a tinkle of glass, but there was not too much noise as the pane shattered. If his captors were asleep, they might not have heard. Jotham stepped down and used the bucket as a tool to clear the glass from the window and remove most of the jagged edges. Once again, he was standing on his toes to reach, but managed to do quite a good job.

Now he had to find a way to climb through the window, but that was easier said than done. Madena had taught him some wall climbing skills. She was a former army officer and that had been a standard part of her basic training.

He positioned the upturned bucket in just the right place. If he took a running leap, he might be able to launch himself high enough to grab the lower ledge. Stepping back, he said a quick prayer and counted to three.

Jotham tried at least twenty times but couldn't make it. Almost ready to give up, he made one last, desperate effort. The space was just out of reach as he jumped up, but then he locked his fingers around the narrow ledge. It felt as if he was dangling but his toes were still touching the bucket. His shoulders hurt like hell.

He cried out in shock as someone or something shoved his backside, propelling him upwards.

A man's voice whispered in his ear and he could feel the outflow of breath. "Time to go. This is my room."

Jotham turned his head and saw the ghostly shadow of a man behind him. "Thank you," he said, and then the figure vanished.

He had never believed in ghosts, but knew in his heart that it was probably a former patient coming to his aid.

Now that he had a firm hold, he brought his left foot to waist height then pushed with his legs and pulled with his arms to drag his body upwards, just as Madena had taught him. Keeping his head forward, he hoisted himself up and then he was climbing out the window.

Tiny shards of glass pressed into his palms as he strained his arm muscles.

He would normally be trying to hoist a leg over, but there was no room to do that: it was head first or nothing.

His head was through the window space and he was moving forward. Feeling as if his arms would be wrenched off, somehow he managed to squeeze his shoulders by twisting his body so that they passed through the opening one at a time. Madena always said that he was a triangle shape, with wide shoulders and narrow hips. He hoped that she was not just flattering him.

His hips slipped through and then he realised he was about to fall skull first into an overgrown shrub. He closed his eyes and held up his hands to shield his face.

As he landed, it felt like a hundred sticks were bashing him at once.

Jotham paused to catch his breath, before he crawled away from the shrub. The burn wound on his arm was radiating pain and he was covered in new cuts and bruises. He knew that he did not look pretty.

He scanned the building, a grim and derelict one-level concrete monstrosity. Even the graffiti on the walls looked faded and worn, as if no one had been near the place for years. He did a quick circuit and noted that there were no vehicles outside, and no lights visible through the windows. There was no sign of the monks, but they might still be inside, along with Silas.

More than half a mile down the road he could see an intersection and a gas station, probably at the edge of a small town. The lights were on over the two fuel dispensers, so it looked as if it were still open. He sprinted down the deserted road, heading straight for it.

There were no customers when he arrived, but inside the store there was a middle-aged woman behind the counter and three small aisles stacked with the usual convenience items.

He strode inside.

The woman's eyes widened at the sight of a man who looked like he'd just been in a war. "Hey there, how's everything?" she asked, playing with a strand of her greasy hair. "Have you been in an accident?"

"Yes, that's right, down the road." He pulled out his wallet and grabbed some muesli bars and a bottle of water, then approached the counter. "Do you

114

know the time?"

"Ten o'clock, honey," she replied, taking a step back.

"Keep the change," he said as he handed her some notes. He opened the bottle and gulped the water.

The liquid helped to revive him and clear his mental fog. If it was ten at night, that meant he'd been out to it for twenty-four hours, which was quite disturbing. Drugged to unconsciousness for that period of time, he was lucky to have woken up at all. He opened one of the muesli bars and took a bite.

"Would you like me to call an ambulance?" asked the woman. "You don't look too good."

"Could I borrow your phone to make a call?" he asked, handing over a fifty-dollar bill.

She handed him her phone. "Please stay here and give it straight back."

"Sure. Where exactly am I?"

"What do you mean?"

"The address of this place."

"Right here," she said, pointing to a sign on the wall.

Jotham dialled Eugene, thankful that he had committed his number to memory, though he was not certain if he'd still be in the country. By now, he might be back in Bristol.

Eugene answered straight away. "Hello."

"Eugene, it's me. Are you in the UK?"

"No, I'm still in San Diego, looking for you. Where are you?"

He recited the address. "Have you heard from Silas?" he asked.

"No, nothing. I'll be right over to pick you up. Anthony and I have been searching for you - and I had to inform Madena."

Jotham's heart sank at the thought of what she must be thinking. Right now, she was probably on her way to America.

He ended the call and handed the phone back. "I'm just waiting for someone to pick me up. I hope you don't mind if I wait by the window."

"Would you like a coffee?" she asked. "You can have a cup on the house."

"I'll just stick with water," he said, opening the second muesli bar.

Jotham stood by the corner window, gazing out at the road while the shopkeeper watched him with saucer eyes.

The shop door swung open and Jotham felt a rush of adrenaline. He swung around, fearing it would be the monks.

But instead of that, a hoodie-clad man in his early twenties ran towards the counter with knife raised.

The woman crouched down in fear.

Jotham reached out and took hold of two soda cans nearby. "Stop right there," he yelled, hurling them towards him. They struck the stranger on the back and he stumbled over. Turning around, he saw Jotham pick up two more cans and aim them.

The woman jumped up with a baseball bat in her hand. "Get out of here before I hit a home run," she said, bending her knees as if ready to pounce.

The thief turned and ran out the door, disappearing into the night at top speed.

The woman smiled weakly at Jotham. "Thanks for your help," she said.

"My pleasure," he replied. "Are you okay?"

"I am now. You're a pretty smooth operator."

Jotham kept his head down while he waited by the window. Finally, he heard the distant sound of a car engine, and a few seconds later he saw the front end of a sedan as it screeched to a halt outside.

Chapter 26

Jotham gulped, hoping that it was Eugene and not the two monks waiting for him in the vehicle. "Thanks for your help," he said to the woman behind the counter.

"That's okay - thank you for your help," she replied. "Good luck."

He opened the door and dashed outside, his heart soaring at the sight of Eugene at the wheel.

Then another face appeared, in the rear passenger window. "Madena!" he cried, jumping into the car beside her. "My love," he said, throwing his arms around her slender waist and drawing her close for a passionate kiss.

She drew back with a concerned frown, and Jotham remembered how bruised and battered he looked. "How did you manage to get here?" he asked.

"It wasn't easy," she replied. "I chartered a jet. Two, in fact, and arrived a few hours ago. But you've been missing for more than twenty-four hours."

"And Belle?" he asked, hugging her again.

"With Cynthia and Felix, in very safe hands."

He nodded. Keeping his eyes locked on her, he tapped Eugene's shoulder. "It's good to see you, Eugene. Thank you for staying here."

It's great to see you," he replied. "But where's Silas?"

"Just down the road in that deserted building, I hope. That's where we were held."

"Then we better go and find him, but you look terrible," said Madena. "What have they done to you?"

"I have felt better, but we can't worry about that now. Two young monks from the Brotherhood drugged and kidnapped us when we went to the Worship Hall."

Madena shook her head in dismay. "And then?"

"They interrogated us, asking what we knew about the Simonian Sect. One of them injected me with something that knocked me out for the best part of a day. I escaped through a window but I'm hoping Silas is still in there somewhere. I have no idea what condition he's in."

"And the monks?"

"They may still be there, so we have to be prepared for anything."

"Was Father Dominic involved?"

"I don't know. He's supposedly dying in a hospice in Sardinia, but someone must be in charge of these goons. I recognised them from that monastery outside Rome. Three years ago, that night when I managed to escape, I briefly saw their faces. When I saw them again, the memories flooded back."

"Do you know their names?"

"They introduced themselves as Brother Sean and Brother Paulo. An Irishman and an Italian. But they're Brotherhood stooges, following orders."

Madena gave him a tender look and examined the wounds on his arms. "Are you sure you're up to this?"

"I'm fine," he replied, trying not to wince when she touched the cuts. "We have to try and find Silas right now. Eugene, take the car just a short distance down the road, and park behind that stand of trees."

"Rightio then," he replied as he drove slowly away.

After parking the car as instructed, they got out and approached on foot. "Madena and I will break in while you keep watch on the outside. But be careful."

"This place really takes the biscuit," said Eugene, as he scanned the grim structure. He touched the sign outside but jumped when part of it snapped off. "The Sisters of Healing Mental Asylum," he recited. "Horrible."

Jotham pointed to the smashed window. "That was courtesy of me. I'll tell you later how I managed to escape and I think I had some help from the resident ghost.

"Don't tell me that," said Eugene, wrinkling up his face.

"He's friendly," said Jotham. "At least, he's helpful."

They sneaked over to the front door. "We'll break down the door, and you shelter behind those shrubs, please, Eugene. Notify the police if we don't return."

Madena looked at him. "We couldn't do this without you here, Eugene. Don't take any risks – the Brotherhood is deadly."

"Best of British luck," he replied, taking out his torch and heading over to his hiding place.

"I've brought a spare torch for you, Jotham," said Madena. "Stay alert."

"Ready if you are." He reached out to touch her face and then they jumped to action.

"I hope your ghost is asleep now," said Madena.

"We may need him."

She looked the building up and down. "I wonder what went on here in the past?"

"You don't even want to know."

They stood on either side of the graffiti-daubed wooden door and held their torches aloft, ready to use as a weapon if necessary.

"Are you okay?" she asked softly.

"Sure," he replied under his breath. "Here goes nothing."

He tensed every muscle and aimed just below the door handle. With a swift kick that used all of his power, the door swung open and the recoil jarred his body. It bashed against the wall, and Jotham hoped that the noise didn't rouse his friends.

They charged inside, beaming the torches around the room. The darkened lobby was eerily quiet, adorned with spiderwebs and the scent of rats. The hairs rose on the back of Jotham's neck as he led the way.

"Stay together," snapped Madena.

They were both familiar with the drill they had practised many times before. Jotham and Madena went from room to room, peering in and prepared to respond if anyone from the Brotherhood appeared.

The first room was the largest. That was where they had been interrogated, and the two wooden chairs were now lying on their side. The portable light and other items were gone. Jotham's breathing rate rose as he shone the torch around.

The next room was locked and, judging by its position, he was sure that it corresponded to his cell with the broken window. Madena pulled across the two heavy latches and pushed the door open. They soon realised that the room was empty, and the only thing in there was the metal bucket.

"Let's leave this to its ethereal occupant," said Jotham.

"A good idea," she replied, her mouth in a grim line as she closed the door.

They continued their search. Most of the interior doors were wide open and the bleak rooms were empty. By the time they reached the end of the dark corridor, they were convinced that the two monks had probably left while Jotham was locked up and unconscious. They began to wonder if they had taken Silas with them.

But then they reached the last door.

It was bolted, just like Jotham's cell, but this time they heard a soft sound inside.

"Someone's in there," said Madena, forcing the bolts across.

Jotham banged on the door "Silas, are you there?"

119

They heard a muffled response. "Jotham, is that you?"

"Stand back from the door," cried Madena.

It was stuck fast, so they both tried to shove hard.

Finally, it swung open, and their torch beams flashed on Silas Conrad, curled up on the floor. Once again, the only furniture was a metal bucket.

Silas struggled to get to his feet in the tiny cell. He looked dishevelled, with sunken eyes. "Am I glad to see you," he muttered.

"Likewise," said Jotham, rushing to his side. Madena took him by the other arm and they helped him to walk out. "Are you okay?"

"I'll be all right. I'm not as bad as I look, but I need water."

"This is my wife and partner, Madena,"

"Pleased to meet you," said Silas, trying to smile as they made it to the front door.

Eugene raced up to them and then tore over to the car. A few seconds later, he drove the vehicle down the road and pulled up in front of them.

"You'll be home soon, and there's some water in the car," said Jotham as he helped Silas into the back seat and sat beside him. He felt a surge of anger at the thought of what might have happened if they hadn't rescued him. Those brutal monks had apparently left them there to die of thirst and hunger.

"Thank God you found me," said Silas, as Madena opened a water bottle and handed it to him. He slurped it loudly as they drove away.

Chapter 27

"This is so good," said Silas as the vehicle sped towards his house, nearly forty minutes away.

Madena turned around and looked at the two men in the back seat. "How bad are your injuries?" she asked.

There are some burn marks on my arm that are painful. Other than that, I don't think I have any lasting damage," said Silas.

"You'll be home soon, and we can dress those wounds," said Jotham.

"Have you informed the police?" he asked.

"No, not yet," said Madena. "But we were getting close to it when we heard from Jotham."

"What about the monks?"

"No, there was no sign of them. They seemed to have cleared out and they left us to rot in there," said Jotham.

Silas started on a second bottle of water. "You have to tell me about the sect. Why were they asking us about that – who are they?"

Jotham cast a glance at Madena. "That's something we need to talk about," he said. "You see, there's a sect that has been trying to undermine the Christian church for centuries. Madena and I are trying to stop them, but so is the Brotherhood. Their tactics are very different from ours, and they're willing to commit any crime to find their opponents and eliminate them."

"Both the sect and the Brotherhood are secret organisations," added Madena.

Jotham watched Silas for a reaction. He looked shocked, as if he'd been oblivious to the existence of both groups.

"I see," said Silas, hanging his head. "I'm afraid that I didn't hold much back. I told those monks everything about the tip of the Holy Spear, and that Goran Novak wanted to meet me in Budapest. I said that he was going to call with his location when we arrived there. And now they have my phone and password, and can answer Novak's call.

"They've go my phone as well," said Jotham, "but it has special security and can't be unlocked."

"Is there anything they don't know?" asked Eugene.

"I didn't tell them that he'd be staying on the Pest side of the riverfront."

Eugene was fast approaching the Conrad house.

"It shouldn't be too hard to find him if he's booked in under that name," said Madena. "Even if he's not, we'll find him somehow."

"Are you still planning to go to Budapest?" asked Silas, turning to Jotham. "I need to get there as soon as possible. So much time has been lost."

"You bet we are," replied Jotham. But I suggest you stay here to recover from your ordeal. Madena and I can go to Budapest."

"You're not going without me," said Silas with a determined look.

"You've been through a traumatic experience," said Madena.

He clenched his fists. "Nothing will stop me."

Eugene turned into the driveway of the Conrad house and the front door was caught in the headlights. Veronica rushed out with Noah close behind her. As the car stopped, she ran with outstretched arms towards her husband.

***

Sardinia to Budapest

The flying time from Sardinia to Budapest was just over two hours, but Father Benjamin took eighteen hours to get there because there was no direct flight. He left Father Dominic at the hospice and drove to the airport at Cagliari. While waiting more than fourteen hours for a connecting flight in Rome, he had plenty of time to reflect on the challenges that awaited him. His intention was to be the next head of the Brotherhood and this would be his first real test.

Tugging at his priestly collar, he glanced around at the other passengers, always on the lookout for any sign of the sect. When he arrived in Budapest, he caught a taxi to his hotel in the city centre. It was one of the more luxurious ones in Vaci Street with all the modern comforts.

It was a huge relief to finally be in the security of his room. He fumbled in his bag for a small wooden crucifix and placed it on the desk. Kneeling in front of it, he raised his eyes heavenward and began to pray as beads of sweat formed on his forehead.

"Dear Lord, help me to do the work you've set for me," he said. "No matter what it takes, no matter how hard it becomes. Do not shine a light on the work of the Brotherhood, exposing us to the world. Help and protect us so that our endeavours remain a secret. We swim against a ferocious tide of evil and you have tasked us with saving the church. Help me to be worthy of that awesome responsibility."

Benjamin raised his arms to the side and thought about how Jesus suffered on the cross. Breathing hard, he prostrated his body on the floor.

Face down, he continued. "I pray that you would help the Brotherhood, each and every one of us," he said. "And as for Jotham Fletcher, who brought that evil Magus into the open, who wrote and lectured about Simon Magus and shone a light on him, I pray that you would deal with him. Destroy all our enemies, Lord.

"Please hear my prayer and give me courage to do whatever is necessary in your name."

***

San Diego

At the Conrad house, the family gathered in the living room with Jotham, Madena and Eugene. The only person not there was Korey, who was in his own apartment. They'd been able to keep him in the dark about the drama.

Anthony Gillam had been checking the plane and arrived a short time later in a taxi. "You never looked so handsome," said Jotham when he walked in.

"Thanks boss, it's great to see you, too," he replied in his British accent. "But you look like you've been in World War Three."

"I'll be fine after a shower. How's the jet?"

"All set and ready to go, we just need the passengers. Are you still planning to go to Budapest?"

They turned towards Silas, who had washed but was now stretched out on the sofa as Veronica tried to administer first aid. "What did they do to you?" she asked, dabbing the crusted burns on his arms.

He grimaced in response. "You don't want to know, honey," he replied.

She stroked his cheek. "I can't believe that monks did this to you."

"Then left us to rot, which is probably worse," said Silas.

"Shocking to think what might have happened," said Noah.

"Thank God Jotham and Madena found you, and Eugene too," said Veronica, smiling at the visitors. "I can't thank you enough."

"The Brotherhood is willing to do anything to find the sect," said Jotham. They don't care who is hurt along the way. They've killed more than once, and not in a nice way."

123

Madena finally convinced Jotham to sit down. "Let me take a quick look at you," she said, checking the wounds on his face and arms.

Jotham glanced over at Silas. "I really think you should consider staying here and seeing a doctor. The sort of experience is very traumatising. Madena and I can go to Budapest and search for Novak."

"I'm okay, and nothing's going to stop me going with you," he replied.

Jotham shrugged his shoulders. "We're planning to leave in half an hour. I want to get to Novak before the Brotherhood do."

"You'll need my help as well," said Eugene.

Jotham exchanged a knowing look with Madena, and she kissed his cheek tenderly. Then he stood and walked over to Eugene. "You really should return to Bristol and get back to university."

The young man took off his glasses. "I don't want to let you down."

"You've already done more than enough," said Madena warmly. "Restoring the computer system and helping to rescue Silas and Jotham. But your studies take priority."

He gritted his teeth. "I have to admit that my big exam is coming up in a few days time - the most important one of the year."

Jotham raised his eyebrows. "Eugene, you should have told us that. You can come with us to the airport, then fly first class back home. If there isn't anything available you can charter a jet."

"Thanks Jotham, that's gobsmackingly good of you – but you haven't heard or seen the last of me."

"I'm sure I haven't," he said. "Now, time for me to have a quick shower."

"Second door at the top of the stairs, there's some towels in there," said Veronica. When he left the room, she took Silas's hand and kissed it. "I'm not sure that you should be going anywhere in your condition, sweetheart. In fact, I want to go in your place."

Chapter 28

Madena saw Silas lying on the sofa and thought he looked haggard and tired. It appeared as if he were about to agree with Veronica's request to go in his place, but then he pursed his lips and stood up. "No way, I'm not letting the Brotherhood anywhere near you and I want to be there to stop them getting their hands on the Holy Spear."

Veronica lowered her head, as if she knew from experience that it was no use trying to argue with him. "Very well, but I'm not happy about it," she said.

Then he put his arm around her. "Did we throw out my old phone?" he asked.

"It's probably in your study. I'll go have a look."

When she left the room, Noah locked eyes with his brother. "Silas, let me go instead."

"No way," he replied with a terse voice. "That's crazy. Your job is to look after Dad, and Veronica needs help to run things here. That's where your skills lie. We'll only be gone a few days at the most."

"I'm younger and fitter than you are," he pleaded but Silas ignored him. Madena couldn't help feeling sorry for Noah. It was clear that he'd been bullied all his life.

Veronica returned a moment later with a phone in her hand. "It still seems to be working. I'll charge it while you get ready."

Noah hadn't finished yet, and glared at his brother. "I mean it Silas, I insist on going. You're not well enough."

Silas dismissed him with a wave of the hand. "Don't be ridiculous. You'd never cope in a high pressure situation like that." There was an embarrassing silence as Noah stormed off and Madena could see that Veronica felt sorry her brother-in-law.

Half an hour later, everyone had packed overnight bags and was ready to leave.

Silas hugged Veronica before he left. "You can make excuses to Dad for me."

"Don't take any risks," she replied. "I want you back in one piece - imagine this place without you."

"Trust me, I won't be doing anything stupid. I've had enough adventures for a while. But try to keep Noah under control."

There were tears in her eyes as she nodded and turned to the others. "Be careful, all of you."

Outside, Jotham slid behind the wheel, ready to drive Silas, Madena and Anthony, as well as Eugene, to the airport in the hire car. Madena peered out the back window to wave as they turned into the street.

Noah was standing next to Veronica near the front door. He frowned when she spoke to him, and then she took out her phone and appeared to be making a call.

***

While Anthony prepared the jet for take off, Silas settled into one of the comfortable leather seats. His eyes were agog as he admired the small cabin. "This is impressive," he said. "What model is it?"

"A Beechcraft Premier One. It's been useful to have our own plane always on hand, as you can imagine."

Anthony's voice came over the intercom as they taxied down the runway. "Please make sure you do up your seatbelts. En route, we'll be stopping in Newfoundland once again to refuel and so that I can get a few hours sleep. I've booked a hotel for us right next to the airport. Then it's straight on to Budapest."

After taking off, Jotham went to the galley and switched on the coffee machine.

"I've never been in a private plane before," said Silas.

Jotham returned to his seat and looked across the narrow aisle. "You must have amassed some wealth as the church expanded."

"Not really. I took wages for Veronica and myself, and invested the rest in infrastructure and growth. It's the German in me, I've always been careful with money, but we don't have any debts."

Madena nestled against Jotham in the seat beside her. "How much are you prepared to pay for the tip of the Holy Spear?" she asked the older man beside her.

Silas paused to think. "To tell the truth I really hadn't thought about it," he said. "But I think I'd be willing to give them everything I have."

***

126

Father Benjamin was in the main boulevard of the city not far from his hotel, enjoying an alfresco lunch of schnitzel with grilled vegetables. The weather was excessively hot and wearing a black priest's suit didn't help. His face was wet with perspiration but at least there was some relief provided by a large aqua fan in the corner that covered him in a continuous spray of water. His smartphone was on the table in front of him and he kept a close eye on it, waiting for a call from Brother Sean. He had Silas Conrad's phone, and was hoping to get a call from the mysterious Goran Novak.

After clearing his plate, he asked for the bill and that was when the phone's screen lit up. He answered it straight away.

"Hello?" he said in a gruff voice.

"Sean here," he replied. "I've had a phone call."

"And?"

"Novak rang and I put on a great American accent; he didn't suspect a thing. Novak says he's staying at the Galaxy Hotel along the riverfront on the Pest side, just near the Chain Bridge. He's staying in suite 709, but his grandmother will meet you in the lobby and take you up to the room. Be there in one hour."

"Is that it?"

"That's it, Father."

"Thank you, but keep me posted if he calls again."

"You can rely on us," he replied, and then he ended the call.

Benjamin waved his hand and the waiter came over. "Can I get you anything?" he asked.

"A glass of red wine," he replied, "but please hurry, I have an appointment in a few minutes."

"Yes, certainly Father," he said, rushing off.

The drink was delivered less than a minute later. Benjamin placed it in the centre of the table and stared at it for at least five minutes as he prayed in silence. *Give me the strength to do your work, to claim this prize for you, to serve the Brotherhood and wipe the evil sect from the face of the earth.*

As he gulped the wine, he thanked God for the blood of his saviour and knew that its potency would provide him with the power that he needed.

He strode more than a mile through the city to reach the riverfront. While he walked, two of the Ten Commandments kept running through his thoughts like a broken record.

You shall not commit murder.

You shall not steal.

The Danube was a breathtaking sight, spanned by several graceful bridges. Although the Pest side of the city was flat, the Buda district on the opposite bank was hilly, with the castle district set on top of a steep cliff. He marched past a series of elegant buildings lining the riverbank and approached the Galaxy Hotel.

As he entered the large, modern lobby, he walked past a sophisticated-looking bar and restaurant. It seemed as if Goran Novak appreciated stylish living.

A petite woman in her late seventies stepped out from behind a column and stood in front of him. "Are you Mrs Novak?" asked Benjamin.

She screwed up her face and nodded. "Follow me," she said, leading him around the corner to the elevators and making no eye contact as they stepped inside. After scanning her keycard, they began to move upwards.

The hallway on the seventh floor was the epitome of restrained opulence. "He's waiting for you," she said slowly, as they walked towards the double doors at the end of the hallway.

A brass plaque on the door announced that it was *Suite 709*. Father Benjamin felt a cold hand grab his stomach and squeeze it tight.

Chapter 29

Jotham, Madena and Silas arrived in Budapest in the early afternoon and headed straight to the Pest side of the riverfront. A tramline ran past grand buildings and tour boats plied the waters, many of them packed with lunchtime diners. Overlooking the scene on the opposite bank was the Buda Castle, perched on top of a hill.

Jotham's goal was to locate Goran Novak, and all they knew was that he was staying in a hotel along the riverfront. They had reached the right area, and now it was time to begin their search.

All of them were dressed smartly so as to blend in, but in shoes and clothes that were comfortable and sturdy enough for them to cope with any physical threat they might encounter. Jotham scrutinised his two companions and knew that there was only one of them that he could trust. Madena's makeup was immaculate and she looked stunning. "You look perfect, Darling," he said. "They'll be eating out of your hand."

"That's good," she replied. "We're going to need all the help we can get."

He turned to Silas. "We'll separate here. Madena can proceed alone to the south and you can stay with me, heading north."

"Why don't we all go alone and get the job done in far less time?" asked Silas.

Madena responded with her firmest voice. "I don't think so. You don't know who you might run into, including one of our Brotherhood friends. They wouldn't hesitate to kill you."

He looked down at the paving. "If you put it like that."

Jotham was prepared to take Silas under his wing, but he was beginning to wonder if he'd been a fool to bring him along. The pair headed north towards their first stop, the elegant Royal Budapest Hotel.

"Why don't you stay out here and stand guard," he said, pointing to a sheltered location close to the entrance. "Look as if you're waiting for someone."

"Good idea," he replied, trying to appear relaxed but failing miserably.

Jotham walked into the Art Deco lobby and approached the small reception desk.

An ageing clerk gave him a haughty look. "Yes, sir, how can I be of assistance?"

Jotham cleared his throat. "Hello, I have a message for Mr Novak. I believe he's staying here.

The man twisted his lips as he searched exhaustively through his registration list, and Jotham marvelled at how long the process took. At this rate, it was going to take all day to visit a few hotels. "We don't seem to have anyone of that name here," he said finally, his eyes narrowed as if he suspected something.

Jotham looked around as if he was confused. "Oh, sorry, I though this was the Marriott."

The man cocked his finger. "That's just down the road, sir."

"Thank you so much," he said, retreating out the door.

***

Madena walked into the imposing lobby of the Galaxy Hotel and scanned the scene. There was nothing suspicious, but she soon noticed that a handsome man of about thirty behind the reception desk was observing her. He flicked back his hair as she approached and gave her a cheesy grin. "Hello, madam, can I help you?"

She flashed a coy smile, fully aware that he had noticed her considerable physical charms. "I wanted to surprise a friend of mine," she said. "But I don't know what room he's in. It's his birthday, you see."

"I understand, what's his name?"

"Goran Novak."

"Mm," he replied, checking the computer system. Madena thought there might be some privacy issues, but to her amazement he didn't hesitate to answer. "Yes, he's in Suite 709. There's a phone over there, you can call his room." He pointed to a guest phone in the corner.

"Thank you so much," she said. "I'm so grateful."

"My pleasure, madam. Let me know if you need any more help."

She sauntered over and picked up the phone, acting as if she was making a call but keeping a close eye on her surroundings. He was in the building, there was no doubt of that, and she needed to notify Jotham urgently and stay alert for any sign of danger.

At first, she nodded her head as if she was chatting, and then pretended to hang up. From there, she strode through the lobby and out into the street, whipping out her phone and texting Jotham.

He and Silas met her around the corner three minutes later.

***

Jotham and Madena quickly formulated a plan and then approached the Galaxy Hotel with Silas.

Madena and Silas stood outside, pretending to be a couple and posing for photographs.

"Now smile," said Silas as he snapped her with the river in the background. All the while, Madena kept a sharp eye on Jotham as he walked into the lobby.

Jotham tried to look relaxed as he sauntered up to the reception desk. Acting had never been his strongest suit, but in the last few years he had pulled off some performances worthy of an international award. He hoped that this would be one of those times.

An attractive young woman was alone behind the counter and greeted him with a suitably gracious smile. "Good morning sir, how can I help you?"

He took a deep breath. "I've just arrived in Budapest and was wondering if you had any rooms available."

"Yes, sir, we have a few vacancies."

Now it was time to come in with the killer line. "I don't suppose..."

"Yes?" she asked expectantly.

"You wouldn't have anything on level seven? I'm superstitious about the number seven."

"Oh, I see," she said with a quizzical look. "Let me check for you." She pressed the keyboard a couple of times and stared at the monitor.

Jotham knew it was time to start praying. Finally, she turned back to him. "Yes?" he asked.

"We do have one available there, but I'm afraid it's one of our most expensive rooms."

"That's fine - I'll take it," he said, pulling out his wallet.

"And what was your name?"

"John McDonald." His favourite alias.

"Could I see your passport?"

He handed over the fake passport, hoping that he was handing her the right one. Two minutes later he had the room key in hand and stood near the elevators.

131

Madena received his text a second later, relieved to realise that they could now access that floor. She looked at Silas. "You can stay out here," she said. "It would be helpful to have you standing guard again."

He answered in a determined voice. "No way, Madena. I'm coming inside with you."

She realised that resistance was futile, but had a sinking feeling that his interference might result in one of them getting hurt. They walked inside, arm in arm like any happy couple and pretended not to know Jotham as they entered the waiting elevator.

Jotham used his keycard to press level seven, and they were whisked upwards. Despite his best intentions, he couldn't help glancing at Madena, and for just a moment she returned his tender look.

The three of them sneaked out of the elevator and pressed their backs against the wall. Suite 709 was easy to see at the end of the wide corridor, and Jotham led the way as they began to move towards it.

It was so quiet that Jotham could hear the sound of his own heartbeat.

Suddenly they heard the sound of a muffled shot and he nearly hit the ceiling. By instinct, they pressed their bodies hard against the wall, but there was no way that Jotham and Madena planned on retreating.

Silas was paralysed with fear, and crouched down behind a narrow side table lining the hallway.

Jotham leapt forward, his body braced for action, but aware that another shot could be the one that hit him. A bullet could easily pass through the locked door. He prayed that God would protect the three of them, but he had to intervene.

He reached the door and assessed the weakest point. Using all the power contained in his tall frame, he kicked it just below the lock.

Chapter 30

The door swung open and crashed against the wall, so that Jotham and Madena could peer into the suite.

A priest of about fifty, in a black suit and clerical collar, was holding a smoking gun. The younger man in the room was bent over and clutching his chest, his face contorted in shock. Blood oozed between his fingers and dripped onto the expensive carpet.

"Goran Novak," cried Madena. His eyes glinted in response as he crumpled to the floor.

At the same time, Jotham jumped forward and leapt on top of the priest like a lion after its prey.

Silas stayed pressed against the wall outside, frozen in fear.

The priest recoiled and pushed Jotham away so that he momentarily lost his balance.

Madena rushed in to help, but he twisted around and threw his arms around in wild gyrations, still holding the pistol. In a single, rapid motion he leaned over and swept up a small box off the floor and into his arms. Leaning his head forward like a rugby player about to do a tackle, he charged towards the door.

The priest was surprisingly fast for his age. Madena and Jotham both reached out to grab him as he ran between them, but he kept the box firmly under one arm and waved the gun at both them.

He reached the door and Jotham wondered if he might shoot Silas as he sprinted past. Alternatively, he hoped that Silas might try to trip him up or push him over.

But instead, he crouched further down with head covered as soon as the priest ran into the hallway. Increasing his speed, he reached the fire escape door, tore it open and headed downstairs, leaving it to slam shut behind him.

"Go after him," said Silas, almost whimpering. "We have to catch him if he has the spear."

Jotham and Madena glanced at each other, both desperately wanting to race after him. But their instincts and training took over and they knew it was their duty to try and render any assistance they could to Novak.

They bent over him on the floor. Jotham felt his neck to search for a pulse, as Madena checked his breathing. But both of them could see that there was a massive wound in his chest around the area of his heart.

Jotham shook his head. Goran Novak was probably in his early thirties, and just a few minutes ago he had been alive and well. "Yet another victim of the Brotherhood," he said.

Madena jumped to her feet. "Let's get after him."

They both turned and headed to the door.

Without pausing, Jotham snapped at Silas as he rushed past him down the hallway. "We'll try and stop him somehow, then come back to search the room. Lay low and stay out of trouble."

"I'll take the elevator," said Madena, recoiling to a stop and pressing the button.

"That leaves me to try the fire escape," he replied. Tearing down the concrete steps three at a time, he focused his mind on the almost impossible task of finding the runaway priest.

***

Father Benjamin bolted out the fire escape door into the street, gasping for breath and clutching at his chest. He was in great shape for his age, one of the reasons he had been selected as a likely replacement for Dominic, and now he realised why that was so crucial.

Madena left the elevator and strode as fast as she dared through the lobby, trying to stay to the side and avoid attracting attention. Marching out into the hot afternoon sunshine and turning to the left, she almost collided with a door as it swung open and Jotham stumbled out of the fire escape.

They scanned the scene. A tram passed by fifty metres away, running on the light rail that was parallel to the riverfront. When it moved on, Jotham's whole face widened. "There!" he cried.

He sighted the priest beyond the track, hurrying off down the path that was on a lower level, right next to the water.

They darted off in pursuit.

There was a low fence on either side of the tram tracks. Jumping over it, they quickly checked to make sure they were not about to collide with another tram. They drew the ire of a guard as they flew across the track and scrambled over the second fence to the stairs that led down to water level. Descending three or four steps at a time, they reached the path where at least five riverboats were berthed, and saw their target in the distance.

Huddles of passengers waited near their luggage to board the riverboats and stared in shock as the black-suited priest ran past. That changed to angry looks as Jotham and Madena tore after him. Some showed their displeasure by yelling out, and they even heard a woman scream.

Hey, look out!

What's going on?

My God, what's happening?

The voices rang in Jotham's ears as up ahead they saw the priest jump onto a small speedboat. The swarthy driver had just started the engine, and he smirked at the visitor. Then he gave an elated smile, probably because he'd been offered a deal too good to refuse.

Before the cleric had a chance to sit down, the boat sped off, leaving behind a vigorous wake.

Jotham and Madena reached the departure point a moment later. Helpless, they stood breathless on the bank, watching as their quarry took out his pistol and tossed it into the Danube.

He waved to them as he disappeared from view, the small box still held tightly under his arm.

Jotham grabbed his own head in frustration, knowing that he was too far away to have any hope of catching him.

"Now what?" asked Madena, catching her breath. "And what was in that box?"

"I hate to think," replied Jotham.

A familiar voice made them turn around. "Sorry I couldn't keep up," said Silas, gasping for breath. "Has he got away?"

"Looks like it," replied Jotham.

His entire body sagged in dismay. "Do you think he has the spear?"

"Highly likely, but we'll think about that later. First, we better double check the hotel room to see if the spear tip might still be there."

Silas screwed up his face in alarm. "With a dead body? We'll be arrested."

"You wait outside the building, please, Silas," said Madena in her most commanding military tone, "and this time we mean it."

He stood up to his full height. "No way, I'm willing to take that risk. I'm staying with you."

"I plan on getting out of Budapest as fast as possible after that," said Jotham. Fear gripped him at the prospect of not returning home soon, and the thought of being separated from little Belle for much longer.

Silas and Madena once again pretended to be a romantic couple and Jotham kept to himself as they headed back into the lobby, ignoring each other as they waited for the elevator. Using the keycard Jotham obtained under the bogus name of John McDonald, they returned to the seventh level.

The elegant hallway was as quiet as ever. "So far so good," said Madena, as they walked sedately towards Suite 709. Silas had shut the door before he left, but Jotham pounded his heel into the weak spot, and Madena and Silas helped by leaning in with their shoulders and pushing hard.

The door flew open, but just then they heard the ping of the elevator. "Level Seven," said the automated voice, and when Jotham turned his head he saw it sliding open.

Someone was about to step out, and they were about to be sprung.

"Quick," snapped Jotham. They scurried inside like terrified mice and closed the door, just in time.

Chapter 31

Now that they were safely secured in the suite, Jotham and Madena walked over to Goran Novak's grotesque body. Lying in the centre of the living room, his skin was now grey and his face devoid of humanity. Silas walked over to the window and stared out at the panoramic view of the Danube, but that was in an effort to avoid looking at the corpse.

"I can't wait to get out of here," said Madena. "We'll do a quick search and then get to the airport."

"I'll look in the bedroom," said Silas.

"We'll finish in here first and then give you a hand," said Jotham. He and Madena checked every square inch of the living room, including the furniture and coffee machine, but found nothing of interest.

Silas went into the bedroom, and his eyes brightened when he immediately saw that one half of the sliding closet door was pulled across. The mini-safe was perched on the centre shelf, and it was unlocked.

He could hardly breathe as he knelt down and looked inside, then used his hand to probe the interior surfaces. He stood up as Jotham and Madena walked in. "It's gone," he said with tears in his eyes.

"We'll have a thorough look in here," said Madena, checking the walls. "We're not finished yet."

Jotham started to inspect the bed, pulling apart the sheets. "But I'm afraid you're right, Silas. It was almost certainly in that box the priest was holding."

That was when Jotham heard the slightest rustling sound.

There was a crash as the bathroom door flew open.

An elderly woman burst into the room, armed with a cattle prod that she held aloft. She stayed silent but was in a frenzy, her yellow teeth bared in a furious grimace.

Silas ran into the other room as she charged towards them, waving the weapon in her outstretched arm.

For someone of her age and size, she seemed able to handle herself well in a fight. Jotham was reluctant to hurt her and although their strength was far superior, she managed to frighten them.

Jotham held his ground and confronted her head on. She hesitated for a fraction of a second as if trying to take aim.

Madena pounced on her from the side and in a single whip-like action, plucked the cattle prod from her hand and disarmed her.

Jotham wrapped his arms around the woman's thin body and held her from behind in a tight hold. He wanted to restrain her without hurting her. "Calm down," he said gently, though he doubted that she would be able to understand his words.

She stopped struggling, probably because of physical exhaustion, but then she broke down into hysterical weeping.

"What will we do?" asked Madena, her face revealing her concern.

The old woman heaved and let out a frightening sob. "Goran, Goran!"

That was when they heard the sound of sirens.

Madena's eyes widened. "Out of here, now," she said.

"She's probably called the police," said Silas from the other room.

"Come with me, Silas, and Jotham can follow us," said Madena, grabbing him by the arm and leading him out of the main door.

Jotham released the woman and stepped back, watching her carefully.

She hobbled over to the body on the floor and fell to her knees beside him. "Goran," she cried, weeping inconsolably.

Jotham turned and ran out after the others. Madena was waiting at the elevator and the door slid open straight away. Walking inside, they realised that all they had to do now was get out of the hotel without arousing suspicion.

Jotham took out his keycard and a bundle of forints, the local currency. "Shame we didn't get to see my room," he said.

In the lobby, the others headed straight to the entrance as Jotham approached the reception desk. Just as they walked out the automatic door, four policemen charged inside through the revolving door adjacent to it.

Jotham walked to the desk, his heart beating fast.

The young man gave him a polite upturn of his lips. "Yes, sir, how can I..."

Jotham didn't wait for him to finish. "I've had a change of plans, this should cover everything," he said, handing him the room keycard and the bundle of notes.

Out of the corner of his eye, he saw that the police had reached the elevator.

The clerk raised his eyebrows. "Thank you, sir. Have a safe journey."

Jotham turned around. With his head lowered, he kept close to the wall as he walked toward the exit. He felt like a taut rubber band that had gone past breaking point. Trying to appear relaxed, he made his way through the revolving door and strolled past the doorman.

He avoided the limousines outside the hotel and strode over to the row of budget taxis in the street. Madena and Silas were already waiting in the back seat of the first one. Jotham ran over and jumped in the front.

The scruffy driver was at least forty. "Can you get us to the airport in fifteen minutes?" asked Jotham. "We'll pay you very well."

"Impossible," he replied. "But I'll do my best." He turned to the passengers in the back seat. "Do your belts up and hang on tight."

He slammed his foot on the accelerator and the tyres squealed as they raced down the street. To avoid the clogged city traffic, he led them through a maze of narrow back lanes. The car twisted and turned, swinging them from side to side as they turned each corner.

Jotham soon realised that he was in the hands of a madman, but took out his phone and held on tight to it as he dialled Anthony Gillam.

"Hello, Jotham," said Anthony, though it was hard to hear him over the cacophony of horn blasts coming from the other vehicles.

"Prep the plane, please, Anthony. We'll be there in ten minutes. Sorry - a sudden change of plans."

"I'm on to it."

Jotham put the phone away and stared at the driver. "Are you having a good day?" he asked.

The man had a firm grip of the wheel, his eyes wide as he zeroed in on the next curve. "It was boring, until you came along," he replied.

"I'm prone to motion sickness," said Silas with a moan.

"Don't worry, we'll be there soon," said Madena, grasping the door handle with white knuckles. "Jotham, what are you planning next?"

He turned his head and locked eyes with her. "I think I know just how to find that priest."

She gave him a sly smile. "Are you thinking what I'm thinking?"

He winked in reply.

Two minutes later, the car stopped with a jerk outside the general aviation terminal. As Jotham handed the driver a wad of notes, a look of joy washed over the man's face. "Anytime," he said.

They scrambled out of the car and Jotham noticed that Silas looked decidedly ashen. "You'll feel better soon," he said, leading them inside and heading towards the jet.

He couldn't help feeling relieved that he would soon be out of

Budapest, but nothing had worked out as expected. Goran Novak's death was a tragedy, and the Holy Spear was probably lost. But there was a slim chance that he might be able to recover it.

***

As Father Benjamin walked anxiously into the terminal at Budapest Airport, he gave a nervous cough.

He already knew the identity of the man who had burst into Goran Novak's suite and disturbed him. Father Dominic had described him in minute detail, and that turned out to be an accurate depiction of all his physical features as well as his ridiculous behaviour.

The man was none other than Jotham Fletcher, and somehow he had managed to turn up in Budapest and interrupt his meeting with the Hungarian.

It could all have ended in disaster.

As he approached the check-in counter, a man in a grey suit approached him. "Excuse me, sir, are you Father Benjamin?" he asked.

He spun around, hairs rising under the back of his collar. "Yes, how can I help you?"

"I'm Mr Pataki. We've been expecting you, and here's your briefcase," he said, handing it over. 'We had our representative collect the luggage from your hotel as you requested. Your suitcase has already been checked in."

"That's excellent," replied Benjamin.

"Your colleague in the Vatican contacted our office in Budapest and said that you were a VIP. Your flight to Rome has been arranged."

"Thank you, that's very kind," he said, as he opened his briefcase and put the box safely inside, then fastened the lock. Benjamin had contacted his former colleague when he was escaping on the speedboat, and he had promised to help him get out of the country straight away. But he had not expected to receive such royal treatment.

"Please come with me," said Pataki in a dignified voice. Benjamin followed the thickset man as he led him through the security barrier and he was allowed to pass through without any checks. Barely able to believe his good fortune, he was led down a long narrow corridor and into a private waiting room.

Pataki opened the door for him. "Just relax in here, Father. Would you like some coffee, perhaps, right now?

"That would be nice," said the priest.

He picked up the phone on the side table and ordered two coffees as Benjamin sat on a comfortable armchair, holding the briefcase close to his chest. But he was surprised when Pataki sat opposite him. "I'll be looking after you till you board the plane, to make sure that you have everything you need," he said.

Benjamin took a moment to collect his thoughts and stared straight ahead. In just a few hours, he would bring the precious object to the Vatican and his future would be secure. The tip of the Holy Spear would soon be entombed under the Dome of St Peter's Basilica, and his own name would be added to the history books. After a short stint as the Head of the Brotherhood, the time would be ripe for him to become a Cardinal.

It was all just as it should be.

He reached into his suit pocket and took out his phone. "Mr Pataki, if you'd excuse me, I really do need to make an important call in private."

"Yes, of course, I'll leave you alone," he replied.

Chapter 32

Pataki sauntered out of the small waiting room and shut the door. Without wasting any more time, Benjamin phoned Father Dominic. He had managed to sneak a phone into Dominic's room before he left so that they could stay in touch.

A croaky voice answered. "Hello?"

"I have the object."

Dominic exhaled. "Praise be to God. Did everything go smoothly in Budapest?"

"Yes, everything went according to plan." He had decided not to mention any of the bloody details, including his encounter with Jotham Fletcher. Their rival had managed to escape and he would have to deal with him another time. It would be better for Dominic if he avoided the subject altogether.

"You've exceeded my expectations."

Father Benjamin gulped, aware that now it was time for the bad news. "I need to let you know that I'm travelling to Rome. I intend to present the object to the Vatican because it's too precious for us to look after."

He did not expect Dominic to be pleased about his decision and he waited for his response.

The sick man gave a strange, frightening moan like an injured animal. "No, I beg you to bring it back to me," he said. "Don't tell the Vatican. Bring it to me first and then you can take it to Rome."

"In Rome, Dominic, it will belong to everyone. Why do you want it so badly?"

Dominic sounded as if he was weeping. "I truly believe that the tip of the Holy Spear would give us the power we need to overcome the sect. If I could touch it, just once, I'm certain that I would live to complete my mission."

Benjamin hadn't expected such an emotional reaction and it had shaken him. Thoughts swirled and collided in the priest's mind, but slowly he began to see a clear path through the traffic jam of ideas. If the spear really had special powers, then it might help him to excel when he became the Head of the Brotherhood. Then his future career path would be assured.

There was no reason why he couldn't bring it to Father Dominic before he delivered it to Rome. He sat back in his chair, smirking at his own cleverness.

"All right, Dominic," he said. "I'll bring the object to the hospice. I know how much it means to you, and after a lifetime of service to the Brotherhood you deserve that chance."

Dominic gasped with relief. "Thank you, Benjamin, you won't regret this," he said.

"But then I want to take it to the Vatican," he said, and ended the call.

Benjamin opened the door and stuck his head out. Pataki was loitering at the end of the corridor and he called out to him. "Is there a booking clerk near here, Mr Pataki?"

"We can call someone," he replied, walking towards him.

"Good. I have a last-minutes change of plans, and I want to book another flight."

***

Father Benjamin was in luck. There was a direct service from Budapest to Sardinia three times a week, and the timing could not have been better. The Air Sardinia flight to Cagliari left at four o'clock and he had to rush to the gate to reach it on time. The airline representative had already begun to close the barrier when he arrived, and his heart rate jumped as he approached.

"You just made it, Father," said the middle-aged woman respectfully as she pulled the cord across the airbridge. Benjamin had a feeling that if he hadn't been a priest he would have been turned away.

As he boarded the jet, a steward saw the business class label on his boarding pass and reached out for his briefcase. "Good afternoon, Father Benjamin, can I put that in the locker for you?"

Benjamin tightened his grip on the handle. "No thanks, I'll keep it with me," he replied. He smiled to himself at the thought of telling him that inside was the tip of the spear that had pierced the side of Jesus Christ.

He put the briefcase underneath the seat in front of him and kept a firm hold of it between his feet. That way, it would stay in his sight throughout the flight.

While the plane waited on the tarmac, he noticed raindrops meandering down the window. He prayed for a safe journey, knowing that in an emergency evacuation he'd be forced to leave the bag behind.

That truly would be a disaster.

Shortly after takeoff, the plane shuddered as it headed into a thick bank of clouds. Benjamin's stomach lurched and he gazed wide-eyed at the mist outside. He was so focused on the window and keeping a firm foothold of his briefcase that he didn't notice the man several rows behind him.

The man was in an aisle seat, and could just see the back of the priest's head and part of his arm. Earlier that day he had seen him running out of the Galaxy Hotel, so he went to the airport in the hope of finding him there. He had almost given up, and couldn't believe it when he saw him walk into the terminal.

Now he had no intention of letting him out of his sight.

***

Jotham, Madena and Silas settled into their seats as Anthony taxied the plane down the runway. The wings oscillated as they left the ground and, up ahead, they saw a wall of grey clouds.

Anthony's voice came over the intercom. "Let me know where we're heading as soon as you make up your mind," he said.

Silas frowned. "He doesn't know where we're going?"

Madena put a reassuring hand on his arm. "Don't worry, he knows we're going to Sardinia," she said.

Silas looked even more concerned. "Sardinia?"

"I think so, if my hunch is correct," said Jotham.

"Where in Sardinia?"

"I need to make a phone enquiry first."

"Would someone please tell me what's going on?"

Jotham whipped out his phone and placed it on the small table between the seats, then searched his contact list.

When he made the call, they heard a woman's voice answer. "*Pronto*," she said.

"*Capitana* Rinaldi, it's Jotham Fletcher here."

"*Si*, Jotham, what can I do for you?" she asked.

He leaned towards the phone. "Maria, you said that Father Dominic is in a hospice in Sardinia – but whereabouts is it?"

She hesitated. "You're not planning to visit him are you, Jotham?"

"No, not at all, I don't want to see him. But I just want to find out about the facility and set my mind at ease."

"I can assure, his health is failing. He's not a danger to anyone any more."

"I'd like to find that out for myself. Do you know the name of the hospital?"

"I think I have access to that. Please hold on, and I'll see if I can look it up, yes?"

She was away from the phone for at least three minutes, and the others stared at Jotham with wrapt attention.

Maria returned to the phone, but her voice was breaking up. "Jotham?" she asked.

"Yes, I'm here."

"He's at the Convent of the Immaculate Conception. They run a hospice there, fifteen miles outside Sassari."

"Thanks for your help, Maria, and how is your *bambino*?

"He's perfect."

Jotham put his phone away and walked up to the cockpit.

Anthony turned his head when the door opened. "Well, are we still heading to Sardinia?" he asked.

"We sure are," replied Jotham. "Close to Sassari, about fifteen miles out of town."

"That's only two hours away, shouldn't be too difficult."

Madena reviewed the location on her device. "Sardinia's second largest city," she said, setting to work. "Let's see if we can find somewhere we can land – I'll talk to Anthony." She walked to the cockpit and closed the door behind her.

Silas appeared to be suitably impressed. "You run a smooth operation here," he said. "How do you manage to have contacts in the Italian police?"

"It's a long story - a very long story," said Jotham. "Maria Rinaldi is with the Caribinieri. We met in Rome about three years ago when I went there to give a lecture on my doctoral thesis about Simon Magus. The next thing I knew I was a murder suspect, although later I was exonerated. Since then, our paths have crossed several times."

"You certainly lead an exciting life," said Silas.

Madena strode back into the cabin, opened the galley compartment door and turned on the coffee machine. "That was when he first found out about the sect and we've been trying to foil their activities ever since. Jotham inherited a fortune from a man who was killed by the Brotherhood."

"So why are we heading to that convent?"

145

Chapter 33

Jotham looked straight at Silas, still wondering if he knew a whole lot more than he was letting on.

"A man called Father Dominic is there. He's been the Head of the Brotherhood for years and he's the most ruthless and violent man I've ever had the misfortune to meet. Now he's supposedly dying of a brain tumour and too ill to be causing any more trouble. But until he's dead and buried, we think he'll be trying to maintain control of the organisation. I suspect that our homicidal priest today belongs to the Brotherhood, and our theory is that he'll be delivering the tip of the Holy Spear to Father Dominic."

Silas sat up straight, his eyes now shining with a spark of hope. "I pray that you're right."

"So do we," said Madena, handing him a coffee.

***

They ate some sandwiches while Madena made the final preparations for their arrival in Sardinia. "There's a disused World War Two airstrip only eight miles from the convent," she said, running a hand through her wavy hair. "When we land, a car will be waiting for us with the keys on the roof, and there won't be anyone else there. We always like to keep our movements under wraps."

Silas had been quiet for more than half an hour, focused on his own dark thoughts but now he started to show an interest. "How did you manage to arrange all that?" he asked.

"With money," replied Jotham. "A fact that still surprises me, but I've learnt that it talks all languages.

"Are you sure the runway will be safe to use?"

Jotham put his arm around Madena. "Apparently it's in quite good condition," she said, "and thankfully, Anthony is a brilliant pilot. We'll be there in less than an hour, so try to get some rest while you can."

"I feel as if my nerves are shot," said Silas. "I might have another coffee to wake me up." He went to the galley and helped himself, then settled back in the seat.

Madena took hold of Jotham's hand and kissed his fingertips. "Belle is probably having her nap right now," she said.

"We'll call home in a few minutes," he replied, and Madena blew a kiss to indicate her approval. They could never predict the outcome of any mission, particularly when Father Dominic and the Brotherhood were involved, so every moment they could spend with their child was precious.

She turned to Silas. "How long have you and Veronica been married?"

"Fifteen years," he replied with a sigh.

Madena glared at Jotham in surprise. "I thought it would be much longer than that," she said. "So Veronica's your second wife?"

"Yes, but I don't usually talk about that. My first wife, Cheryl, was killed by a drunk driver when my daughter was just a baby. Veronica's the only mother they can remember."

"That's tragic, but so good that you found happiness again."

"My whole life changed when Veronica came along. I'd just taken over from my father when I met her, but it was only the small church that he'd started outside San Diego. Veronica had been reading about the Holy Spear and told us about its power. I prayed about it and introduced some of her ideas. After that, the church really took off and began to grow."

"So you owe her a great deal," said Madena.

"Veronica's everything to me, but now I'm afraid I might lose her."

She raised her eyebrows. "Why would you think that?"

"I don't know why, but I have a sense of foreboding. What if something goes wrong in Sardinia? I might never see her again."

She noticed then that he looked pale and clammy, and knew that having a sense of impending doom could be a sign that he was about to have a heart attack. "Silas, are you okay?" she asked.

"I feel a bit queasy."

Jotham picked up on her signals and strode over. "I'll get you some water," he said. He quickly poured a glass and rushed back to Silas, who took a few sips. As he rolled his head back, Jotham felt for a pulse.

"Slow and steady breaths," said Madena, putting a hand on Silas's shoulder. "Your pulse is racing, just relax."

After a couple of minutes, his breathing became shallower and his colour began to improve. "I feel a bit better now," he said.

"You may have just been anxious," said Jotham, concerned about how Silas might react in a confrontation with the Brotherhood. A panic attack was the last thing they needed.

Silas waved away his concerns. "It's happened before, I'll be fine in a few minutes. Don't worry about me."

"Just take it easy, we'll be landing soon," said Jotham, exchanging a worried look with Madena. "We'll see how you're feeling then."

***

Sardinia

Father Benjamin picked up his briefcase as soon as the flight touched down at Cagliari Elmas Airport. He kept a white-knuckled grip on the handle as he flowed with the tide of travellers who trundled off the plane and through the airport concourse.

All through his adult life he had attracted stares because of his clerical clothing. The collar and black suit marked him as a man who separates himself from normal people. There were always smiles or occasional respectful nods, but today he ignored them and kept a lookout for anything suspicious. All he wanted was to keep his mind on the task at hand, and that was to transport the relic to safety.

He didn't see the person who trailed far behind him, watching his every move and being sure not to let him out of his sight. His objective was to follow him, no matter where he went.

Father Benjamin had already made a booking for a hire car. He approached the counter, the first one in a row of six booths, and waited while the clerk took an interminable time to deal with the three customers ahead of him.

The man following him walked past the next two booths and found a company that could serve him straight away.

Father Benjamin completed the tedious paperwork and marched off towards the car park.

By that time, his shadow was ready to follow him with his own set of car keys in hand. He kept just far enough back to avoid being noticed. His biggest challenge now was to find his own vehicle and stay on the priest's tail. But even if he lost sight of him for a while, he had a fair idea of where he was headed.

As he drove away, he blinked nervously and gripped the steering wheel tight.

Father Dominic was sitting in his armchair when Benjamin walked into the room. He was struck by how much worse he looked after just a few days, his once powerful body even thinner and his cheeks sunken. Sister Alicia was expertly adjusting some cushions to help make him more comfortable.

Dominic's dull eyes sparked to life as soon as he saw him. "Benjamin, what do you have for me?" he asked, stretching out his arms.

"I'll leave you two alone to talk," said Sister Alicia. "But could I please have a word with you first, Father Benjamin?"

He followed her outside and shut the door. "I'm glad to see you back, Father," she said. "I'm afraid that Dominic's condition has deteriorated in the last couple of days."

"Do you mean that he's dying?" asked Benjamin, trying to adopt a concerned expression.

"He's not there yet, but his sense of balance is affected and he's had trouble with pins and needles in his arms and legs. Anyway, I'm sure that he'll be pleased to see you. Did you have a successful trip?"

"Yes, it went very well, thank you, Sister." She walked off and he returned to the room.

Dominic was silent but watched closely as Benjamin sat down and removed the weathered box from his briefcase. "You've brought it," he said, his eyes full of hope.

Benjamin slowly unlatched the lid and opened it.

Though he appeared to be in pain, Dominic sat up straight and gazed at the object as if it was a newborn baby. "The tip of the spear that pierced the side of Christ. This humble object touched our Lord's flesh."

"Yes, I believe so," said Benjamin.

Dominic looked heavenward with moist eyes and began to pray. "Thank you for bringing the Holy Spear to me, Lord. Give me the strength to defeat our enemies and wipe the Simonian Sect from the face of the Earth."

He blinked and appeared to be struggling for breath. "My pain is easing," he said, his mouth gaping.

"That's the healing balm of prayer," replied Benjamin.

Chapter 34

Father Dominic looked up at Benjamin. "The Holy Spear will cure me and I'll be able to complete my mission. There'll be nothing to stop us now and the evil sect will be destroyed."

Benjamin took the object out of the box and held it in the palm of his hands. Warmth radiated up his arms, as if he'd brought his hands close to a blazing fire.

Leaning forward, he brought the tip of the Holy Spear so close to Dominic's face that he was able to kiss it.

After that, he carefully replaced it in the box and secured the lid.

Dominic sat there for a minute in silent meditation and then looked at him with wide eyes. "I feel stronger already," he said, grabbing hold of Benjamin's hands so tightly that he flinched.

"You're feeling better?" asked Benjamin.

"It's a miracle, I'm sure of it. But it will take a while for me to experience the full effects."

Benjamin put the box down on the bedside table, then stood up and paced the floor.

"Sit down with me, we need to pray together," said Dominic. "The Lord won't complete a miracle unless voices are raised in fervent prayer."

Benjamin looked out the small window at the gently rolling hills beyond the stucco wall that encircled the convent. "Yes," he said, turning around. He was stunned to see that Dominic's face had relaxed as if he was in less pain and his skin colour was improving. "But I'm the man who will defeat the Simonian Sect. There's no way that you can be cured."

Dominic wrinkled up his face in shock. "Why not - why would you say that?"

"From now on, I'll be in charge of the Brotherhood."

Dominic barked at him. "How dare you speak to me like that? There's been a miracle - you can't deny it. God wanted you to bring the Holy Spear to me."

Benjamin charged at him, his eyes blazing. "You're time is over," he said.

Dominic's face twisted in fear. He braced his once-powerful frame and tried to stand up.

In one rapid motion, Benjamin picked up the pillow on the bed and pressed it over Dominic's face.

He may have just received a miraculous cure, but the ravages of disease had whittled away most of Dominic's strength. Now faced with the threat of death, he tried to draw on every ounce of energy in his body. He strained each muscle to the point of agony as he tried to fight back with flailing limbs.

Benjamin exerted all the power he could muster to wrest control of the Brotherhood, but his victim put up an almighty struggle that was nothing short of incredible. Benjamin was about to collapse with the strain and began to wonder if he would succeed in killing him.

If he didn't, he would have to come up with a good explanation.

At last, after several minutes of struggling, Dominic stopped moving.

Benjamin maintained his pressure on the pillow for a while longer. Finally confident that there was zero chance of survival, he took it away, fluffed up the feathers and placed it back on the bed.

Father Dominic stared at him with dead eyes.

***

Jotham saw the runway come into view, cutting a swathe through the undulating grazing land. Madena was next to him and he cupped his hand around hers. Although generally fearless she could be a nervous flyer, especially at landing time. "I have no control over the situation, that's what scares me," she said, just as the wheels hit the ground.

The landing on the disused runway was relatively smooth, which was remarkable considering the poor condition of the tarmac. When the plane finally came to a halt, Silas slumped in relief. "We made it, I don't believe it," he said.

Jotham gave him a half-smile. "I told you Anthony was a brilliant pilot."

A grey BMW was waiting for them, fifty metres away. Anthony stayed with the plane but the others headed straight to the vehicle and stepped inside.

"Now for the Convent of the Immaculate Conception," said Jotham as he switched on the ignition. "I'm sure Father Dominic will be delighted to see us."

With Madena as navigator, he drove eight miles along narrow roads, cutting through a landscape of gently rolling hills. Turning a sharp corner, they finally saw the convent up ahead. The Romanesque building was set by itself in a valley surrounded by farming land.

"Rather a grim exterior," said Madena, casting her eyes over the well-worn white walls surrounded by a stucco fence.

A cold chill raced down Jotham's spine. "What's grim is the thought of Father Dominic somewhere inside that building. This could be very dangerous, Silas. I want you to keep well back and let us do the talking."

Silas pursed his lips. "Whatever you say, Jotham."

They stopped in the small parking area at the front and then walked inside. The lobby was austere, with a crucifix and three religious paintings hung on the whitewashed walls. The only furniture was a desk in the corner, in front of a door marked *Madre Superiora*. A young guard in a white uniform was sitting there and looked as if he were surprised to see them. "*Bongiorno*," he said.

Madena sauntered up to him with an alluring smirk. "Hello, do you speak English?" she asked. "I want to visit a patient."

The door behind him opened and a trim, middle-aged nun walked out, straightening her crisp white habit. "No he doesn't, but I do," she said. "How can I help you? This isn't visiting hours."

Jotham extended his hand. "How do you do, I'm John McDonald," he said. "We're here to see Father Dominic, if we could. I'm an old friend of his - he was like my uncle."

She looked him up and down. "I'm Sister Alicia, the manager. You should have let me know you were coming. He's very ill, and right now he's with Father Benjamin."

Jotham adopted a glum expression. "I'm on vacation here with my wife and friend. We heard about Dominic's illness and just wanted to pay our respects."

"I see," she said, her face softening a little. "Father Dominic's under special restrictions, as you no doubt know, but he's very weak these days." Jotham twisted his face to convey his despair, and he could see the spark of sympathy in her eyes. "Perhaps you could visit him for just a few minutes. He doesn't normally have any visitors, apart from Father Benjamin. He was away for a couple of days but he arrived back just a little while ago."

"*Grazie*," said Madena, gently wringing her hands in a show of gratitude.

Jotham briefly exchanged a knowing glance with her, and saw the spark of recognition in her eyes. They had been right. Father Benjamin was likely to

152

be the man they encountered in Budapest - Novak's killer. And last time they saw him, he was holding a gun.

"Follow me. I'm sure he'll be pleased to have some visitors," said Sister Alicia as she led them down the corridor towards his room.

Jotham could hear the pulse pounding in his temple as he tried to stay in front of Madena. She gestured for Silas to keep well back.

Alicia fumbled with the keys in her pocket and unlocked the door. Without looking too obvious, Jotham and Madena tried to stand on either side of it for protection.

She knocked and opened the door slightly. "Excuse me, Father Dominic, you have some visitors." Pushing it open, she walked over to him.

Jotham and Madena peered in to check before venturing inside. Just then, Sister Alicia shrieked and threw her hands in the air.

Chapter 35

Dominic was sprawled across the armchair, his right arm dangling down and his head cocked at an awkward angle. He stared back at them with mouth gaping open.

"Father Dominic," said Sister Alicia in shock. She set to work without a moment's thought, checking his vital signs as her instincts as a nurse took over.

Jotham and Madena rushed in, while Silas stayed at the door.

They all knew straight away that there was no hope for him, but needed to go through the motions of being sure that he was dead.

As Sister Alicia did her work, Madena examined his face. "His skin's blotchy," she said.

"It looks red and blue," added Jotham. They both knew what that meant: he was cyanotic.

Madena leaned over him and scrutinised his face and neck, pointing to some pinpoint spots of blood. "Do you think these are petechial haemorrhages?" she asked.

"Sister Alicia, does that indicate he's been smothered?" asked Jotham.

She looked at both of them with frantic eyes, shaking her head. "Father Benjamin, where is he? I didn't see him leave, but he could have gone out the back."

Jotham was suddenly struck hard by the fact that Father Dominic was dead. He studied the grotesque body and shock washed over him. He'd seen terrible sights like that before, but this time the impact seemed to immobilise him.

This was personal.

He recalled Dominic's past, though he had only encountered him several times over the last three years. All of those events were bad memories. Tortured by him, he was lucky to have escaped with his own life. He had seen the body of more than one man that Dominic had killed, and Jotham referred to him as the homicidal priest. Most terrible of all, he was responsible for the deaths of Jane and William, his first wife and baby son.

It was hard to comprehend that such a strong and brutal figure was now dead.

Sister Alicia regained her professional composure as she realised that there was no hope for her patient. "I'll have to call the police. Father Benjamin arrived an hour ago, but could he responsible for this?"

Jotham remained frozen, bracing himself against the bed so that he didn't fall over.

Madena spoke to Sister Alicia. "Who's Father Benjamin, where does he come from?"

"He's Italian and worked at the Vatican in a senior position, but they sent him to help look after Father Dominic. He's been counselling him over the last couple of weeks."

"I see," said Madena with a glance at Jotham. Benjamin had become involved with the Brotherhood at the behest of the Vatican. Perhaps they wanted him to get rid of Dominic.

The sound of screeching tyres made them jump, and that brought Jotham to his senses. "What was that?" he yelled as he spun around.

He and Madena brushed past Silas as they raced down the corridor and into the lobby. Through the window they could see the parking area out the front of the building.

A sedan had just passed through the front gate and was speeding down the quiet road.

"That's him, that was the priest!" cried Madena, just as Silas and Sister Alicia joined them.

Jotham turned to Alicia. "That's Father Benjamin?" he asked.

"*Si, si*," she replied.

"Our man in Budapest," said Silas.

Madena cocked a finger at him. "Stay here, please, Silas. This is going to be dangerous."

At that moment, they saw another car move forward and tear out of the car park. The driver appeared to be a male, and he was obviously on the priest's tail.

Silas let out a guttural cry as a dark shadow slid across his face. "No!"

"What is it?" asked Jotham, startled by the strange sound.

"That was Noah," he replied, choking on his words.

"Your brother?" asked Madena, and then she realised that was true. "Yes, I think it was - you're right."

Jotham glared at Sister Alicia. "Has that man been to visit Dominic?"

She shook her head. "No, I haven't seen him before. Father Benjamin was the only visitor."

All the while, the young man behind the desk in the lobby had been watching them. Sister Alicia marched over to him and snapped instructions in

Italian. "Piero, please call the police."

"*Si, si,*" he replied, nervously picking up the phone.

"Let's not waste any more time," said Jotham.

He and Madena bolted out the door. They ran over to the BMW parked not far from the gate. "My turn to drive," said Madena, heading to the left side.

Silas was right behind them. He jumped in the back seat before they could stop him, but there was no time to argue.

"Okay Silas, keep down and make sure you do up your belt," said Jotham.

Although he knew how to drive fast, Jotham had to admit that Madena was master of the game. Before they had even settled in their seats, she was accelerating through the gate and down the road. Jotham braced his hands against the dashboard as she skidded around the first corner.

Madena was driving fast, but the two cars far in the distance were doing a frightening speed. They swung around a sharp bend and vanished from sight.

Madena pressed her foot on the pedal and tried to close in on them but Jotham felt a rush of panic. "Try not to take the bend too fast," he said.

"I didn't know you were a backseat driver," she snapped but then steadied her pace. "I guess there's no sense killing ourselves. They can't keep up that speed for long." Her eyes were centred on the road ahead, reflecting the total focus of her mind.

Silas was gripped with fear and held on tight to the seat in front. He tried to avert his eyes from the road, but the shaky view of the countryside as they rushed past only made him feel worse. Besides, he was mesmerised by the two cars which then accelerated out of sight. "Perhaps it isn't Noah," he said, still trying to come to terms with what he had seen. "I mean, how could he possibly be here?"

"That's what we want to know," said Madena. "Hold tight."

Coming over the crest of a blind hill, they saw them far ahead – and both were travelling at a frightening pace.

"If it's him, he must be here to protect me," said Silas.

"Where did he learn to drive like that?" asked Jotham, straining his eyes to sharpen his view. Madena upped her pace but was still not closing in on them.

The two fleeing vehicles were close to maximum speed. But in one fraction of a second, everything changed.

The second car swerved to the left, becoming parallel to the first one -

and then hit it with a sideswipe.

At that instant, Father Benjamin's car skidded, sparks flying as the two cars collided metal on metal. In a deafening squeal followed by a thud, it twirled one hundred and eighty degrees in a semi-circle and ran off the road, coming to a halt in a shallow ditch.

The second car turned in a complete and uncontrolled circle with tyres squealing, then slid down the road. It smashed to a stop further along the same ditch, coming to rest against a small boulder.

Finally, both cars had been brought to a stop - and they did not look as if they would be moving anytime soon.

Madena pressed gently on the brakes to bring their car to a safe stop. She wanted to keep well back from the two smashed vehicles.

A vice-like knot squeezed Jotham's stomach. He held his body taut, automatically prepared for the explosion that might be about to happen - and he recalled the terrible fireball that killed his wife and child. The driver that time was a hit and run assassin who was sent by the Brotherhood. Then, three years later, a car that was pursuing him and Iago Visser, near the estate in the Peak District, had crashed down an embankment and burst into flames.

Now it could be about to happen again, or perhaps Silas Conrad was about to find out that his brother had been killed or injured.

Madena slowed down as she and Jotham cast their eyes over the scene. They would need to help the two drivers, but their first job was to assess the situation for any signs of danger. The priest could have a gun and they didn't know what weapons Noah might have.

But then they saw movement.

Father Benjamin struggled to open the dented left side door of his car, then quickly climbed over to the passenger seat, opened that door and ran away.

Noah opened the driver's window of his car and managed to clamber out. Slow and limping, he struggled to chase after the priest.

By the time Madena stopped the car, both men were running towards the only building in the rural landscape: an old church a few hundred metres away.

Madena had parked well away from the accident scene and she turned around to Silas. "We don't know what's happening and this will be dangerous; please stay here and get down.

"Both of them could be armed," said Jotham.

"The priest threw his gun into the Danube," said Silas, preparing to get out.

"But he could have got his hands on another one. Does Noah know how to use a gun?"

"No, he hates them."

Madena flicked her hair out of her face as she prepared to move. "Let's hope his attitude hasn't changed. When we get out of the car, we're going to be fair game."

Jotham locked eyes with Madena for just a moment. "I love you," he said. The look in her blue eyes told him that she felt the same way.

They both vaulted out of the car.

Chapter 36

Father Benjamin felt every bone in his body jar when his car came to a dramatic stop. After being thrown forward and then recoiling, he breathed a sigh of relief to find that he was still conscious and seemed to be in one piece. His head ached as if it were caught in a vice, but he could move his arms and legs without experiencing any severe pain and didn't appear to be trapped.

He blinked and observed the green, hilly landscape. In the distance he could see a flock of sheep, but his mouth dropped open when he realised that, right in front of him, was a sight he knew very well.

By the side of the road was the church and ruined cloister of *Santissima Trinity di Saccargia*. His parents had brought him to Sassaria every year for their annual vacation, and they always visited the Romanesque church that was located twelve miles outside the city. It was built one thousand years ago in striking black and white stripes, and the most remarkable feature was a tall campanile.

He had clambered up that bell tower so many times as a child, and every square inch was familiar to him.

Those memories helped him to instantly formulate a plan. If he could lure his enemy there, he should be able to defeat him.

Benjamin leaned over and felt a twinge of pain in his ribs. Catching hold of his briefcase, he pulled out the small wooden box and tucked it firmly under his left arm. His job was to protect the tip of the Holy Spear and deliver it to the Pope, no matter what the cost.

The driver's door was smashed in, but he clambered over the central console between the front seats. A spasm of agony charged across his ribs as he pushed open the passenger door, just wide enough to squeeze out.

His pursuer in the other car looked as if he were in much worse condition. He was in his late thirties with curly brown hair, and there was blood streaming down what looked like an otherwise handsome face. Benjamin couldn't resist the chance to rejoice in God's power at work. "Vengeance is mine," he shouted, and he could tell that the other man heard him.

Then he noticed the three people in the vehicle that was further down the road, and he recognised them straight away. Somehow, Jotham Fletcher and his friends, including Silas Conrad, had managed to track him down. But how did they know he would be in Sardinia? They must have known that Father Dominic was there, and guessed that he would turn up.

The three of them were jumping out of their car. He looked up at the church's bell tower, and moved towards it as fast as he could.

***

Jotham and Madena saw the unfolding drama as they exited their car.

Just as Father Benjamin set off in the direction of the church, Noah Conrad managed to climb out the driver's side window head first, but his face was squeezed tight in pain. He let out a spontaneous moan as he struggled to his feet, and there was blood flowing onto his shirt from a head gash.

He staggered after the priest but was limping, clearly affected by some injuries.

Jotham and Madena ran after them, but Silas trailed behind, unable to keep up their pace. It didn't help that he was in a state of distress about his brother, and he yelled out to him. "Stop, Noah. What are you doing?"

The ear-piercing cry reverberated through the tranquil countryside, but his brother didn't even look back.

Father Benjamin, meanwhile, ran into the church and turned towards the bell tower. His head was spinning after hearing Silas Conrad call out his brother's name. *Noah*. He had read about the Conrad family, but hadn't seen a photograph of the younger man.

So that was the maniac who had almost killed him in the car.

When he reached the crumbling spiral staircase, he began the steep ascent to the top of the tower. When he was a child he had practised running up and down those steps a thousand times. Now, with their deep treads, it seemed far more of a challenge, but he surprised himself at how fast he moved.

He was halfway to the top when Noah Conrad entered the building. Benjamin looked down and saw him approach the first step. His injured leg was clearly causing him distress and his limp was becoming more pronounced. Despite the pain, it appeared that sheer determination was driving him to keep on going.

Benjamin heard him moan as he began the climb, but the man was trying to move as fast as he could.

Jotham and Madena were still outside but had almost reached the entrance to the church. When they finally got there, they ran around to the exterior of the bell tower and looked up. Through the small windows that zigzagged down the wall, they could see the heads of the two men as they

160

moved up the staircase.

Silas caught up with them a moment later.

"If we run up there, we'll have no room to manoeuvre," said Jotham.

"This is exactly what happens in all those movies," said Madena. "Running up stairs to escape from someone is a really dumb idea."

Jotham nodded. "Unless you have an extra card up your sleeve."

"So what do we do now?" pleaded Silas.

"Keep close to the wall so that we don't get shot," said Jotham, "or get hit by buckets of boiling oil."

When Father Benjamin reached the upper level of the bell tower he was panting for breath despite being very fit. With the box under his arm, he unlatched the small wooden door that led to the terrace. The first thing he noticed when he walked out there was that the timber slats beneath his feet were weathered and some were split. He prayed that God would protect him.

He wanted to collect his thoughts for a moment and went to lock the door behind him to keep his followers at bay. But when he tried to pull the latch across he realised that he was too late.

Noah was there already and pressing against the door with all his weight. As it flew open, Benjamin stepped back just in time to avoid being knocked over.

He retreated to the opposite corner of the terrace, trying hard to avoid the broken timbers.

Noah chased after him, but stopped when one plank snapped under his feet with a crunch. He stopped and scowled at Benjamin, facing him off from several metres away.

Far below them, Silas emitted a desperate cry. "Noah, what are you doing here?"

Noah held his body rigid and kept his eyes on Benjamin, but shouted back to his brother. "We can't let it slip through our fingers," he said. "This will give us power that we've only dreamed about before."

Benjamin glared at Noah. "I know who you are, what you are," he said, narrowing his eyes to thin slits.

"I'm you're brother, stop this madness," yelled Silas from below.

Noah roared back. "We need to protect the Holy Spear and keep it safe."

Jotham signalled to Madena by touching her hand. She raised an eyebrow in response, to indicate to him that they were both on the same wavelength. He felt the rush of an adrenaline surge through his body as he prepared for a showdown.

Silas had come here to protect the Holy Spear, so why had Noah come all this way in secret to intervene?

He felt as if a blindfold had fallen from his eyes, and he was finally seeing the truth through a haze of confusion.

Jotham bellowed at Noah, his voice like thunder. "You belong to the Simonian Sect."

Everything was becoming clear. Noah Conrad was in the Simonian Sect and he was there to find the Holy Spear and take possession of it – for the sect.

The members of the Simonian Sect trusted in magic, and probably believed that the Holy Spear would give them unlimited power. Their goal was to fulfil the Magus Covenant – a vow to destroy the Christian church. With the power of the Holy Spear, it might be possible to achieve their goal at last.

Jotham clenched his fists and braced himself, knowing that he would need to race up the staircase and intervene. He turned to the others with his jaw held firm. "I'll have to go up there. Madena, please keep Silas down here."

"No I'm coming with you," snapped Silas.

Jotham barked back at him. "Stay here."

Silas stepped back in alarm. "Very well," he replied, finally agreeing to do as he was told.

Jotham glanced at Madena one last time, knowing that there was always the chance that he might never see her again. He turned and raced inside the church.

"Be careful, my love," she called after him.

Silas sneered and changed his mind on the spot, deciding that he was not going to be stopped. He moved to head off, but Madena was watching. She jumped in front of him to block his way and grabbed his right arm, twisting it backwards so that he was held in a rear wrist lock, and pushing him against the wall.

"You're a pain in the neck, Silas," she said. "You could be killed, do you realise that?"

He tried to struggle for a moment, but then calmed down. "You can let me go," he whimpered.

She relaxed her grip slightly but still kept him in the wrist lock. "You're staying right here."

Chapter 37

Father Benjamin stood with his back pressed against the balustrade of the terrace. He glanced down at the ground more than thirty metres below and wondered whether he could survive a fall from that height. That would require a spectacular miracle, but he was holding one of the world's most sacred relics.

Noah Conrad took a step towards him, his well-muscled arms outstretched and his hands fully extended as if he was determined to grab the Holy Spear. "Give that box to me," he said, baring his teeth.

"Don't come near me," snapped Benjamin. "I know who you are."

Noah glowered at him and dropped his arms to his side. He lowered his head and braced his shoulders, then charged forward as if he were about to tackle him.

With saucer eyes, Benjamin watched as Noah closed in on him. Holding the box close to his chest, he raised his free arm to deflect him just as the full force of Noah's powerful body struck him.

Benjamin was pushed backwards and fell down. Automatically, he raised both arms in an effort to defend himself. "You're in the evil sect," he cried with a booming voice.

Noah, so much younger and stronger, made a lightning fast movement and grabbed the box. Smirking at the realisation that the Holy Spear was in his hands, he stepped back and swung around. Ignoring the danger posed by the worn timbers on the floor, he dashed towards the exit.

Just then, Jotham reached the top of the stairs inside the tower, but found the door bolted.

His stomach lurched. He was determined to break through the barrier, but two dangerous men were waiting for him on the other side and there was no way of knowing what might happen in the next few minutes. His life could be changed forever.

Jotham pressed his shoulder into the door and aimed his body so that the momentum would target the weakest spot.

He pushed once, then twice, to no effect.

Finally, he leaned in with a final application of force and the door swung open. His body recoiled like a tight spring.

Distracted for a moment by the sound of the crashing door, Benjamin took his chance. He leapt forward with arms wide and seized Noah by his shoulders. Catching him in a tight hold, he spun him to the right and pushed him against the balustrade.

Jotham burst onto the terrace and saw the two men, but he stopped dead in shock.

Benjamin was holding Noah against the railing. The top half of his body was extended backwards in midair. He was hanging thirty metres above the ground, but still he was managing to keep a tight hold of the small wooden box.

"You serve the Simonian sect," said Benjamin as if he were in a wild delirium.

"Help me," yelled Noah, his blood-covered face twisted in terror as Benjamin pushed him further over the edge.

On the ground, Madena was still holding Silas in a wrist lock, but both were craning their necks to look upwards.

Silas tried to break free and cried out in anguish. "Noah!"

After taking in what was happening, Jotham dashed towards the two men. "Stop, let him go," he shouted, and kicked out his leg to try and push Benjamin out of the way.

He struck his hip and Benjamin stumbled - but he remained standing.

Jotham then took a step back, lunged forward again and shoved him hard.

Benjamin was in such a rage that his strength was superhuman and the impact didn't move him. Noah hung precariously over the edge, his face wide in horror as he tried to repel his attacker. Still, he kept hold of the box.

With one final thrust, Benjamin pushed Noah further over the edge of the railing. This time he had gone too far.

Noah was about to fall and Jotham saw again that look of innocence in his eyes, a look that didn't reflect his heart.

Jotham leaned forward and tried to grab hold of his arms to save him. At the same time, Benjamin reached out to snatch the box.

But Noah was already in the air and, with a blood-curdling shriek and wild flailing of his arms and legs, he plummeted to the ground.

Finally, he let go of the wooden box and it free fell beside him.

"No!" roared Benjamin as he watched the precious object land at the same time as Noah.

Jotham leaned over the edge and peered down, his heart thumping and the taste of vomit in the back of his throat.

The scene was sickening. Noah lay on the ground with blood oozing from the back of his head. He stared up with eyes open wide and mouth agape.

The box appeared to have made a safe landing and was on the grass beside his right hand.

Silas moaned in anguish and repeated his brother's name over and over. "Let the power of the Holy Spear heal him, Lord," he cried. Madena released him and he rushed over, grabbing his own head in despair as he fell to his knees beside Noah.

Jotham recalled how Simon Magus had come to the same gruesome end two thousand years ago in Rome. He was reputed to have levitated high in the air and then fallen to his death.

Benjamin was panting for breath. "A fitting end for someone in the sect," he said. "But now I have to retrieve my property."

He turned as if he were about to run out.

Jotham refocused his thoughts and knew he had to stop Benjamin. He braced himself, preparing to grab him as he ran past.

Instead, Benjamin hurtled straight towards him and managed to clutch the collar of his shirt. His eyes blazed with hatred and he screeched at him. "You, Jotham Fletcher, are the enemy of the Brotherhood." He swung him to the side and, with the natural advantage of centripetal force, hurled him towards the edge of the balcony.

Jotham slammed into the railing and was stunned for an instant. He almost catapulted over the edge, but grabbed hold of a column and managed to stop himself.

Madena was watching from the ground and he heard her call out in alarm. "Jotham, I'm coming up."

As he leaned over the edge, time seemed to stand still. The momentum was propelling him on, and he needed all his strength to come to an abrupt halt. If Benjamin shoved him a second time, he would succeed in killing him.

But Benjamin's priority was to retrieve the precious box. He ignored Jotham and bolted towards the door. After reaching the spiral staircase he began the descent, half running and half sliding down. He was like a wild animal trapped in a cage who sees a chance to escape, and nothing was going to stop him.

Jotham cried out to Madena. "No, stay there and grab the box. Watch out, he's coming down."

Despite what he said, she was determined to stop Benjamin. Silas had fallen to his knees beside his brother in a state of shocked disbelief. He was both useless and defenceless at that moment.

165

Madena scooped up the box and steeled herself ready to deal with Father Benjamin. The last thing the world needed was a replacement for Father Dominic who had the same ruthless and murderous approach.

She raced around the corner and headed inside the church.

Madena bounded up the first ten steps inside the bell tower and reached a small landing. She held the wooden box behind her back with one arm, keeping the other one free to defend herself.

Just then, Benjamin came tearing down the unstable staircase and met her head on. Hoping that he wouldn't notice the box, she clenched the fist of her other hand and punched him as he came towards her.

Benjamin was struck full in the stomach and moaned in response, but he pushed her against the wall and kept on moving. Her strategy had worked. He didn't see the box, but would either escape or return in search of it.

He was out the door and ran over to Silas Conrad, who was still distraught and kneeling over his dead brother.

Benjamin expected to find the box on the ground, but was stunned to find that it was nowhere to be seen. "Where is it?" he roared at Silas, his face creased in panic.

Silas responded with a confused look and then stumbled back in fear, falling over in the process.

Benjamin turned around and saw Madena standing there with the box in her arms.

Jotham ran out of the church just a few seconds behind her, and he was fast approaching. "The police are on their way," he yelled, jumping in front of Madena to help shield her.

Benjamin gasped, his face reddening as he weighed up his options. If arrested, he could face a long spell in jail – a gross indignity after such a stellar career. He realised that he wouldn't get his hands on the precious object this time, but vowed that he would return one day to collect it. Like a hare being chased by hounds, he pivoted around and sprinted off, heading towards the nearby hills that were covered in thick forest.

Chapter 38

Jotham wrapped his arm around Madena and held her tall and slender body close to his. They gazed at each other, knowing that they had survived yet another almost-fatal skirmish.

"Do you want to go after him?" she asked.

Jotham shrugged his shoulders. "There was no sign that he had a gun, but there's still that possibility. We have what we wanted."

"The police should catch up with him," said Madena. "Especially if we give them an anonymous tip off. We need to concentrate on getting safely out of here."

Silas was still beside his brother, but slowly rose to his feet.

Jotham and Madena strode over and worked together to check if Noah was showing any signs of life. But after checking his vital signs, they both nodded. After falling from such a great height, death was almost inevitable.

"I'm afraid there's no hope, he's gone," said Jotham.

"This is all my fault," said Silas.

Walking away from the body, they turned their attention to the wooden box. Madena examined the exterior surface. "This is remarkable," she said. "There might be some minor damage, but it appears to be intact."

"Open it, please," said Silas in a reverent tone as he walked over. "We need to be certain."

She carefully pulled the small latch and lifted the lid. Inside, the broken tip of an iron spear was resting on a cushion of ancient cloth. The object was crude, but there were no signs of damage.

Silas walked back to his brother and knelt down, then turned to the others. "Please, bring the box over here and hold it over his head," he said.

Jotham brought the box over and held it above Noah's forehead.

With tears streaming down his face, Silas prayed. "Lord, let the Holy Spear heal my brother. Bring him back to life." He repeated those words ten times, and then slumped his shoulders and broke down into sobs.

"I'm sorry, Silas," said Madena, putting a hand on his shoulder.

Jotham secretly wondered if God had chosen not to perform a miracle because Noah was in the sect.

Silas looked at both of them. "I still have faith in the Holy Spear," he wailed. "But what will I say to Veronica and my father?"

That was when they heard a dull wail. Barely imperceptible at first, they all recognised the sound of distant sirens.

Madena widened her blue eyes. "The police," she said.

***

Jotham cocked his ear. "They're headed our way," he said, the rising tension hitting him like a shovel. "Courtesy of Sister Alicia, no doubt, but I'm hoping they'll catch Father Benjamin."

"If they don't catch us first," said Silas.

Madena looked at Jotham and rolled her eyes. They were both aware of their dire predicament. There was a real possibility that the three of them could spend years inside a Sardinian jail. "Lets get out of here," she said.

"Time to go, Silas," said Jotham, putting a comforting hand on his shoulder. As a priest, he had often counselled people at the most tragic times of their lives. "Let's get in the car."

"Do we have to leave Noah behind?"

"Yes, and we need to move fast. The police will deal with his body."

Silas stamped his foot. "I can't leave him," he said, his eyes filled with pain. "You go on and leave me here."

"We don't have a choice," snapped Madena. "The authorities will contact you when you're back home. If we don't leave now, we'll be accused of having a hand in his death."

"They're almost here. We're going," said Jotham, running out of patience.

The sirens were louder, and that meant they were closing in.

Fear finally brought Silas to his senses. He literally jumped and the three of them were ready to move. They sprinted across the field and a hundred metres down the road to the hired BMW. Jotham pressed the key long before he reached the vehicle and jumped in the driver's seat.

Madena gave Silas a shove to speed up his entry into the rear seat and then she leapt in the front. "I'll ask Anthony to get the plane ready," she said, taking out her phone.

The tyres screeched as Jotham tore off, racing along the quiet country road for over a mile. Suddenly he slammed on the brakes and slowed to a sedate pace.

"What's going on?" asked Silas, his tight throat choking his words.

"Don't worry, it's all under control, I hope," he replied, pulling a face at

Madena.

She raised her eyebrows in reply, just as Anthony Gillam answered her phone call.

The pulsing beat of the sirens rang in their ears. Ten seconds later, two police cars appeared at the end of the road after passing over the crest of a hill. They were heading towards them.

"Keep your heads down and look the other way," said Jotham. As the patrol cars sped past on the other side of the road, he drove slowly and tried to avoid attracting their attention.

He glanced in the rear vision mirror as they disappeared from sight. They were headed in the direction of the convent, four miles away.

When the wailing could no longer be heard, Jotham pressed on the accelerator and sped towards the remote runway. "There's nothing to stop us now, I hope," he said.

Madena's phone beeped and she read a message. "Good news. Anthony should be ready to leave by the time we get there."

They were more than a mile away when Jotham thought he heard the sound of a siren. "Uh-oh," he said as he felt the intoxicating rush of an adrenaline surge. He had two simple choices: he could either fight or flee. This time, with Madena and Silas in tow and his little girl waiting for him at home, he was definitely choosing flight.

The noise was increasing, and it sounded as if there were more than one siren.

"Hang on, everyone," he said.

He floored the pedal and charged forward to a winding section of road. The engine almost redlined as he skidded the car through three tight curves. Madena clung to the grab handle and dashboard as they were thrown from side to side.

All the while, the ear-splitting wails grew louder. The police had turned around, and they were closing in on them.

At that speed, Jotham needed to maintain total concentration on the task at hand. In the distance, he could see the plane. One more kilometre and they would be there.

Nothing was going to stop him now. They reached maximum speed and Silas yelled out in fear, but Jotham could see the finish line.

Finally, he slowed down and raised dirt as the car skidded to a stop.

They were just a few metres from the cabin door, and Anthony was waiting for them. "I'll start the engines," he shouted, and darted towards the cockpit.

Gasping for breath and head pounding, Jotham turned to Madena and Silas. "Let's go." They jumped out of the car, raced over and ran up the airstairs into the cabin. He secured the cabin door as Madena yelped in relief.

She was still holding the wooden box.

They sat in the leather seats and secured their belts as Anthony began to taxi the plane down the runway.

Jotham peered out the window and saw two police cars racing down the road. They were headed straight towards them with lights flashing and sirens wailing.

Just then, the plane's wheels left the ground and they were airborne.

Jotham and Madena reached out to hold hands as they rose in the air.

"We're going to be arrested," replied Silas, with beads of perspiration on his pale skin.

"We should be out of range of their guns by now," said Jotham.

Madena gave Silas a comforting look. "Don't worry. Anthony will turn off the radio and we'll be out of Italian airspace soon. They won't be able to track us. We've done this before."

Silas leaned against the back of his seat, breathing heavily.

Jotham pressed his face against the window. The two police cars stopped on the runway next to the hired BMW, and the four officers jumped out and waved their fists in the air.

He slumped in relief to see them growing smaller with every passing second.

"Looks like we made it," said Madena.

"And we have the tip of the Holy Spear," said Silas.

***

Anthony Gillam threw open the cockpit door and called out. "I've turned off the radio so there's no way they can contact me."

"Thanks Anthony," replied Jotham, sitting back in his seat.

"At the moment I've set a course towards the UK. Let me know if you change your plans."

"Will do, that's what we need to discuss," said Madena, standing up. "We'll get back to you soon." She closed the cockpit door for him and, as

170

usual, switched on the coffee machine.

Silas was in a deep gloom. "Do you really think they'll contact us about Noah's body?" he asked.

Madena sat beside him and put a comforting hand on his arm. "You and Korey are his next of kin, so the police should contact you so that his remains can be brought back to America – unless you want to bury him in Sardinia."

Silas frowned. "No way, I want him brought home."

In an effort to distract him, Jotham handed him the wooden box.

Silas sighed as he placed it on the small table between the seats. Despite his feelings of despair, he couldn't resist the chance to examine the contents again. He opened the box with reverential care and gazed at the humble object inside with love, as if he were staring at the face of Jesus. "It's perfect," he said, and then carefully secured the lid.

Chapter 39

Jotham knew that time was running out to decide on their next destination. He cleared this throat as he sat opposite Silas. "We need to have a talk," he said.

"I can't believe that my brother belonged to a sect," he replied, with a look of despair. "Why would he have wanted the Holy Spear? Perhaps he wanted to destroy it."

Madena went over to pour the coffee and ran a hand through her hair as she sat down. "We think that Noah wanted to obtain the spear for the sect," she said, pursing her lips. "The Simonian Sect has always been obsessed by magic. The leader might see it as a way to obtain more power."

"They'd regard it as a magical object," said Jotham.

Silas nodded. "Noah was always fascinated by the story of the Holy Spear, almost as much as Dad."

Jotham spoke in a low voice. "Your father's going to take his loss very hard. Do you have any idea when Noah might have joined the sect - has he always lived with you?"

Silas gave that some thought. "When he was twenty-two, he was having a difficult time. He'd already dropped out of college. He went away for a couple of years, backpacking and working around Europe, just after I met Veronica."

Jotham realised that they could be on to something. "Did you hear from him much during that time?" he asked.

"No, only occasionally, just to let us know that he was okay. They weren't long phone calls."

"That could very well be the time when he was inducted into the sect."

Silas put his head in his hands. "What will I say to Veronica?"

"Do you think they were very close?" asked Madena.

They both jumped when he let out a frightening sob. "I think they were having an affair."

Jotham's mouth dropped open. "Why would you think that?" he asked.

"I saw the way they looked at each other. I've noticed for the last three years, but I was too afraid to ask her in case she said yes."

Jotham could tell by Madena's shocked face that she hadn't suspected either. He thought the charming, demure Veronica was a loyal wife. She appeared to be begrudgingly kind to Noah, but there were a few moments when he sensed that they were close. He was certainly younger and better looking than his brother, and now it seemed likely that he'd been in the Simonian Sect for many years.

The fog was beginning to clear in Jotham's mind and he locked eyes with Silas. "Now you have what might be the tip of the Holy Spear."

Silas's face sagged. "Yes, that was the most important thing in the world to me. But after losing Noah, it doesn't seem to matter as much. I should ask God's forgiveness for saying that, because I believe that the Lord has led me here and wants me to protect it."

Jotham cast his eyes down. "I think that the search for the Holy Spear has already led to enough deaths and done enough harm."

Silas scrunched up his face. "What do you mean?" he asked.

"My suggestion is that we shouldn't tell anyone about the spear, including Veronica. What do you think, Madena?"

"I agree with you," she replied, picking up on his thoughts. "Something tells me that you're planning something."

"I don't understand, why should I lie to my own wife?" asked Silas.

"I think that we should return the spear to its rightful place," said Jotham, "beneath the monastery of Saint Dimitrios in Greece. We should go back there and bury it."

Silas jumped to his feet, his face reddening. "No, that's out of the question," he said. "Absolutely no way."

Jotham was taken aback by his anger and squeezed his hands tight, ready to respond if things became even more heated. "Think about it, Silas," he said. "We'll be the only people who know the location. Look at the damage that's already been done because people wanted to possess it."

Silas paced the small aisle. "You want us to hide it so that no one ever finds it again?"

"That right," replied Jotham. "Hidden from the world forever."

He glared at Madena. "What do you think?" he asked, his voice husky.

"I think Jotham's right. In my view, no individual or organisation should have the Holy Spear as a possession, or even on display in a museum. It should stay where it's been resting peacefully for hundreds of years."

He gazed out the window at the wall of grey clouds and sadness darkened his features. "You're right, Jotham," he said finally. "I was wrong to think that it should belong to me, or my church."

"So where shall we go now?" asked Madena.

173

"Korey and Veronica have to be told about Noah," said Silas. "And I need to make arrangements for the funeral."

Jotham looked at a map on his device. "We want to return home ourselves. But first, we can fly to Greece and bury the Holy Spear. We're not that far away."

"You want to go there right now?" asked Silas.

Jotham thought he could detect a hint of suspicion in his voice. "If that's okay with you. We'll only be delayed by one or two days. Then you can fly back to San Diego and we'll go home."

"Wait, please," he said, with a panicked voice. "I'm willing to agree to your proposal, but first I've got one request."

"And what's that?" asked Madena.

"I want a chance to see if the Holy Spear can cure my father's blindness."

Jotham was becoming impatient. "You want to test its magic," he said, with more than a hint of sarcasm.

"Not magic, Jotham - miraculous power. You and I both believe that God can perform miracles."

"Yes, but not an inanimate object. God can perform a miracle if we have faith in him." Jotham felt the hairs on the back of his neck stand up, realising that the man couldn't let go of his obsession.

"This object pierced our Saviour's side. When blood dripped onto a Roman soldier, God cured his sight."

Madena raised an eyebrow. "If we take the object to San Diego then Veronica will know about it, and so will your father."

"I can keep it hidden," replied Silas. "Neither of them needs to know."

The plane shuddered as it hit some turbulence and they all resumed their seats and buckled up. Anthony Gillam's voice came over the intercom. "We'll be through this in a couple of minutes. Do up those belts if you haven't already."

Jotham tried to ignore the stomach-lurching vibrations and focused on his thoughts. He felt as if he were performing the role of priest, trying to guide a member of his flock along the right path. He wanted to convince Silas that he would be setting things right with God by taking the Holy Spear back to Greece.

But there were seeds of doubt planted in his mind. Perhaps the object did have miraculous healing powers, and he would be denying an old man the chance to see again - a man who was about to find out that his younger son was dead.

He looked at Silas and an ice-cold chill swept over him. Perhaps he was the one who belonged to the Simonian Sect. For two millennia, its members had undermined the church by leading people astray. They were experts at corroding the truth and polluting people's minds.

Two thousand years ago, Simon Magus created a farcical belief system that thousands of people followed. And that was exactly what Silas Conrad had done. He was just like Magus.

Noah might have discovered the truth, and came to Sardinia to stop him getting his hands on the Holy Spear. Or perhaps both brothers were in the sect.

The shuddering stopped just as his thoughts cleared. Jotham knew that he had to find out the truth, and the only way he could do that was to take Silas back to San Diego.

Silas continued to plead with him. "I'll keep it hidden and lock it in my safe. Then we'll take it back to Greece together. That's all I'm asking for, Jotham: a chance to restore my father's sight.

"That will prove if you've been right all along," said Jotham quietly.

"Yes, I suppose it will, but then I swear that I'll go with you to Greece."

Jotham locked eyes with him. "There's an even greater danger that I have to warn you about. If Father Benjamin manages to escape from Sardinia, he'll probably realise that you now have the Holy Spear, and you're likely to bring it home. He could alert members of the Brotherhood in California. Those two monks might be waiting for us, or whoever else he wants to employ to track you down.

Silas's face turned dark with fear. "That would happen even if we take it to Greece. They'll always think I have the Holy Spear. I'll never be safe."

Chapter 40

Jotham knew that Silas was probably right and the Brotherhood would continue to pursue him. He was also still traumatised by his encounter with Brother Sean and Brother Paulo.

He had to offer to help him. "I'll go back to San Diego with you now, and deal with the Brotherhood. Then I'll return the spear to Greece."

"Thank you, Jotham," said Silas, clutching his face in relief.

Madena was still gripping the armrests. "Silas, let Veronica know that you're coming home and that Noah has been killed," she said, "but don't say anything about the spear."

"I'll call her soon," he replied.

"Once you're home, Veronica will need you there," said Jotham. "I can take the box back to Greece by myself." He took hold of Madena's slender hand and kissed her fingertips. "You can return home to the UK, and I'll go on to San Diego with Silas."

"There's more work to do, isn't there?" she asked, her smile fading as he nodded. She knew what that meant – Jotham still had concerns about Silas that he wanted to investigate, and their mission was not finished yet. "Then I really think I ought to stay with you."

Jotham knew how much she wanted them to work as a team, always watching each other's back. That was how they'd always operated, but now they had a child to think about. "Belle needs you right now more than I do," he said.

She shrugged her shoulders. "Then where to head from here?" she asked.

"Let's talk to Anthony," he said. "Excuse us, Silas."

He nodded in reply, then stared out the window and wiped away a single tear.

Jotham and Madena stood up and walked into the cockpit, shutting the door behind them.

"What's happening, Jotham?" asked Anthony, his eyes fixed on the windscreen.

Madena put her arm around Jotham. "I think I know what you're planning," she said. They both knew that if they flew back to the Peak District, then Silas would be aware of where they lived. There was no way that could be allowed to happen.

"Could we drop Madena off at a private jet airport, perhaps in France?" asked Jotham. "She can charter a plane and go home from there. Then I'll go straight on to San Diego with Silas."

"Sure, whatever you say," said Anthony, scratching his head. "If we're going to California, we'll need to overnight in Newfoundland again."

"That's fine. It should be a brief visit, one or two nights, and then I'm heading to Greece before finally returning home."

Anthony rolled his eyes. "Even I'm confused, but consider it done."

Jotham wrapped his arms around Madena. "Darling, you could fly back to Sheffield Airport. Felix can pick you up from there and you'll be back home in no time."

She gave that some thought. "Perhaps I should stay with you. I don't want you over there without me."

"I need you, but Belle needs you even more," he said. As Jotham pressed his lips against hers, Anthony gave a fake cough.

"Sorry, Anthony, but we just have to do this," said Madena, returning Jotham's kiss. They all knew that there was always the possibility that this could be their last embrace.

***

Silas gazed out the window and stayed quiet for half an hour. Finally, Jotham reminded him that he needed to phone Veronica. "I can help explain the situation," he said, trying not to show how much he was dreading the conversation.

"I suppose it's for the best," said Silas, his eyebrows furrowed. "Thank you for agreeing to my terms." Madena patted him on the shoulder as he put his phone on the small table and switched it to speaker mode.

The phone buzzed three times before Veronica answered. "Silas, how are you?" she asked straight away.

"I'm fine," he replied with a weak voice. "But we've run into some difficulties."

She jumped in before he could say any more. "Wait, sweetheart, there's something I haven't told you."

"What is it?" he asked, his eyes ricocheting between Jotham and Madena.

177

Veronica sighed. "After we said good bye, Noah said that he needed to get away for a few days. He packed a bag and left. I haven't been able to contact him and he hasn't been answering his phone."

"That's what I was about to tell you," he said.

"What - have you heard from him?"

"Noah came over to Sardinia."

Silas stared at the phone waiting for her to answer. "No, that's crazy," she said finally.

"It's true, Veronica. We saw him."

At that point, Jotham decided to intervene. "We don't fully understand the details, but we think Noah may have secretly belonged to a sect."

She raised her voice, clearly agitated. "Silas told me that you're some sort of sect hunters. But it's madness to say that Noah belonged to anything other than our church. Where is he now?"

"Noah's been killed," said Silas, his lips trembling. "He's dead."

Veronica burst into a flood of tears. "No, don't tell me that," she moaned.

"I'm sorry, honey."

"What happened to him?"

"You know that the spear was stolen by a priest in the Brotherhood, and Noah followed him, just like we did, to Sardinia. I don't know how he knew about the location. That man was trying to escape and Noah was chasing him. He fled into a church and ran up to the top of a bell tower. They were fighting and the priest pushed him off the edge. No one could survive a fall from that height."

Veronica cried out. "What - he fell to his death?"

"We'd just arrived and saw everything. It was horrific, but he died instantly."

"Noah's really dead?"

"Yes, my love, I'm sorry." She descended into vehement sobs, and tears streamed down Silas's face at the same time. "I'll be home soon," he muttered.

After a couple of minutes, she calmed down enough to speak. "What happened to that priest?"

Jotham cut in. "We tried to stop him, but he managed to escape with the spear."

"Are you telling me that he's stolen it?"

"Yes, unless the police catch him. He said he was going to throw it into

178

the ocean. I'm afraid that it's almost certainly lost forever." Jotham was stunned by his own ability to tell a lie. Madena glanced at him with raised eyebrows but a sly half-smile slid across her face.

Silas lowered his head with a guilty look.

Veronica now sounded more composed. "Did you try to chase him?" she asked.

Silas answered her. "Noah had just fallen and we had to stay and try to help him. But there was no hope at all."

"After that, we had to get out of there before the police arrived," said Jotham, "or we might have been implicated in his death."

Veronica cried out in anguish, a horrifying sound that gave Jotham goosebumps. "So you left him there?" she asked.

"I'm sure the police will contact you to notify you about his death and make arrangements for his body."

"What about Korey - what will I tell him?"

"Please don't breathe a word about any of this to him," said Silas. "Wait till I get home so that I can talk to him myself."

She sighed again. "This is a terrible day."

"I love you, Veronica," said Silas, and a moment later he ended the call.

**

After dropping Madena at an airport not far from Lyon, Anthony Gillam took off with only Jotham and Silas onboard. They were heading towards San Diego, but planned to stop and refuel in Newfoundland so that Anthony could get some rest before the final leg of the journey.

As the plane reached cruising altitude, they could hear the steady thrum of the engines when Anthony walked into the cabin. "I've booked two hotel suites for us close to the airport," he said. "We can all do with a few hours sleep."

Jotham was already starting to feel the effects of exhaustion. He turned to Silas and could see that his face was clouded with sadness. "If we can be up at six o'clock in the morning, we can make an early start on the flight," he said.

"That won't be a problem," replied Silas. "I can't wait to get home."

"Before then, I hope to hear that Madena's back with Belle."

179

Chapter 41

The Peak District

Madena was the only passenger in a small charter jet and the flight seemed very lonely without Jotham by her side. Her heart skipped a beat to see the landscape of England come into view.

She was pleased to see Felix Young waiting for her outside the small terminal. He was always a dour Scotsman, but couldn't resist a subtle smile as he talked about Belle. "The wee pet has been so good and happy," he said as he placed Madena's bag in the boot of the Mercedes.

He whizzed along the highway at high speed and continued to maintain a fast pace along the narrow, winding roads closer to their home.

Madena couldn't help but admire the beautiful countryside of the region that was now her home, but she and Jotham could never relax. Her eyes were always peeled, on the lookout for any sign of danger. The lanes near their estate would be the perfect place for an ambush, if the Brotherhood or the Simonian Sect were to become aware of their location.

Her mouth went dry as the car passed the point in the road where Iago Visser was assassinated just three years ago. Although she had never met him, Jotham had told her every detail about the tragic event.

As soon as the entrance gates swung open, Cynthia rushed out of the house to greet them. Little Belle was in her arms, waving and blowing little kisses as she squealed in delight. Madena marvelled at how much she seemed to have grown in her short absence.

The next few hours passed so quickly, filled with the joy of hugs and kisses, playtime, bath time and reading stories. When Belle fell asleep, Madena stood beside her cot for a long time and watched her steady breathing.

***

John Pedersen was in bed, but he'd been lying awake for hours. He couldn't forget the sickening thud as the bus hit Kowalski, and he kept replaying the accident in his mind. That was despite his delight at being rid of the unwanted visitor.

At three in the morning, the ringtone sounded on his phone and he almost knocked it off the bedside table in his haste to answer the call.

He recognised the number straight away. "Yes," he said curtly. He listened to the brief message, and immediately felt as if a brick wall was collapsing right on top of him. "I don't believe it, that can't be possible."

The caller whispered a reply. "I'm sorry."

Frustration and rage spewed from him. "Is that all you've got to say? We're relying on you to find out the truth. Don't let me down, I'm warning you."

He ended the call, and then heard Zykov's heavy footsteps, followed by a tap on the bedroom door. "What's wrong, John, can I help you?" he asked.

Pedersen snapped back at him. "Go back to bed. You've already done enough."

"Okay," he said. "See you in the morning."

At the sound of his retreating footsteps, Pedersen threw his head back on the pillow, and wondered if anything else could go wrong. So far, one sect member had been killed, the Holy Spear supposedly lost, and he'd achieved absolutely nothing.

Not a good look for someone who wanted to be the next Leader.

***

San Diego

Jotham exhaled in relief when the jet finally touched down in San Diego. "Home at last," he said to Silas, who stared back at him with sunken eyes.

"Yes, but I still don't know what I'm going to say to Veronica," he replied. He checked his briefcase before they disembarked as if he feared the Holy Spear may have vanished during the flight.

"As long as it's not the truth," said Jotham, feeling a pang of guilt as he said those words.

Anthony Gillam was planning to stay close to the airport, and Jotham stuck his head in the cockpit to speak to him before they left.

Anthony spoke in a low voice. "I'll keep my phone with me, don't hesitate to call if there's any sign of trouble."

Jotham could tell that he didn't trust Silas, but put a hand on his shoulder. "Thanks Anthony. If I need help, you'll definitely be the first to know." He had no intention, no matter what happened, of putting him in any danger. Whatever happened, he wanted to deal with it by himself.

Anthony inclined his head towards the cabin, where Silas was now double-checking his suitcase. "Something doesn't feel right. I'm not happy about leaving you alone. Are you sure you don't want me to come with you?"

Jotham nodded, but wondered if Anthony could sense his lack of conviction. He really had no idea how things would develop when he reached the Conrad house. "You look after the plane," he said. "I'll give you a call later today."

He shrugged his shoulders and continued his shutdown checks.

Jotham and Silas walked away from the plane and headed straight to the hire car that was already waiting for them – a silver Lexus sedan with the keys on the bonnet. Jotham scanned the surroundings as he opened the door, looking in every direction for any sign that that they were being watched.

They both got in the car and did up their seatbelts. "Keep your eyes peeled the entire time," said Jotham. "I'll be doing the same thing. If you notice anything at all suspicious, tell me straight away."

"Okay," replied Silas with a strained expression, and Jotham noticed that his hands were shaking. But his fear was not surprising. Silas's encounter with the two monks had definitely been the most terrifying of his life, and he was well aware that they might be in danger again. He placed his briefcase on the floor between his feet, and strained his leg muscles to keep a firm hold of it.

Jotham started the engine and drove off. His goal was to get to the Conrad house as fast as possible, but at the same time he needed to keep a lookout in every direction. He stayed silent, wanting to maintain his focus on those two tasks.

As they left the outskirts of the city, Jotham pressed his foot on the accelerator. As the engine hummed, he glanced in the rear vision mirror, and that was when he saw the old van closing in on them.

"There they are," he said, trying not to shout but finding it hard to speak in a normal voice.

Silas jumped in shock and looked back. "My God, it's them," he said, eyes wide in fear. "Sean and Paulo."

Jotham had to appear to be calm and in control for Silas's sake, but knew that this could be the end for both of them.

Dark-haired Paulo was at the wheel, demonstrating his best Italian driving skills, and beefy Brother Sean was next to him.

Jotham felt an adrenaline rush at the realisation that he only had one chance to stop them. He was relieved to see that there were not many cars on the road and the traffic up ahead was clear. "Hang on tight, Silas," he said. "I'm going to outrun them. They'll never catch up with us."

He had to put as much distance between them as possible. There was every chance they were armed and they might even use their vehicle as a battering ram if they came close enough.

No matter what, their main objective would be to get their hands on the Holy Spear.

Silas let out a stifled moan and shrank down in his seat. "Don't do anything too crazy," he said.

"I can't make any promises," he replied.

Jotham slammed his foot on the accelerator and pushed towards top speed. He knew that would be about one hundred and forty miles an hour. Soon afterwards, he redlined the engine as he reached maximum revs.

The old van should not be capable of keeping up with them.

Silas turned back to check, but tried to keep his head down at the same time. "We'll be home soon," screeched Silas, hanging on as the Lexus tore down the road.

Jotham applied more pressure to the accelerator and braced himself. His every sense was on maximum acuity and his heart was thumping. He was sure that his adrenaline levels had soared so high that they must be close to maxing out.

What happened after that, he had no idea.

Despite his best efforts, the van kept moving forward at unbelievable speed, despite looking like an old rust bucket.

Cars honked their horns all around them as they sped past, though luckily the traffic was thin. Jotham kept listening, expecting to hear the sound of sirens. When the police caught up with them, he would have to do a lot of explaining.

But so far, there was no sign of them.

Jotham's brain was in overdrive, trying to think of what to do next. Then, in an instant, everything changed.

Chapter 42

In the rear vision mirror, Jotham watched as events unfolded, hundreds of yards behind them.

The van drove over an oil slick and spun out of control. Gyrating in wild circles with tyres bursting, it crashed head on into the side barrier.

In that brief moment of time, the front half of the van crumpled to a dented, twisted mass of metal.

The traffic behind it came slowly to a halt.

Jotham's heart sank at the sickening sight. He gradually slowed the Lexus to a more reasonable speed and kept on moving forward.

Silas's face was contorted in horror. "Should we go back?" he asked.

"There's nothing we can do," said Jotham, inwardly reproaching himself. His instinctive reaction to any crisis was always to lend a hand. "Those other drivers will call for help," he said.

But he hit his hands against the steering wheel in frustration.

"What is it, Jotham?" asked Silas.

"I've seen too many incidents like that, and now it's happened again," he said with a despairing look. "More death and destruction."

"It was their choice to chase us," said Silas.

"I know that. God help them, I'd be surprised if they're still alive."

They drove on for several more miles. Silas's face lifted as soon as they turned into his street. "Home never looked so good," he said, with a sad smile.

Jotham drove through the gate and came to a stop near the front door. His whole body sagged and he rested his head on the steering wheel, as if his adrenaline levels were plummeting.

"Are you okay?" asked Silas, with a concerned frown.

"I feel like I've just been in a prize fight," he replied, sitting up again.

Silas picked up his briefcase and held it firmly. "You have. And somehow you won."

Jotham felt a huge sense of relief to have reached the house in one piece.

He glanced at Silas, but a saw a look of dread slide across his face. "Will the Brotherhood come back?" he asked.

Jotham knew there was every chance that might happen, and tried to think of a solution. "Silas, when this is all over, I'll get a message to them somehow," he said. "They'll find out that the Holy Spear has been laid to rest forever, and that you have no idea of the location."

Silas looked hopeful. "Do you really think that will satisfy them?"

Jotham nodded emphatically. "Yes. The Brotherhood's only objective is to hunt down the Simonian Sect. They'll soon forget about you and the Holy Spear, and move on to their next challenge - wherever there's the least hint that anyone might belong to the sect."

***

Jotham's heart rate was almost back to normal, but began to increase as they walked to the front door. Silas took out his key, but the door flew open before he had time to use it.

Veronica stood there, smartly dressed as usual in a blue skirt and floral blouse, but her makeup was smudged and her eyes were red and puffy. "How could this have happened?" she asked. "I can't believe that Noah won't be coming home."

Silas walked inside and threw his arms around her. They burst into sobs and Jotham stood back, well aware of the pain of their grief. There was no doubting that they had both loved Noah.

Veronica finally raised her head and looked up at Silas. "The police in Sicily contacted me an hour ago," she said, her lips trembling. "Let's go to the living room."

Jotham followed as she led them there and shut the door. "Who spoke to you?" asked Silas as they sat down.

"I've written his name down," she said, pulling up a note on her phone. "Capitana Venturi. He spoke quite good English and said that Noah's body had been found. He apparently fell from the steeple of a church and they think it may have been an accident."

"Did they say how they reached that conclusion?" asked Jotham.

"They said the car he was driving had crashed into another vehicle, and that he may have fought with the other driver. One or both of them ran into the nearby church and up the tower. Perhaps he might have been trying to get away from the other man, or maybe there was a struggle."

"That was the priest we told you about," said Silas. "So you didn't say you'd already heard about him?"

She shook her head in reply.

"Have they caught him?" asked Jotham.

"They're still looking for him. They want him in connection with another matter." She looked at both of them. "Do you know anything about that?"

Jotham lowered his eyes. "We think he killed the man that we were trying to see – Father Dominic. He was the head of the Brotherhood, but when we got there we found him dead."

Tears streamed down her face. "Are you going to tell the police about all this?"

"If we do that, then we might be implicated in the deaths," said Jotham. "We have to keep our mouths shut. I hope the police catch Father Benjamin, and he should be facing a murder charge. But they may not be able to prove he killed Noah."

"Does Dad know about Noah?" asked Silas.

"He just knows that Noah went away for a few days. Some of the staff have been helping me look after him."

"We'll have to find someone to help care for him now."

Veronica crinkled her forehead. "He's been asking for Noah."

"I'll talk to him now."

She reached out to him. "Has the Holy Spear really disappeared?"

"The priest grabbed it and ran off, yelling that he was going to throw it in the ocean," said Jotham, trying not to show the guilt he felt at fabricating a lie.

Veronica widened her eyes. "You didn't chase him?"

Silas took hold of her hand. "We told you, sweetheart, we had to stay with Noah, to see if there was anything we could do for him."

She wiped away some tears. "Are you going to tell Korey now?

"Yes, I think I better," he said, turning around. "Jotham, would you come with me? I might need your help."

"That's a good idea," said Veronica.

"Yes, certainly," replied Jotham. Silas was sure to be concerned about his father's health and might even ask him to help break the news. There was no telling how the old man would react.

But Jotham knew there was another reason for the request. The tip of the Holy Spear was hidden in his briefcase and he wanted to see the effect that would have on his father. A knot tightened in his stomach as he wondered if there really would be a miracle.

With his briefcase in hand, Silas led Jotham to the north wing. The door to Korey Conrad's apartment was ajar and as they knocked and walked in, they saw him listening intently to a news bulletin on television.

"Dad, how are you?" asked Silas.

Korey spoke without turning his head. "Hello who's that - is that you, Noah?"

"It's me, Silas."

"You're finally back home. Where are you?"

"Right here," he said softly, striding over and putting his hand on the old man's arm. "Jotham Fletcher's with me."

"Hello, Jotham," he replied. "I'm glad you've brought one of my sons home."

Silas picked up the remote control and turned off the television.

"I was listening to that," snapped Korey.

"I'll turn it back on soon," he said, putting his briefcase down on a chair. He opened it and reached into the bottom of a zippered compartment. Then he took out the small wooden box and placed it on the coffee table next to his father.

"Have you seen Noah?" asked Korey. "Veronica said he went away for a few days."

Jotham expected Silas to talk to his father about Noah and knew that his world was about to be torn apart. He had experienced for himself the gut-wrenching agony of losing a child, and that was a pain that never went away.

But instead, Silas leaned over the box and carefully unlatched the lid.

Jotham frowned. "Are you sure you want to do this first?" he asked.

Silas glared back and put a finger across his own mouth to silence him.

Jotham, his heart thumping, watched as Silas picked up the tip of the spear and cradled it in his hands. "Let's pray together, Dad," he said. Holding his arms aloft, he brought the object close to his father's face.

Chapter 43

Korey had no idea what was happening. "Where are Noah and Veronica?" he asked in a gruff voice. "I need them."

Silas gently touched the object with his lips and held it next to his father. "Let's just say a word of prayer first." He closed his eyes with a devout look. "Lord, please help my Father. Let the power of the Holy Spear restore his sight."

Korey shrugged. "I'm too old for miracles," he said. "Pray for someone who can be cured, or for Noah to come home and for me to be granted eternal rest. Ask God to forgive my sins while you're at it. I know that I haven't always been a good man."

Jotham silently prayed that both men would find peace and that their faith would be renewed.

Silas lowered his head and recited the same phrase over and over. "Let the power of the Holy Spear restore his sight." His hands were shaking and Jotham held his breath, afraid that he would drop it. Finally, after more than a minute, he placed the spear back in the box, closed the lid and pulled the tiny latch across.

Korey jumped. "What was that noise?"

"Nothing Dad," said Silas. "I just need to put some papers in my safe, I'll be back in a couple of minutes."

"A good idea, I'll stay with your father," said Jotham, nodding as Silas put the box in his briefcase and strode out of the room.

"I'm not a child, you know," said Korey. "So how was this important trip of yours?"

"Very eventful," said Jotham, sitting next to him.

"Don't tell me about it, I'm too old to hear about people's travels."

"How have you been while we've been away?"

He coughed. "Missing both my sons. I don't understand why Noah went away."

Silas came back into the living room a moment later and shut the door. He looked grim, knowing that he would now have to tell his father about Noah. But as he walked up to him, his eyes searched his face. "How are you feeling now?" he asked.

Korey raised his head and blinked several times as if there was grit in his eyes. "Is that you, son?"

Silas stopped dead in his tracks. "Yes, Dad."

He paused for half a minute. "I think I can see you."

Jotham jumped to his feet.

Silas threw his hands over his mouth. "You can see me?"

Korey stared straight at him. "Yes, I'm sure I can, and you look so much older."

Silas flew over to his father, fell to his knees and took hold of his hands. "Can you still see me?"

He raised his eyebrows in reply. "Your eyes are sparkling. Praise God."

"You can say that again. This is a miracle."

Jotham was amazed to see Korey break into a happy smile, such a contrast to his normal demeanour. "This is wonderful," he said, but his head was spinning and thoughts were crashing through his mind at a hundred miles an hour.

Korey looked straight at him. "You're a handsome man," he said with tears in his eyes. "Silas, God has been very good to me. I shouldn't ask him for anything else, but I want to see Noah. Do you know where he is?"

Silas glanced at Jotham with a dark expression. He was clearly not keen to reveal the truth at that moment.

Korey realised something was wrong. "What is it - have you heard from him?"

"No, I haven't," he replied. "Let me tell Veronica about you, she'll be thrilled."

"Yes, I want to see her," he said.

***

Jotham followed Silas to the central part of the house and walked upstairs to where Silas and Veronica each had their own office.

Veronica's office door was wide open and she was meeting with two of the senior staff members. They all had grave faces and were wiping away tears.

Silas knocked and walked straight in. "Excuse me, honey, could I speak to you for a moment?"

She gave him a wan smile. "Sure. I've just been informing Dean and Stacy about Noah. They want us to hold a staff meeting later and tell everyone the news."

"We'll talk to you later," said Dean, lowering his head as the two of

189

them walked out of the room. "If there's anything we can do, just let us know."

"I'm so sorry, Silas," said Stacy.

"Thank you both," he replied. "We'll be needing your help to get through this."

They walked down the stairs as Silas shut the office door.

Jotham looked around at the sleek, spacious suite – the model of a well-organised workspace. There was a flattering portrait of Silas and Veronica on the wall, and next to it a framed photograph of the entire family, including Noah and Korey. Everything else was the epitome of restrained minimalism.

"Have you told him yet?" asked Veronica. "I'm surprised you left him alone."

"Not about Noah."

She wrinkled up her face. "Then what have you been doing?"

"We'll tell him soon, but something incredible has happened." A look of joy slid across his face. "There's been a miracle. While I was talking to him, Dad said that he could see me."

She lifted an eyebrow. "See you?"

"Yes, he's regained his sight."

Her jaw dropped. "There must be some mistake."

"No mistake, and he wants to see you."

She gave him an excited smile and wasted no time in walking towards the door. "I better take a look for myself," she said, and proceeded down the stairs.

Jotham spoke to Silas before they left her office. "Did you put it in your safe?" he asked.

"Yes, locked tight, so don't worry."

"I want to leave for Greece first thing tomorrow, but perhaps you ought to stay here with Korey. He'll need you by his side when you break the news about Noah."

"We'll discuss it later, but I want to be with you when you return it," he said, twisting his mouth as if he was agitated. "I never really expected a miracle. Just think of what we could do with the help of that relic. You could defeat the sect and the Brotherhood, and I could use it to help my church, to help cure the sick."

Jotham spoke to him firmly. "It was God who performed a miracle today. The Holy Spear is not a magic wand."

Silas paced the floor for a moment. "I'm having second thoughts;

190

perhaps if we just wait a few days. Think of the power we would have, Jotham, and what we could achieve."

"You're sounding like someone who wants absolute power," said Jotham. "That quotation has proven true time and time again: *absolute power corrupts absolutely*. Is that what you really want?"

He downcast his eyes and looked like a puppy that had just been scolded. "Let's join Veronica," he said.

They strode back to the north wing and found Korey's apartment door wide open. As they walked into the small living room, Jotham froze in the shock of disbelief.

The old man was in his wheelchair but looked as if he was sound asleep, his head rolling forward onto his chest. Jotham recalled how his own grandfather often nodded off in the same position.

"Strange," said Silas. "He looks dead to the world – at a moment like this?"

Jotham felt his head spin. "He sure does," he replied, racing over to him.

Then they saw Veronica, whose features were contorted into a look of horror.

Jotham was the first to reach him. Gently pushing his head back, he palpated his neck to check for a pulse. Korey's mouth dropped open, and his eyes were wide open and staring into space.

"Dad, what's happening?" asked Silas in a panicked voice.

"Call an ambulance," said Jotham. "I'm afraid he's gone."

Veronica came to her senses. "I found him like this, sweetheart. I'm so sorry – I'll call the ambulance." She took out her phone and walked quickly out of the room.

Silas howled - a long, low noise that made Jotham's blood run cold. "No, not now, please God," he moaned. Reaching out, he took hold of his father's bony wrist and tried to feel for a pulse himself, then pressed against his chest to search for any indication of heartbeat or breathing.

"Let's pray," said Jotham. He made the sign of the cross before reciting the same prayer he had often used as a parish priest. "Into your hands, Lord, we humbly entrust our brother, Korey Conrad."

"Amen," said Silas.

Jotham closed the old man's eyes. "I'm so sorry about this."

Silas nodded, now slightly calmer. "Perhaps this is a blessing. Now he never needs to learn that his son is dead."

"I'll try to find Veronica and find out what's happening with that ambulance," said Jotham. "Can you stay here with your father?"

"Of course I will, and thank you," he replied with a choked voice. As Jotham strode out of the room, he turned back and saw him lean over to gently kiss his father's forehead, then pull out a tissue to wipe away his own tears.

Jotham had a flash of insight that grabbed his stomach and squeezed it tight. He pulled the door almost closed then ran as fast as he could towards Silas's office.

He felt as if scales had just fallen from his eyes.

Chapter 44

When Jotham reached the top of the stairs, he could see that Silas's office door was shut. He tiptoed down the corridor, hoping that he was not about to discover a creaky floorboard, and when he reached it he wrapped his fingers around the lever doorknob.

He pushed down on it so slowly that the movement to an observer would be imperceptible, then inched the door open so as not to make a sound.

When the gap was just wide open enough for him to see inside a segment of the room, he sensed that someone was in there. It was like the feeling that a mouse was about to scurry across the floor, and the hairs on the back of his neck stood up.

Now was the moment for him to spring to action. With one swift shove, he pushed the door wide open.

He could see the entire room. Veronica Conrad was standing behind the desk with her back to him, and the wall safe in front of her was open. She had taken the wooden box out and was holding it, gazing at the contents.

She didn't turn around despite the crash of the door. Instead, she picked up the tip of the iron spear and held it in her hands.

"Don't move, Veronica. Put that back in the box and don't even think about touching it again."

She swung around and glared at him, her eyes full of hate.

He was struck with a sudden thought. Had he been wrong about Noah? Perhaps Veronica had only used him as a stooge.

Jotham braced his body, prepared to deal with whatever was about to happen. At that instant, he had no inkling of what that might be. "It was you all along, Veronica, and I should have guessed that. Did Noah find out about you?"

The hard look on her face softened slightly at the mention of his name. "We loved each other. He's always been in love with me, but he was no genius. I told him that you and Silas were in that sect and he believed me. He was trying to stop the two of you getting your hands on the spear, and he was planning to bring it back to me."

"So you could hand it over to the Simonian Sect, to become the perfect addition to their arsenal of magic."

"You must think that you're very clever," she said, placing the box on the desktop but keeping hold of the relic.

Jotham took a step towards her. "Not clever enough to save Noah."

"You know how upset I am about his death, but this object is more important than that. This will give us more power than we've ever had before. Knives have always been an integral part of our ceremonies, our daily mantra. Now we have the perfect weapon for our Leader to use – the tip of the spear that pierced the side of Jesus Christ."

"When did you join the sect?" he asked, hoping to distract her but also realising this might be the only chance he had to find out what he wanted to know.

"I was twenty years old, and living on the streets."

"The sort of people the sect always likes to prey on."

He saw her eyebrows move in a nervous twitch. "Be quiet."

"And they sent you to undermine Silas's church. Ever since you met him, you've been pushing those beliefs in the power of the Holy Spear."

"I never expected to have a chance to possess it. I did love Silas, in a way."

"But why did you kill Korey?" he asked.

She gave a contemptuous laugh. "I didn't do anything. The magic killed him. I walked in and he was able to see me for the first time in several years. I prayed over him, prayed for the magical power of Simon Magus, and then his heart suddenly stopped beating."

"I saw the shocked look on his face," said Jotham, a cold shiver racing down his back.

"Korey was very fond of me. We had a special understanding and I was able to influence him in my work against the church. I was forever feeding his mind with stories about the Holy Spear, just like Silas, until they finally thought it was all true. Senior people in the sect fed ideas to me.

"What did Korey say when he saw you today?"

"He realised that something was wrong. He threatened to tell Silas that he didn't trust me, and that was when I said my prayers."

Jotham shuffled forward by a shoe length, his breathing rate rising.

Veronica ran her slender fingers over the surface of the spear tip and sneered. "Now I can recite our mantra using the Holy Spear, and that will be perfect. I'm going to deliver this to the Leader and then take my place by his side. After all these years in the wilderness I'll finally have my reward."

"I've seen other members say the mantra," said Jotham. "A sickening spectacle."

She raised the spear tip high in the air, as if she was about to strike.

"The first part of our ceremony is always to take knife or dagger and thrust it down five times.

Veronica did that once to demonstrate, and Jotham shuddered to see the Holy Spear in her hands. "Put it on the table," he said, trying to calm her down and prevent it being damaged.

He wondered if she would dare to use it as a weapon. That would not be the first time he had fought off a stabbing attack from a member of the Simonian Sect.

She continued her explanation, but now there was a terrifying mania in her voice. "And then we say the mantra:

The Father's mind produced the first thought to create the angels,
Then they created the visible universe.
Praise be to Simon Magus for his words.
We must follow the Magus Covenant,
A solemn promise to destroy the Christian Church."

"You've spent you're life trying to destroy your husband and his church," said Jotham.

She glared back at him. "I'm stronger than I look, you know."

Suddenly she grabbed a heavy glass paperweight from the desk, aimed and hurled it at Jotham's head.

He jumped to the side, just in time to avoid the impact.

But she picked up the empty wooden box and threw that as well, with even more force.

Jotham raised his arm to shield himself. Somehow, he managed to reach out and grab the box just as it began the parabolic fall towards the ground. Thanks to him, it remained intact. The tip of the spear had been stored inside it for hundreds of years, and he hoped that it would continue forever.

He placed it on a chair that was right beside him, and his attention was focused on that for a fraction of a second.

But at the same moment, she tore open a desk drawer and whipped out Silas's handgun: a SIG Sauer P320. "Put your hands in the air," she said.

Jotham complied, and felt a pulse in his forehead pounding. There were few things more terrifying than the sight of a gun barrel pointed in your direction, especially when you know the person holding it is desperate.

"I was wrong about you," he said calmly, taking another step towards her.

He tried to focus his mind on everything he knew about situations like this. There was the combat training that Madena had given him, and his own experience as a parish priest needing to deal with any situation that might arise. He was also relying on his own gut instincts.

He could hear Madena's words in his head: *defuse the situation and avoid a deadly confrontation.*

Thoughts of Madena and Belle swirled through his mind, and more than anything in the world he wanted to hold them in his arms again.

Veronica held the gun firmly with both hands, her jaw set firm as she took aim.

Jotham gulped. "You're not a murderer. You never expected Noah to be killed."

Her lower lip trembled. "That wasn't my plan. I loved him. If anyone had to die it should have been Silas. I wanted Noah to escape with me."

"Did he have any idea that you were in the Simonian Sect?"

"All he knew was that he loved me, and he would do anything at all to please me. In the sect we're free to love each other without any inhibitions."

Do you plan on shooting me, and then perhaps killing Silas?

"I have my orders," she said. "The spear brings us the power we need to finally defeat the Christian Church. Once and for all time. I'm sorry to have to kill you but I can't let you interfere."

"What will you say to Silas?"

"That shooting you was an accident. No one would think that I was capable of a crime - the charming wife of Pastor Silas Conrad."

She held firm and moved her finger against the trigger.

Jotham leaned forward slightly, and then was almost close enough to pounce.

Gritting her teeth, Veronica closed her hands on the gun and fired.

Chapter 45

Jotham lunged towards her just as the shot was fired. At the same time, he veered to the side but felt the burning blast of the bullet as it grazed his arm. With a swift movement of his left leg, he kicked the gun out of her hand.

Veronica let out a yelp as the gun hit the ground, her eyes as wide as saucers.

Jotham leant over and swept it up, stuffing the weapon in his trouser pocket. He expected a rush of pain in his left arm, but was surprised to find that he could still use it. The bullet may have missed him, or perhaps a huge body rush of adrenaline masked the pain. No doubt, he would soon find out.

Jotham stretched out and grabbed hold of Veronica's arm. Twisting her around, he tried to take hold of the spear tip.

But she raised it high in the air with her free hand, then brought it down in a flash and stabbed him in the right forearm.

The sharp agony came in an instant, but he steeled himself and didn't even flinch.

Now she headed towards the french doors that led to the balcony, but Jotham was after her with blood dripping from his arm.

He moved at rapid pace and, despite the injury, took hold of her arm and pulled it upwards. That meant she was held in a wrist lock. She moaned as she lost her grip on the spear tip and it fell to the ground.

Veronica tried to fight against his hold, leaning forward in an attempt to pick up the spear.

"Leave it alone," said Jotham in his firmest voice. He pushed her against the wall for support, despite the pain in his arm.

"Let me go," she demanded, trying to break free.

"I'm making a citizen's arrest, for theft, conspiracy and attempted murder. And perhaps even the murder of Korey Conrad."

She shook with fury. "You can't do that. You know that'll destroy Silas's precious church. Imagine the scandal."

"I'm glad you still care about that," he said, struggling to hold her steady despite the fierce spasms in his arm. "But you've been trying to wreak havoc on the church since you married him – for fifteen long years."

"Yes, but I'm sure you don't want to see it destroyed."

"No, but I have no choice. At least you and the sect will be out of Silas's life."

She stopped struggling and spoke in a defiant tone. "Let me take the spear now and I'll disappear."

Jotham felt his anger rising. "You're crazy if you think I'm going to hand over the Holy Spear to the Simonian Sect."

He suddenly realised that the stab wound was causing him to weaken his grasp.

At that moment, she spun around like a whip and broke free of his hold. She bent down to pick up the spear tip, but he managed to push her away just in time and grabbed it.

Now he held the object tight behind his back with his injured arm. Shafts of pain radiated from the wound.

Veronica stepped back and stared at him as if she was searching for a chance to snatch it.

Jotham glared at her with one eye narrowed. "Something tells me, you'd rather give up on the Holy Spear if that meant you could stay out of jail."

She paused to think, as if balancing the pros and cons of his suggestion. That gave him another chance to act.

He collared her with his free arm and pushed her against the wall again, trapping her arm in another wrist lock. "You've got ten seconds to make up your mind. Jail - or leave right now with nothing."

Her body relaxed under his grip and she took a heavy breath. "I don't want to go to jail," she said. "I'll go now and never come back."

A whirlwind of thoughts circled around in Jotham's brain. Silas had already lost his brother, and now his father was dead. If Veronica left, then it meant that he would lose his wife as well. He also knew that a scandal could destroy the Holy Spear Pentecostal Church.

But there was no other choice, and it would be much worse if she stayed.

"Are you really prepared to do that?" he demanded.

She nodded firmly. "Yes, I swear."

He let her go, still keeping a firm hold on the tip of the spear. At the same instant, he withdrew the gun from his pocket and aimed it straight at her.

Veronica immediately put her arms up.

"Do you have your car keys?" he asked.

"There's a spare set in the drawer, and some cash," she said, inclining her head to indicate the desk.

"Then take them. Get into your car now and drive away. I'll tell Silas that you were in the sect, and that you're gone forever."

"What will you do with the spear?" she asked, still trying to outsmart him.

He roared back an answer. "I'm taking it where no one will ever find it again. Walk away right now before I call the police."

"Can you make sure that Silas doesn't follow me?"

"I guarantee it. He'll never want to see you or think about you again. He's already suffered enough. Walk straight out that front door right now, and don't speak to anyone. I'll be right behind you, watching you."

Tears streamed down her face as she headed straight towards the door. Then she stopped and turned around, her eyes boring into him. "Tell Silas that I did love him once."

"Get out," said Jotham.

He trailed Veronica as she marched downstairs and straight out the front door. Without saying a word, she opened the garage door, climbed into the grey sedan and backed out. A few seconds later, the vehicle passed through the front gate for the last time.

When he could no longer see her, Jotham sprinted inside and up to Silas's office. He put the gun back in the desk drawer, hoping and praying that he had seen the last of Veronica Conrad.

He opened his fist and gazed down at the spear tip that was still in his hand.

With great reverence, he placed the ancient object inside the box where it had been stored for hundreds of years.

He clutched his bleeding forearm as he raised his head and stared out the window at the empty road. For a moment, he wondered if Veronica would turn around and drive straight back. But there was no sign of her.

That was when he heard the sound of a siren and recognised it straight away.

Just then, Silas strode into the room. "Sounds like the ambulance is almost here," he said. "But I thought I heard a loud noise. Did you hear a car backfiring?"

Jotham swung around, still gingerly clutching his arm. "It wasn't a car, I'm afraid. We need to have a talk."

Silas screwed up his face at the sight of the blood soaking through his shirt.

After that, a look of horror slid across his face. "Jotham - why is the

199

safe wide open?"

Chapter 46

La Jolla, California

Veronica drove in the direction of Los Angeles, but after half an hour she pulled in at the seaside village of La Jolla and parked next to the beach. She sat there mesmerised by the waves lapping on the rugged shoreline for at least ten minutes, tears streaming down her face. Finally, she summoned the courage to get out her phone.

She quickly dialled the number she had memorised and there was an answer after two beeps. "Hello," said a man's voice.

"John, it's me," she replied.

Pedersen recognised the Californian accent, just like his own, straight away. "Well, Veronica. Tell me the good news. You have it, don't you?"

She could hear the anticipation in his voice, and she felt her throat tighten so that she could hardly talk. "There's no good news," she said. "It's over – I was forced to leave, just walk out the door with nothing except my car. If I go back they'll arrest me, and I might even face a murder charge. You need to get me out of the country."

He took a minute to digest what she had just said and his body began to tremble with an upsurge of rage. "I knew the time had come to leave your husband. But what about the Holy Spear?"

She gulped. "There's nothing I can do about that. Jotham Fletcher destroyed it, I saw him with my own eyes."

"What do you mean by that – what happened?"

She prayed to Simon Magus that her lies would sound convincing. Her normal confidence had vanished. "He said it was an idol, a fake relic. He hit the spear tip with a hammer until it was pulverised, and then he threw it in the ocean. After that, he threatened to kill me if I didn't leave Silas straight away."

She heard a thud as he slammed his fist on the table. "Fletcher is responsible for all of this?" he asked, his voice like thunder.

"Yes," she said weakly, now truly afraid of what her future might hold.

Pedersen was in a furious rage. "I'm warning you, you better not let me ever set eyes on you again, or I'll kill you myself. I'm sending you out of the country, that's for sure. You can go to meet the Leader and give him a full explanation."

That thought horrified her, but she almost felt relieved that she would not have to confront John Pedersen in his current frame of mind. At least on her way there she would have time to invent a convincing story. Just a smidgeon of her confidence returned. "I've done my duty towards the sect all these years," she said.

"And achieved nothing," he replied, abruptly ending the call.

***

John Pedersen saw Zykov standing in a corner of the living room with wide eyes transfixed on him as he spoke to Veronica. John raised his arm, contorted his face and threw the phone against the wall, missing him by inches. They both watched it shatter, just like his dreams.

***

San Diego

Jotham delayed the trip to Greece by one day because of his stabbing injury. Using his favourite alias of John McDonald, he spent the night in the emergency ward of Sharp Memorial Hospital. Silas wanted to be with him, but Jotham insisted that he needed to stay home and get some rest. Instead, Anthony Gillam joined him and did what he could to keep up his morale.

A doctor injected a local anaesthetic so that she could explore the wound, which at least made it stop hurting like hell. Afterwards, they bandaged his arm and he was expected to make a full recovery.

He phoned Madena at ten o'clock at night, which was just before dawn in the Peak District.

She was horrified to hear that he'd been hurt, and to find out the truth about Veronica. "This is my fault, I should never have left you alone," she said. "When we meet in Thessaloniki, we need to have a serious talk."

Jotham knew by her tone that she was determined to go with him to bury the Holy Spear. "I haven't had a chance to speak to Silas," he said.

"I think he needs to stay at home now and get his life sorted out. Our mission is over, I hope, or at least it will be when we return the spear."

"I won't be alone - Anthony can come with me," he said. But it was beginning to dawn on him that resistance was futile – especially now that he was in a slightly weakened state. He was longing to see her again.

"Straight after breakfast, I'll charter a jet to take me to Greece," she

202

said. "Felix can drive me to the airport. When you arrive, I'll be there – and by the way, I can't wait to see you."

"This whole episode will be over soon," he said, wincing as a spark of pain flashed down his arm.

Jotham was released from the hospital at six o'clock in the morning, and he and Anthony caught a taxi back to the Conrad house. "We can take my hire car back to the airport when we leave," he said as they approached the front door. "Frankly, I can't wait to get out of here."

Silas greeted them in his bathrobe and Jotham and Anthony joined him for breakfast. He looked relieved that the pressures of the last few days were over, and instead he could focus on dealing with his own heartache.

"I need to arrange a memorial service for Noah and Korey," he said, toying with the scrambled eggs on his plate. "I'm finding it hard to believe that my marriage was a lie."

"Have you thought much about the future?" asked Jotham, sipping a double-strength coffee.

He looked at them with sad eyes. "First of all I have tell my kids about Veronica. Then I'm planning to address the congregation. I've been awake all night, making plans."

"I guess there'll be some big changes," said Anthony.

"You said it. First, I intend to change the name of the church, although I haven't chosen anything yet. But that's only the start. I'm going to renounce all the doctrine relating to the Holy Spear."

Jotham was pleased to see the tension appear to melt from to his face. "Back to first principles," he said. "That's wonderful news."

"Yes, Jotham, that's right - and you've led me back to the truth. I feel so ashamed, to think that I allowed myself to be dragged down the wrong path like that for so many years. And leading so many others there as well."

"Don't blame yourself. Much greater minds than ours have been led astray by the Simonian Sect. They've had two thousand years of practice at undermining Christianity."

He massaged his own forehead. "Why didn't I realise that something was wrong a long time ago? Instead of that, because of my pride and vanity, I allowed Veronica to poison my mind."

Anthony looked at Jotham with eyebrows raised, and he nodded in reply. He knew that it was time to say farewell to Silas Conrad.

"Silas, I really think that it's time for us to leave. Madena's flying to

203

Greece and wants to join me there. We intend to return the Holy Spear to its proper resting place."

"But I wanted to help you do that," he said with a frown. "I feel as if it's my duty."

Jotham stood up and locked eyes with him. "Forget about the Holy Spear, put that behind you and tend to your flock. They're the ones who need you now."

Silas cast his eyes down. "So what should I do?"

"I think you should stay here," continued Jotham. "Madena and I came here to complete a mission, and once we visit Greece then we can return home satisfied."

Silas rose to his feet. "I'll get the box for you."

Jotham put a hand on his shoulder. "Thank you," he said. "We'll leave this morning, and we won't be back unless you need our help again."

Chapter 47

En route to Greece

Two hours later, Anthony Gillam powered the plane down the runway. Jotham gazed out the cabin window as the wheels lifted off the ground, and he breathed a sigh of relief to be leaving San Diego behind. The spear tip was secured inside his suitcase, and that was now in the luggage storage area behind his seat.

The mission was drawing to an end. His major regret was that too many people had suffered and too many had died. That included his former adversary, Father Dominic. Silas had lost three family members, but his church would now take a different course and his flock would be guided back to the truth. The future looked brighter.

He phoned Madena, who was about to board the jet that she'd chartered. On the small screen, he looked into her blue eyes and his heart skipped a beat. "I'll be with you soon, my darling," he said.

"I can't wait," she replied. "Now that Dominic's dead, it remains to be seen if Father Benjamin resurfaces."

"And whether he'll be the new Head of the Brotherhood. He might be even more destructive than his predecessor."

She looked to the side as if she was being called, and blew Jotham a parting kiss. "Soon this will all be over."

They needed to stop in Newfoundland again for a few hours, mainly so that Anthony was able to refuel the jet and have some sleep. The final leg of the journey ended when he brought the plane in to land at Thessaloniki Airport.

Madena was waiting for Jotham when he exited the plane. Throwing her arms around him, they held each other tight for more than a minute.

She picked up her backpack and put it over her shoulders. "I've got some equipment in here, but are you sure you're feeling all right to proceed?"

"Absolutely," he replied as she helped him put on his own backpack. He had the wooden box inside, as well as a torch and other equipment.

A late model BMW was waiting for them nearby, and Madena was quick to take the car keys. "You can't drive with that arm," she said as she went to the left side.

"I think I could manage," he replied, but climbed in the passenger seat and cradled the backpack in his arms. "Now we're this close, I don't want to let this out of my sight."

"Before we go any further, I'd like to take a look at your wound," said Madena. "I've been so worried about you. Would you mind?"

Jotham looked at her tenderly. "Of course not," he said, holding up his arm.

She inspected the bandage and began to unwrap it. "Does it hurt very much?" she asked.

"Only when I laugh too much," he replied as a burst of pain radiated down to his fingertips. He averted his eyes as she exposed the suture line. "How does it look?" he asked.

"You must have had a good doctor," she said. "The suture line is already healed."

Jotham jerked his head down and stared at his arm, then wondered if he was dreaming. A day ago there had been a gaping wound but now there was a neat pink line underneath the row of stitches. "That's miraculous," he said.

Madena nodded, her eyes wide in astonishment. "Yes, it really is."

"But it still hurts, so I hope that improves."

"I'm sure that it will. I'll do up the bandage for now, but when we finish here you may not need it any more."

"There's something I didn't tell you, darling. Veronica stabbed me with the tip of the spear."

Madena gasped and, still holding his arm, she gazed into his eyes. "That probably explains everything. You really are the most extraordinary man I've ever met."

Jotham gulped. "Do you really think we're doing the right thing bringing the spear back here?"

"Definitely," she said emphatically. "Let's go."

Madena adjusted the navigation system, then turned the key and the engine sparked to life. Making her way through the crowded town, she knew that it was the perfect opportunity to discuss something. "Jotham, I don't think you would have been injured if I'd been there."

He nodded. "Perhaps, but it could have been worse. Veronica fired a gun and I was lucky that the bullet only grazed my arm. If you had been there, you might have been killed." His blood ran cold to think about that.

She pursed her lips as she focused her attention on negotiating the narrow streets. "I think we both realise that we always need to cover each other's back. From now on, we should stay together when we go on a mission –

for the entire duration."

Jotham knew that she was right. He'd been trying to protect her because she was the mother of his child, but they'd always been equal partners, and that was why he loved her so much. "One day we really will defeat the Simonian Sect," he said.

"I hope so," she replied, shrugging her shoulders as they headed into the countryside.

For the first two hours of the journey they were on main roads that cut through rugged countryside. But for the final hour, the road became increasingly narrow with treacherous curves. Madena drove with consummate skill, keeping the vehicle centred in her lane with deft turns of the steering wheel.

Jotham held the backpack even closer to his chest, reminding himself that inside was the tip of the Holy Spear. They turned a blind corner and, for the first time, glimpsed the monastery of Saint Dimitrios in the last rays of daylight. The sight was awe-inspiring, a complex of buildings set on top of a steep hill.

Five minutes later they entered the small village of Dimitrios. That was situated at the base of the hill, and consisted of one small taverna and a few dusty streets. They drove past tiny red-roofed houses with faded white walls covered in peeling white paint.

They headed up the steep path that led to the monastery as darkness fell. When they were well away from the village, Madena veered off the road. She parked the car so that it was concealed behind a thick stand of shrubs.

They climbed out and put their backpacks on, but before moving any further Jotham took her hand. He kissed her fingertips tenderly and then held her close for a moment.

Gazing up, they could just see the monastery towering far above them. The hill was covered in dense scrub, so they had plenty of cover. "There are meant to be hundreds of caves around here," said Jotham. "We shouldn't have any trouble finding a place to bury the box." They took out their torches.

Despite his bandaged arm, Jotham was able to keep up with Madena as they began the hike up the hill. After almost an hour, they both felt exhausted despite being in peak physical condition. Jotham didn't reveal that with each step, the throb in his arm increased so that by the time they were halfway up, he needed to stop. He sat on a rock for a short break, and Madena helped to take the backpack off his shoulders.

"Perhaps you should have left this for me to do," she said.

"I'm fine," he replied, hoping she wouldn't notice his grimace. "I really don't think that we need to go much further."

"You stay here and let me look around," she said. She walked off, but as soon as she disappeared from view, Jotham had second thoughts and wanted to stay with her. He picked the backpack up and held it with his hands as he trailed after her.

A second later he caught up, though she was half-hidden by some overgrown bushes. "Take at look at this, darling," she said.

He rushed over, but the prickly branches cut him as he slipped past. As soon as he joined her there, his face brightened. She was standing in front of a narrow, tunnel-like opening into a cave. "Madena, you're a genius," he said.

"Thank you," she replied, giving him a peck on the cheek.

"This looks ideal, but I'm not looking forward to crawling through that space."

Jotham put his backpack on the ground and unzipped it, then pulled out and the wooden box. Madena took out two scooped trowels. "We're going to need these," she said.

"Better than using hands," he replied, still inspecting the cave opening. He knew how much Madena hated tight spaces, and he tried to hide his own reluctance. "Just breathe deeply and relax. I'll go first."

She frowned. "It looks like a tomb, but don't worry. I'll use psychology and talk myself through it."

They both crouched down. Jotham led the way as they crawled through the narrow tunnel that was more than a metre long.

"This is like being trapped in a collapsed building," said Madena with a moan.

A few seconds later, Jotham reached the inside of the cave. It was only about one and a half metres high, so he had to remain crouching. He used his torch to inspect the walls, ceiling and floor of the small space. But that was when an awful stench hit his nostrils.

Chapter 48

Madena was still in the tunnel, but contorted her face in disgust. "What is that smell?" she asked.

"Maybe a dead rat or some other animal," he replied with a splutter. "Perhaps a few of them – and they died a painful death." Jotham continued to inspect the cave. Shining the torch towards the right hand corner, he saw what looked like the opening to a second chamber, but a rock pile barred the way. "Looks like there's been at least one cave-in here."

"I think we'll have to get out of here and bury it someplace else," she said.

"I agree. That smell is a killer."

Madena struggled backwards through the narrow opening at a pace she would not have believed possible, and a moment later she was outside. Jotham was close behind her, pausing only to flash his torch on the rock pile one final time. Two minutes later, they were in the fresh air.

Madena coughed to clear her lungs. "I wonder if all the caves smell like that," she said.

"I hope not," replied Jotham. "But why don't we try walking towards the monastery? We might find just the right place for the burial somewhere in the grounds."

She came up close to him. "Yes, that sounds like a good idea."

They headed uphill but the path become progressively steeper and soon they were both panting. About two hundred metres from the top, they could see the monastery buildings towering over them. "It's very imposing," said Madena as they came to the edge of a tiny clearing that was a few metres wide.

But before they had time to think, they heard the sound of footsteps approaching.

They came to an abrupt stop and sheltered behind some bushes just as an old man appeared. He was dressed in a rough grey habit with a gold cross around his neck, so it was obvious where he had come from. He approached the cliff face, holding a torch to light his way, and walked straight up to a small area of bare rock. Jotham could just make out a crude cross etched on it, about thirty centimetres high.

The priest stood in front of it and made the sign of the cross, then fell to his knees and appeared to be praying.

Jotham whispered to Madena. "I might speak to him."

She locked eyes with him to indicate her agreement. "I'll stay here," she replied.

After ten minutes, the man rose to his feet and turned around. Jotham's heart thumped as he took a step into the clearing.

The man stepped back, clearly frightened, and snapped at him in Greek.

"I'm sorry, I didn't mean to startle you," said Jotham. "Do you speak English?"

"I'm Father Lambros, the abbot," he replied.

"I'm John McDonald, a tourist, just out for an evening hike."

"In the dark, that's very dangerous. You could fall and kill yourself."

"Yes, perhaps it wasn't a good idea. Is this a shrine, Father?"

"Just for myself. I come here sometimes to pray for the Holy Spear. They say that it's buried somewhere on the hillside." He looked as if he was reluctant to say any more, and tried to change the subject. "Do you need help to get back to the village, Mr McDonald?"

"No thank you, I'll be fine - I'm heading back now."

"If you don't need my help, I must return to the monastery before I'm missed. Please don't tell anyone about what you just saw."

"I promise that I won't. Good night, Father."

"God bless you, my son."

Father Lambros shuffled off. Madena waited a few more minutes to be sure that he was gone and then stepped into the clearing.

"This would be the perfect place," she said, her eyes sparkling.

Jotham smiled. "Yes, my darling." He walked over and wrapped his arms around her. "Let's get to work, and hope that Father Lambros doesn't decide to return."

They knelt down in front of the humble shrine and set to work, digging a narrow hole and continuing until it was at least a metre deep. "We'll have to make sure that no one notices this," said Jotham. Although his wound appeared to be healed, burning pain radiated down his arm.

Despite the cool evening air, both of them were soaked in sweat. "Are we ready now?" asked Madena as she took the box out of the backpack, adopting an air of decorum for the burial ceremony.

Jotham nodded. They bowed their heads and he prayed that the Holy Spear would remain safe forever. Madena leaned forward and placed the wooden box carefully in position at the bottom of the hole. Then they worked to shovel the pile of dirt on top of it.

When that was done, Madena smoothed the soil on the surface and then roughened it up so that the area looked the same as the rest of the ground.

Jotham added some final touches of his own to make the area look as natural as possible. "No one would know that anything had happened here," he said as he admired their handiwork. "The Holy Spear can rest in peace forever."

They stood up and walked to the edge of the clearing. Jotham stopped and waved his torch around the area for a final look. He remembered Goran Novak, and wondered if he had come here and how he had managed to find the relic. He'd either stolen it or fooled someone into selling it. The abbot certainly didn't seem to know anything.

"We're finished," said Madena softly.

"Amen to that," he replied, and noticed that the pain in his arm had vanished. "Now let's go home."

They hiked back to their car, both of them feeling as if an impossible burden had been eased from their shoulders. Jotham took the wheel this time and drove straight to Thessaloniki Airport. Anthony Gillam had prepared the plane and was waiting for them.

***

The Peak District

Jotham saw his own landing strip come into view, and felt a huge surge of relief. He reached out to Madena and took hold of her hand. "It's all over," he said.

Felix was waiting for them with the Mercedes. "Belle's been an angel," he said. "Such a beautiful child."

"We're so happy that you and Cynthia could look after her," said Madena as they jumped in the car.

"We love it," he replied.

Felix sped along the narrow roads that led to the estate, as Jotham and Madena held hands in the back seat. "Such a beautiful day," said Jotham, but they both looked in every direction, searching for any sign of danger.

It still took his breath away to realise that he now had a beautiful wife and daughter. After Jane and William died, he never thought he would be happy again. They were buried in the little graveyard of the church where he had been a parish priest in Canberra. Soon, he would make his annual visit to Australia to

211

lay flowers on their grave, and then quickly return home to his new family.

He knew that his happiness would only be complete if he could achieve his goal of defeating the Simonian Sect and the Brotherhood. Then he and Madena could live in peace and safety, but he doubted that he would ever achieve that goal. He frowned as they passed the spot where the Brotherhood had assassinated Iago Visser.

As they turned a sharp corner, Jotham jumped when he heard his phone buzz. He smiled when he saw who was calling, and pressed the answer button. "Eugene, how are you, my friend?" he asked, switching to videophone.

Eugene's boyish face grinned back at them. "Are you safe home now?" he asked.

"Almost there. I'll tell you all about it next time we meet."

"That would be gobsmackingly good. I have some news to tell you."

"Really?" asked Madena. "Don't keep us in suspense."

"It's just about my exam results. I came first in the major exam."

"Passed with flying colours," said Jotham. "Congratulations, Eugene, that's wonderful."

"We said that you were destined for great things," said Madena. "And what about Emily?"

"She came second."

Jotham sighed. "I think that sounds like true love."

They ended the call just as the massive wall around the estate came into view. The entrance gates opened and a moment later the Mercedes came to a halt near the front door.

Cynthia Young strode out to greet them with Belle in her arms.

Jotham felt joy wash over him as he raced over and swept Belle up in his arms. Madena joined them and they walked inside.

"I'll make you a nice cup of tea," said Cynthia, heading towards the kitchen. "And I've made some of my shortbread."

When they were alone in the living room, Jotham began to waltz his wife and daughter around the room.

"I'm glad that Eugene's found a smart girlfriend," said Madena, with a dazzling smile. "Speaking of second, I think we ought to think about baby number two very soon."

"Yes, how about tonight?" he said, planting a kiss on Belle's soft cheek.

"I was going to suggest the same thing myself."

***

THE END

***

A Note from the Author

Thank you very much for reading HOLY SPEAR OF MAGUS, Book 4 in *The Jotham Fletcher Mystery Thriller Series*. If you enjoyed it, please tell your friends and spread the word on your favourite social media sites – including Facebook, Goodreads and Twitter.

Would you be able to take a moment to review this book on Amazon and share your opinion? That allows me to hear your views and also helps other potential readers. If you've never written an Amazon review before, please consider making this the first time.

My Amazon Author page is an easy way to access all my books, including the rest of *The Jotham Fletcher Mystery Thriller Series*:

Book 1 - THE MAGUS COVENANT

Book 2 - THE ROCK OF MAGUS

Book 3 – THE MAGUS EPIPHANY

I'm aso the other of two non-fiction books. THE ONE WAY DIET is a no-nonsense guide to losing weight and coping with the journey. HAPPY TRAVELS 101 is a short book of tips for anyone who wants to travel overseas. If you would like to see some of my travel photos, here is my Instagram page: @authorlovestravel.

You can read more about me and HOLY SPEAR OF MAGUS on my website at www.tonipike.com. I would be delighted to hear from you, and please let me know if you would like to be added to my email list.

Yours sincerely,

Toni Pike

Made in the USA
Lexington, KY
30 December 2018